# A COLLECTION OF SHORT-STORIES

## By Lemuel Arthur Pittenger

**NATAL PUBLISHING LLC**
*ARS LONGA, VITA BREVIS*

# A PREFATORY NOTE

This collection of short-stories does not illustrate the history of short-story writing, nor does it pretend that these are the ten best stories ever written, but it does attempt to present selections from a list of the greatest short-stories that have proved, in actual use, most beneficial to high school students.

The introduction presents a concise statement of the essentials of the history, qualities, and composition of the short-story. A brief biography of each author and a criticism covering the main characteristics of his writings serve as starting points for the recitation. The references following both the biography and criticism are given in order that the study of the short-story may be amplified, and that high school teachers may build a systematic and serviceable library about their class work in the teaching of the story. The collateral readings, listed after each story, will aid in the creation of a suitable atmosphere for the story studied, and explain many questions developed in the recitation. Only such definitions as are not easily found in school dictionaries are included in the notes.

# INTRODUCTION

# HISTORY OF THE SHORT-STORY

Just when, where, and by whom story-telling was begun no one can say. From the first use of speech, no doubt, our ancestors have told stories of war, love, mysteries, and the miraculous performances of lower animals and inanimate objects. The ultimate source of all stories lies in a thorough democracy, unhampered by the restrictions of a higher civilization. Many tales spring from a loathsome filth that is extremely obnoxious to our present day tastes. The remarkable and gratifying truth is, however, that the short-story, beginning in the crude and brutal stages of man's development, has gradually unfolded to greater and more useful possibilities, until in our own time it is a most flexible and moral literary form.

The first historical evidence in the development of the story shows no conception of a short-story other than that it is not so long as other narratives. This judgment of the short-story obtained until the beginning of the nineteenth century, when a new version of its meaning was given, and an enlarged vision of its possibilities was experienced by a number of writers almost simultaneously. In the early centuries of story-telling there was only one purpose in mind—that of narrating for the joy of the telling and hearing. The story-tellers sacrificed unity and totality of effect as well as originality for an entertaining method of reciting their incidents.

The story of *Ruth* and the *Prodigal Son* are excellent short tales, but they do not fulfill the requirements of our modern short-story for the reason that they are not constructed for one single impression, but are in reality parts of possible longer stories. They are, as it were, parts of stories not unlike *Dr. Jekyll and Mr. Hyde* and *A Lear of the Steppes*, and lack those complete and concise artistic effects found in the short-stories, *Markheim* and *Mumu*, by the same authors. Both *Ruth* and the *Prodigal Son* are exceptionally well told, possess a splendid moral tone, and are excellent prophecies of what the nineteenth century has developed for us in the art of short-story writing.

The Greeks did very little writing in prose until the era of their decadence, and showed little instinct to use the concise and unified form of the short-story. The conquering Romans followed closely in the paths of their predecessors and did little work in the shorter narratives. The myths of Greece and Rome were not bound by facts, and opened a wonderland where writers were free to roam. The epics were slow in movement, and presented a list of loosely organized stories arranged about some character like Ulysses or AEneas.

During the mediaeval period story-tellers and stories appeared everywhere. The more ignorant of these story-tellers produced the fable, and the educated monks produced the simple, crude and disjointed tales. The *Gesta Romanorum* is a wonderful storehouse of these mediaeval stories. In the *Decameron* Boccaccio deals with traditional and contemporary materials. He is a born story-teller and presents many interesting and well-told narratives, but as Professor Baldwin[1] has said, more than half are merely anecdotes, and the remaining stories are bare plots, ingeniously done in a kind of scenario form. Three approach our modern idea of the short-story, and two, the second story of the second day and the sixth story of the ninth day, actually attain to our standard. Boccaccio was not conscious of a standard in short-story telling, for he had none in the sense that Poe and Maupassant defined and practiced it. Chaucer in England told his stories in verse and added the charm of humor and well defined characters to the development of story-telling.

In the seventeenth century Cervantes gave the world its first great novel, *Don Quixote*. Cervantes was careless in his work and did not write short-stories, but tales that are fairly brief. Spain added to the story a high sense of chivalry and a richness of character that the Greek romance and the Italian novella did not possess. France followed this loose composition and lack of beauty in form. Scarron and Le Sage, the two French fiction writers of this period, contributed little or nothing to the advancement of story-telling. Cervantes' *The Liberal Lover* is as near as this period came to producing a real short-story.

The story-telling of the seventeenth century was largely shaped by the popularity of the drama. In the eighteenth century the drama gave place to the essay, and it is to the sketch and essay that we must go to trace the evolution of the story during this period. Voltaire in France had a burning message in every essay, and he paid far greater attention to the development of the thought of his message than to the story he was telling. Addison and Steele in the *Spectator* developed some real characters of the fiction type and told some good stories, but even their best, like *Theodosius and Constantia*, fall far short of developing all the dramatic possibilities, and lack the focusing of interest found in the nineteenth century stories. Some of Lamb's *Essays of Elia*, especially the *Dream Children*, introduce a delicate fancy and an essayist's clearness of thought and statement into the story. At the close of this century German romanticism began to seep into English thought and prepare the way for things new in literary thought and treatment.

The nineteenth century opened with a decided preference for fiction. Washington Irving, reverting to the *Spectator*, produced his sketches, and, following the trend of his time, looked forward to a new form and wrote *The Spectre Bridegroom* and *Rip Van Winkle*. It is only by a precise definition of short-story that Irving is robbed of the honor of being the founder of the modern short-story. He loved to meander and to fit his materials to his story scheme in a leisurely manner. He did not quite see what Hawthorne instinctively followed and Poe consciously defined and practiced, and he did not realize that terseness of statement and totality of impression were the chief qualities he needed to make him the father of a new literary form. Poe and Maupassant have reduced the form of the short-story to an exact science; Hawthorne and Harte have done successfully in the field of romanticism what the Germans, Tieck and Hoffman, did not do so well; Bjornson and Henry James have analyzed character psychologically in their short-stories; Kipling has used the short-story as a vehicle for the conveyance of specific knowledge; Stevenson has gathered most, if not all, of the literary possibilities adaptable to short-story use, and has incorporated them in his *Markheim*.

France with her literary newspapers and artistic tendencies, and the United States with magazines calling incessantly for good short-stories, and with every section of its conglomerate life clamoring to express itself, lead in the production and rank of short-stories. Maupassant and Stevenson and Hawthorne and Poe are the great names in the ranks of short-story writers. The list of present day writers is interminable, and high school students can best acquire a reasonable appreciation of the great work these writers are doing by reading regularly some of the better grade literary magazines. For a comprehensive view of specimens representing the history and development of the short-story, students should have access to Brander Matthews' *The Short Story*, Jessup and Canby's *The Book of the Short-Story*, and Waite and Taylor's *Modern Masterpieces of Short Prose Fiction*.

NOTE: [1] *American Short-Stories*, by Charles Sears Baldwin, New York: Longmans, Green, & Company, 1904.

# QUALITIES OF THE SHORT-STORY

It was not until well along in the nineteenth century that any one attempted to define the short-story. The three quotations given here are among the best things that have been spoken on this subject.

"The right novella is never a novel cropped back from the size of a tree to a bush, or the branch of a tree stuck into the ground and made to serve for a bush. It is another species, destined by the agencies at work in the realm of unconsciousness to be brought into being of its own kind, and not of another,"—W.D. Howells, *North American Review*, 173:429.

"A true short-story is something other and something more than a mere story which is short. A true short-story differs from the novel chiefly in its essential unity of impression. In a far more exact and precise use of the word, a short-story has unity as a novel cannot have it.... A short-story deals with a single character, a single event, a single emotion, or the series of emotions called forth by a single situation.—Brander Matthews, *The Philosophy of the Short-Story*.

"The aim of a short-story is to produce a single narrative effect with the greatest economy of means that is consistent with the utmost emphasis."—Clayton Hamilton, *Materials and Methods of Fiction*.

The short-story must always have a compact unity and a direct simplicity. In such stories as Björnson's *The Father* and Maupassant's *The Piece of String* this simplicity is equal to that of the anecdote, but in no case can an anecdote possess the dramatic possibilities of these simple short-stories; for a short-story must always have that tensity of emotion that comes only in the crucial tests of life.

The short-story does not demand the consistency in treatment of the long story, for there are not so many elements to marshal and direct properly, but the short-story must be original and varied in its themes, cleverly constructed, and lighted through and through with the glow of vivid imaginings. A single incident in daily life is caught as in a snap-shot exposure and held before the reader in such a manner that the impression of the whole is derived largely from suggestion. The single incident may be the turning-point in life history, as in *The Man Who Was*; it may be a mental surrender of habits fixed seemingly in indelible colors in the soul and a sudden, inflexible decision to be a man, as in the case of *Markheim;* or it may be a gradual realization of the value of spiritual gifts, as Björnson has concisely presented it in his little story *The Father*.

The aim of the short-story is always to present a cross-section of life in such a vivid manner that the importance of the incident becomes universal. Some short-stories are told with the definite end in view of telling a story for the sake of exploiting a plot. *The Cask of Amontillado* is all action in comparison with *The Masque of the Red Death. The Gold-Bug* sets for itself the task of solving a puzzle and possesses action from first to last. Other stories teach a moral. *Ethan Brand* deals with the unpardonable sin, and *The Great Stone Face* is our classic story in the field of ideals and their development. Hawthorne, above all writers, is most interested in ethical laws and moral development. Still other stories aim to portray character. Miss Jewett and Mrs. Freeman veraciously picture the faded-put womanhood in New England; Henry James and Björnson turn the x-rays of psychology and sociology on their characters; Stevenson follows with the precision of the tick of a watch the steps in Markheim's mental evolution.

The types of the short-story are as varied as life itself. Addison, Lamb, Irving, Warner, and many others have used the story in their sketches and essays with wonderful effect. *The Legend of Sleepy Hollow* is as impressive as any of Scott's tales. The allegory in *The Great Stone Face* loses little or nothing when compared with Bunyan's *Pilgrim's Progress*. No better type of detective story has been written than the two short-stories, *The Murders in the Rue Morgue* and *The Purloined Letter*. Every emotion is subject to the call of the short-story. Humor with its expansive free air is not so well adapted to the short-story as is pathos. There is a sadness in the stories of Dickens, Garland, Page, Mrs. Freeman, Miss Jewett, Maupassant, Poe, and many others that runs the whole gamut from pleasing tenderness in *A Child's Dream of a Star* to unutterable horror in *The Fall of the House of Usher*.

The short-story is stripped of all the incongruities that led Fielding, Scott, and Dickens far afield. All its parts harmonize in the simplest manner to give unity and "totality" of impression through strict unity of form. It is a concentrated piece of life snatched from the ordinary and uneventful round of living and steeped in fancy until it becomes the acme of literary art.

# COMPOSITION OF THE SHORT-STORY

Any student who wishes to express himself correctly and pleasingly, and desires a keener sense for the appreciation of literary work must write. The way others have done the thing never appears in a forceful light until one sets himself at a task of like nature. Just so in the study of this text. To find and appreciate the better points of the short-story, students must write stories of their own, patterned in a small way on the technique of the masterpieces.

The process of short-story writing follows in a general way the following program. In the first place the class must have something interesting and suggestive to write about. Sometimes the class can suggest a subject; newspapers almost every day give incidents worthy of story treatment; happenings in the community often give the very best material for stories; and phases of the literature work may well be used in the development of students' themes. Change the type of character and place, reconstruct the plot, or require a different ending for the story, leaving the plot virtually as it is, and then assign to the class. Boys and girls should invariably be taught to see stories in the life about them, in the newspapers and magazines on their library tables, and in the masterpieces they study in their class work. After the idea that the class wishes to develop has been definitely determined and the material for this development has been gathered and grouped about the idea, the class should select a viewpoint and proceed to write. Sometimes the author should tell the story, sometimes a third person who may be of secondary importance in the story should be given the rôle of the story-teller, sometimes the whole may be in dialogue. The class should choose a fitting method.

Young writers should be very careful about the beginning of a story. An action story should start with a striking incident that catches the reader's attention at once and forecasts subsequent happenings. In every case this first incident must have in it the essence of the end of the story and should be perfectly logical to the reader after he has finished the reading. A story in which the setting is emphasized can well begin, with a description and contain a number of descriptions and expositions, distributed with a sense of propriety throughout the theme. A good method to use in the opening of a character story is that of conversation. An excellent example of a sharp use of this device is Mrs. Freeman's *Revolt of Mother*, where the first paragraph is a single spoken word.

Every incident included in the story should be tested for its value in the development of the theme. An incident that does not amplify certain phases of the story has no right to be included, and great care should be used in an effort to incorporate just the material necessary for the proper evolution of the thought. The problem is not so much what can be secured to be included in the story, but rather, after making a thorough collection of the material, what of all these points should be cast out.

The ending must be a natural outgrowth of the development found in the body of the composition. Even in a story with a surprise ending, of which we are tempted to say that we have had no preparation for such a turn in the story, there must be hints—the subtler the better—that point unerringly and always toward the end. The end is presupposed in the beginning and the changing of one means the altering of the other.

Young writers have trouble in stopping at the right place. They should learn, as soon as possible, that to drag on after the logical ending has been reached spoils the best of stories. It is just as bad to stop before arriving at the true end. In other words there is only one place for the ending of a story, and in no case can it be shifted without ruining the idea that has obtained throughout the theme.

There are certain steps in the development of story-writing that should be followed if the best results are to be obtained. The first assignment should require only the writing of straight narrative. *The Arabian Nights Tales* and children's stories represent this type of writing and will give the teacher valuable aid in the presentation of this work. After the students have produced simple stories resembling the Sinbad Voyages, they should next add descriptions of persons and places and explanations of situations to develop clearness and interest in their original productions. Taking these themes in turn students should be required to introduce plot incidents that complicate the simple happenings and divert the straightforward trend of the narrative. Now that the stories are well developed in their descriptions, expositions, and plot interests they should be tested for their emotional effects. Students should go through their themes, and by making the proper changes give in some cases a humorous and in others a pathetic or tragic effect. These few suggestions are given to emphasize the facts that no one conceives a story in all its details in a moment of inspiration, and that there is a way of proceeding that passes in logical gradations from the simplest to the most complex phases of story writing.

Franklin and Stevenson knew no rules for writing other than to practice incessantly on some form they wished to imitate. Hard work is the first lesson that boys and girls must learn in the art of writing, and a systematic gradation of assignments is what the teacher must provide for his students. Walter Besant gave the following rules for novel writers. Some of them may be suggestive to writers of the high school age, so the list is given in its complete form. "(1) Practice writing something original every day. (2) Cultivate the habit of observation. (3) Work regularly at certain hours. (4) Read no rubbish. (5) Aim at the formation of style. (6) Endeavor to be dramatic. (7) A great element of dramatic skill is selection. (8) Avoid the sin of writing about a character. (9) Never attempt to describe any kind of life except that with which you are familiar. (10) Learn as much as you can about men and women. (11) For the sake of forming a good natural style, and acquiring command of language, write poetry."

# SHORT-STORY LIBRARY

***BOOKS FOR REFERENCE*:**
*American Short-Stories*, Charles Baldwin, Longmans, Green, & Co.
*A Study of Prose Fiction*, Chapter XII, Bliss Perry, Houghton, Mifflin Co.
*Composition Rhetoric*, T.C. Blaisdell, American Book Co.
*Forms of Prose Literature*, J.H. Gardiner, Charles Scribner's Sons.
*Materials and Methods of Fiction*, Clayton Hamilton, The Baker and Taylor Co.
*Principles of Literary Criticism*, C.T. Winchester, The Macmillan Co.
*Short-Story Writing*, C.R. Barrett. The Baker and Taylor Co.
*Specimens of the Short-Story*, G.H. Nettleton, H. Holt & Co.
*Story-Writing and Journalism*, Sherwin Cody, Funk & Wagnalls Co.
*Talks on Writing English*, Arlo Bates, Houghton Mifflin Co.
*The Writing of the Short-Story*, L.W. Smith, D.C. Heath & Co.
*The Philosophy of the Short-Story*, Brander Matthews, Longmans, Green, & Co.
*The World's Greatest Short-Stories*, Sherwin Cody, A.C. McClurg & Co.
*The Short-Story*, Henry Canby, Henry Holt & Co.
*The Short-Story*, Evelyn May Albright, The Macmillan Co.
*The Book of the Short-Story*, Jessup and Canby, D. Appleton & Co.
*Modern Masterpieces of Short Prose Fiction*, Waite and Taylor, D. Appleton & Co.
*The Short-Story*, Brander Matthews, American Book Co.
*Writing the Short-Story*, Esenwein, Hinds, Noble & Eldredge.
*A Study of the Short-Story in English*, Henry Seidel Canby, Henry Holt & Co.

## COLLECTIONS OF SHORT-STORIES:

*American Short-Stories*, Charles S. Baldwin, Longmans, Green, & Co.
*Great Short-Stories*, 3 vols., William Patten, P.F. Collier & Son.
*Little French Masterpieces*, 6 vols. Alexander Jessup, G.P. Putnam's Sons.
*Short-Story Classics* (American), 5 vols., William Patten, P.F. Collier & Son.
*Short-Story Classics* (Foreign), 5 vols., William Patten, P.F. Collier & Son.
*Stories by American Authors*, 10 vols., Charles Scribner's Sons.
*Stories by English Authors*, 10 vols., Charles Scribner's Sons.
*Stories by Foreign Authors*, 10 vols., Charles Scribner's Sons.
*Stories New and Old* (American and English), Hamilton W. Mabie, The Macmillan Co.
*World's Greatest Short-Stories*, Sherwin Cody, A.C. McClurg & Co.
*The American Short-Story*, Elias Lieberman.

# THE FATHER[1]

*By Björnstjerne Björnson (1838-1910)*
The man whose story is here to be told was the wealthiest and most influential person in his parish; his name was Thord Överaas. He appeared in the priest's study one day, tall and earnest.
"I have gotten a son," said he, "and I wish to present him for baptism."
"What shall his name be?"
"Finn,—after my father."
"And the sponsors?"
They were mentioned, and proved to be the best men and women of Thord's relations in the parish.
"Is there anything else?" inquired the priest, and looked up. The peasant hesitated a little.
"I should like very much to have him baptized by himself," said he, finally.
"That is to say on a week-day?"
"Next Saturday, at twelve o'clock noon."
"Is there anything else?" inquired the priest,
"There is nothing else;" and the peasant twirled his cap, as though he were about to go.
Then the priest rose. "There is yet this, however." said he, and walking toward Thord, he took him by the hand and looked gravely into his eyes: "God grant that the child may become a blessing to you!"
One day sixteen years later, Thord stood once more in the priest's study.
"Really, you carry your age astonishingly well, Thord," said the priest; for he saw no change whatever in the man.
"That is because I have no troubles," replied Thord. To this the priest said nothing, but after a while he asked: "What is your pleasure this evening?"
"I have come this evening about that son of mine who is to be confirmed to-morrow."
"He is a bright boy."
"I did not wish to pay the priest until I heard what number the boy would have when he takes his place in the church to-morrow."
"He will stand number one."
"So I have heard; and here are ten dollars for the priest."
"Is there anything else I can do for you?" inquired the priest, fixing his eyes on Thord.
"There is nothing else."
Thord went out.

Eight years more rolled by, and then one day a noise was heard outside of the priest's study, for many men were approaching, and at their head was Thord, who entered first.

The priest looked up and recognized him.

"You come well attended this evening, Thord," said he.

"I am here to request that the banns may be published for my son: he is about to marry Karen Storliden, daughter of Gudmund, who stands here beside me."

"Why, that is the richest girl in the parish."

"So they say," replied the peasant, stroking back his hair with one hand.

The priest sat a while as if in deep thought, then entered the names in his book, without making any comments, and the men wrote their signatures underneath. Thord laid three dollars on the table.

"One is all I am to have," said the priest.

"I know that very well; but he is my only child; I want to do it handsomely."

The priest took the money.

"This is now the third time, Thord, that you have come here on your son's account."

"But now I am through with him," said Thord, and folding up his pocket-book he said farewell and walked away.

The men slowly followed him.

A fortnight later, the father and son were rowing across the lake, one calm, still day, to Storliden to make arrangements for the wedding.

"This thwart[2] is not secure," said the son, and stood up to straighten the seat on which he was sitting.

At the same moment the board he was standing on slipped from under him; he threw out his arms, uttered a shriek, and fell overboard.

"Take hold of the oar!" shouted the father, springing to his feet, and holding out the oar.

But when the son had made a couple of efforts he grew stiff.

"Wait a moment!" cried the father, and began to row toward his son.

Then the son rolled over on his back, gave his father one long look, and sank.

Thord could scarcely believe it; he held the boat still, and stared at the spot where his son had gone down, as though he must surely come to the surface again. There rose some bubbles, then some more, and finally one large one that burst; and the lake lay there as smooth and bright as a mirror again.

For three days and three nights people saw the father rowing round and round the spot, without taking either food or sleep; he was dragging the lake for the body of his son. And toward morning of the third day he found it, and carried it in his arms up over the hills to his gard[3].

It might have been about a year from that day, when the priest, late one autumn evening, heard some one in the passage outside of the door, carefully trying to find the latch. The priest opened the door, and in walked a tall, thin man, with bowed form and white hair. The priest looked long at him before he recognized him. It was Thord.

"Are you out walking so late?" said the priest, and stood still in front of him.

"Ah, yes! it is late," said Thord, and took a seat.

The priest sat down also, as though waiting. A long, long silence followed. At last Thord said,—

"I have something with me that I should like to give to the poor; I want it to be invested as a legacy in my son's name."

He rose, laid some money on the table, and sat down again. The priest counted it.

"It is a great deal of money," said he.

"It is half the price of my gard. I sold it to-day."

The priest sat long in silence. At last he asked, but gently,—

"What do you propose to do now, Thord?"

"Something better."

They sat there for a while, Thord with downcast eyes, the priest with his eyes fixed on Thord. Presently the priest said, slowly and softly,—

"I think your son has at last brought you a true blessing."

"Yes, I think so myself," said Thord, looking up, while two big tears coursed slowly down his cheeks.


# NOTES


[1] This story was written in 1860. Translated from the Norwegian by Professor Rasmus B. Anderson. It is printed by permission of and special arrangement with *Houghton Mifflin Co.*, publishers.

[2] 3:28 thwart. A seat, across a boat, on which the oarsman, sits.

[3] 4:21 gard. A Norwegian farm.

# BIOGRAPHY

Björnstjerne Björnson, Norse poet, novelist, dramatist, orator, and political leader, was born December 8, 1832, and died in Paris, April 26, 1910. From his strenuous father, a Lutheran priest who preached with tongue and fist, he inherited the physique of a Norse god. He possessed the mind of a poet and the arm of a warrior. At the age of twelve he was sent to the Molde grammar school, where he proved himself a very dull student. In 1852 he entered the university in Christiana. Here he neglected his studies to write poetry and journalistic articles.

In politics Björnson was a tremendous force. Dr. Brandes has said; "To speak the name of Björnson is like hoisting the colors of Norway." He was honored as a king in his native land. He won this recognition by no party affiliation, but by his natural gifts as a poet. His magnetic eloquence, great message, and sterling character compelled his countrymen to follow and honor him. He says of his success in this field: "The secret with me is that in success as in failure, in the consciousness of my doing as in my habits, I am myself. There are a great many who dare not, or lack the ability, to be themselves." For his views on political issues the following references may well be used: *Independent.* January 31, 1901, pp. 253-257; *Current Literature*, November, 1906, p. 581; and *Independent*, July 13, 1905, pp. 92-94.

Björnson and Ibsen, the two foremost men of Norway, were very closely associated throughout life. They were schoolmates, and both were interested in writing and producing plays. Ibsen's son, Dr. Sigurd Ibsen, married Björnson's daughter, Bergilot. These two great writers were direct contrasts in nearly everything: Björnson lived among his people, Ibsen was reserved; Björnson played the rôle of an optimistic prophet, Ibsen, that of a pessimistic judge; the former was always a conciliatory spirit, the latter a revolutionist; and Björnson proved himself a patriotic Norwegian, Ibsen, a man of the entire world.

Lack of space forbids the inclusion of a list of Björnson's writing's. High school teachers will find suitable selections in the list of collateral readings that follows. Those who wish a complete bibliography of his works will find it in *Bookman*, Volume II, p. 65. Translations of his works by Rasmus B. Anderson, Houghton Mifflin Co., and Edmund Gosse, the Macmillan Co., will furnish students extensive and standard readings of this master story-teller.

# CRITICISMS

Björnson, in his masterly character delineations, seldom produces portraits. He gives the reader suggestive glimpses often enough and of the right quality and arrangement to produce a full and vigorous conception of his characters. His female parts are especially well done. His characters present themselves to the reader by unique thinking and choice expressions. Students should analyze *The Father* for this phase of character building. Note also the simplicity of the words, sentences, paragraphs, and complete story arrangement, the author's originality of story conception and expression, his short, passionate, panting sentences, the poetic atmosphere that sweetens and enriches his virile writing, and the correct, religious pictures he paints of his beloved northland.

After having read a number of selections from Björnson, students will see that he has a wonderful breadth of treatment for every imaginable subject. He is so universal in his choice of subjects that Lemaître in his *Impressions of the Theatre* half-humorously and half-ironically puts these words in Björnson's mouth, "I am king in the spiritual kingdom," and "there are two men in Europe who have genius, I and Ibsen, granting that Ibsen has it."

# GENERAL REFERENCES

*Adventures in Criticism*, A.T.Q. Couch.
*Essays on Modern Novelists*, William Lyon Phelps.
"Björnsoniana," *Dial*, January 16, 1903, pp. 37-38.
"Prophet-Poet of Norway," *Cosmopolitan*, April, 1903, pp. 621-631.
"Three Score and Ten," *Dial*, December, 1902, pp. 383-385.

# COLLATERAL READINGS

*Lectures*, Volume I, John L. Stoddard.
*The Making of an American*, Chapters 1, 7, and Jacob Riis.
*Myths of Northern Lands*. Guerber.
*Synnove Solbakken*, Björnson.
*A Happy Boy*, Björnson.
*The Fisher Maiden*, Björnson.
*The Bridal March*, Björnson.
*Magnhild*, Björnson.
*A Dangerous Wooing*, Björnson.
*The Eagle's Nest*, Björnson.
*The Bear Hunter*, Björnson.
*Master and Man*, Leo Tolstoi.
*The Doll's House*, Henrik Ibsen.
*The Minister's Black Veil*, Nathaniel Hawthorne.
*The Ambitious Guest*, Nathaniel Hawthorne.
*The Beeman of Orn*, Frank R. Stockton.
*A Branch Road*, Hamlin Garland.
*Mateo Falcone*, Prosper Mérimée.
*The Death of the Dauphin*, Alphonse Dadoed.
*The Birds' Christmas Carol*, Kate Douglas Wiggin.
*Tennessee's Partner*, Bret Harte.

# THE GRIFFIN AND THE MINOR CANAAN[1]

*By Frank R. Stockton (1834-1902)*

Over the great door of an old, old church which stood in a quiet town of a far-away land there was carved in stone the figure of a large griffin. The old-time sculptor had done his work with great care, but the image he had made was not a pleasant one to look at. It had a large head, with enormous open mouth and savage teeth; from its back arose great wings, armed with sharp hooks and prongs; it had stout legs in front, with projecting claws; but there were no legs behind,—the body running out into a long and powerful tail, finished off at the end with a barbed point. This tail was coiled up under him, the end sticking up just back of his wings.

The sculptor, or the people who had ordered this stone figure, had evidently been very much pleased with it, for little copies of it, also in stone, had been placed here and there along the sides of the church, not very far from the ground, so that people could easily look at them, and ponder on their curious forms. There were a great many other sculptures on the outside of this church,—saints, martyrs, grotesque heads of men, beasts, and birds, as well as those of other creatures which cannot be named, because nobody knows exactly what they were; but none were so curious and interesting as the great griffin over the door, and the little griffins on the sides of the church.

A long, long distance from the town, in the midst of dreadful wilds scarcely known to man, there dwelt the Griffin whose image had been put up over the churchgoer. In some way or other, the old-time sculptor had seen him, and afterward, to the best of his memory, had copied his figure in stone. The Griffin had never known this, until, hundreds of years afterward, he heard from a bird, from a wild animal, or in some manner which it is not now easy to find out, that there was a likeness of him on the old church in the distant town. Now this Griffin had no idea how he looked. He had never seen a mirror, and the streams where he lived were so turbulent and violent that a quiet piece of water, which would reflect the image of anything looking into it, could not be found. Being, as far as could be ascertained, the very last of his race, he had never seen another griffin. Therefore it was, that, when he heard of this stone image of himself, he became very anxious to know what he looked like, and at last he determined to go to the old church, and see for himself what manner of being he was. So he started off from the dreadful wilds, and flew on and on until he came to the countries inhabited by men, where his appearance in the air created great consternation; but he alighted nowhere, keeping up a steady flight until he reached the suburbs of the town which had his image on its church. Here, late in the afternoon, he alighted in a green meadow by the side of a brook, and stretched himself on the grass to rest. His great wings were tired, for he had not made such a long flight in a century, or more.

The news of his coming spread quickly over the town, and the people, frightened nearly out of their wits by the arrival of so extraordinary a visitor, fled into their houses, and shut themselves up. The Griffin called loudly for some one to come to him, but the more he called, the more afraid the people were to show themselves. At length he saw two laborers hurrying to their homes through the fields, and in a terrible voice he commanded them to stop. Not daring to disobey, the men stood, trembling.

"What is the matter with you all?" cried the Griffin. "Is there not a man in your town who is brave enough to speak to me?"

"I think," said one of the laborers, his voice shaking so that his words could hardly be understood, "that—perhaps—the Minor Canon—would come."

"Go, call him, then!" said the Griffin; "I want to see him."

The Minor Canon, who filled a subordinate position in the church, had just finished the afternoon services, and was coming out of a side door, with three aged women who had formed the week-day congregation. He was a young man of a kind disposition, and very anxious to do good to the people of the town. Apart from his duties in the church, where he conducted services every week-day, he visited the sick and the poor, counseled and assisted persons who were in trouble, and taught a school composed entirely of the bad children in the town with whom nobody else would have anything to do. Whenever the people wanted something difficult done for them, they always went to the Minor Canon. Thus it was that the laborer thought of the young priest when he found that some one must come and speak to the Griffin.

The Minor Canon had not heard of the strange event, which was known to the whole town except himself and the three old women, and when he was informed of it, and was told that the Griffin had asked to see him, he was greatly amazed, and frightened.

"Me!" he exclaimed. "He has never heard of me! What should he want with *me?*"

"Oh! you must go instantly!" cried the two men.

"He is very angry now because he has been kept waiting so long; and nobody knows what may happen if you don't hurry to him."

The poor Minor Canon would rather have had his hand cut off than go out to meet an angry griffin; but he felt that it was his duty to go, or it would be a woeful thing if injury should come to the people of the town because he was not brave enough to obey the summons of the Griffin.

So, pale and frightened, he started off.

"Well," said the Griffin, as soon as the young man came near, "I am glad to see that there is some one who has the courage to come to me."

The Minor Canon did not feel very courageous, but he bowed his head.

"Is this the town," said the Griffin, "where there is a church with a likeness of myself over one of the doors?"

The Minor Canon looked at the frightful creature before him and saw that it was, without doubt, exactly like the stone image on the church. "Yes," he said, "you are right."

"Well, then," said the Griffin, "will you take me to it? I wish very much to see it."

The Minor Canon instantly thought that if the Griffin entered the town without the people knowing what he came for, some of them would probably be frightened to death, and so he sought to gain time to prepare their minds.

"It is growing dark, now," he said, very much afraid, as he spoke, that his words might enrage the Griffin, "and objects on the front of the church cannot be seen clearly. It will be better to wait until morning, if you wish to get a good view of the stone image of yourself."

"That will suit me very well," said the Griffin. "I see you are a man of good sense. I am tired, and I will take a nap here on this soft grass, while I cool my tail in the little stream that runs near me. The end of my tail gets red-hot when I am angry or excited, and it is quite warm now. So you may go, but be sure and come early to-morrow morning, and show me the way to the church."

The Minor Canon was glad enough to take his leave, and hurried into the town. In front of the church he found a great many people assembled to hear his report of his interview with the Griffin. When they found that he had not come to spread ruin and devastation, but simply to see his stony likeness on the church, they showed neither relief nor gratification, but began to upbraid the Minor Canon for consenting to conduct the creature into the town.

"What could I do?" cried the young man, "If I should not bring him he would come himself and, perhaps, end by setting fire to the town with his red-hot tail."

Still the people were not satisfied, and a great many plans were proposed to prevent the Griffin from coming into the town. Some elderly persons urged that the young men should go out and kill him; but the young men scoffed at such a ridiculous idea. Then some one said that it would be a good thing to destroy the stone image so that the Griffin would have no excuse for entering the town; and this proposal was received with such favor that many of the people ran for hammers, chisels, and crowbars, with which to tear down and break up the stone griffin. But the Minor Canon resisted this plan with all the strength of his mind and body. He assured the people that this action would enrage the Griffin beyond measure, for it would be impossible to conceal from him that his image had been destroyed during the night. But the people were so determined to break up the stone griffin that the Minor Canon saw that there was nothing for him to do but to stay there and protect it. All night he walked up and down in front of the church-door, keeping away the men who brought ladders, by which they might mount to the great stone griffin, and knock it to pieces with their hammers and crowbars. After many hours the people were obliged to give up their attempts, and went home to sleep; but the Minor Canon remained at his post till early morning, and then he hurried away to the field where he had left the Griffin.

The monster had just awakened, and rising to his fore-legs and shaking himself, he said that he was ready to go into the town. The Minor Canon, therefore, walked back, the Griffin flying slowly through the air, at a short distance above the head of his guide. Not a person was to be seen in the streets, and they proceeded directly to the front of the church, where the Minor Canon pointed out the stone griffin.

The real Griffin settled down in the little square before the church and gazed earnestly at his sculptured likeness. For a long time he looked at it. First he put his head on one side, and then he put it on the other; then he shut his right eye and gazed with his left, after which he shut his left eye and gazed with his right. Then he moved a little to one side and looked at the image, then he moved the other way. After a while he said to the Minor Canon, who had been standing by all this time:

"It is, it must be, an excellent likeness! That breadth between the eyes, that expansive forehead, those massive jaws! I feel that it must resemble me. If there is any fault to find with it, it is that the neck seems a little stiff. But that is nothing. It is an admirable likeness,—admirable!"

The Griffin sat looking at his image all the morning and all the afternoon. The Minor Canon had been afraid to go away and leave him, and had hoped all through the day that he would soon be satisfied with his inspection and fly away home. But by evening the poor young man was utterly exhausted, and felt that he must eat and sleep. He frankly admitted this fact to the Griffin, and asked him if he would not like something to eat. He said this because he felt obliged in politeness to do so, but as soon as he had spoken the words, he was seized with dread lest the monster should demand half a dozen babies, or some tempting repast of that kind.

"Oh, no," said the Griffin, "I never eat between the equinoxes. At the vernal and at the autumnal equinox I take a good meal, and that lasts me for half a year. I am extremely regular in my habits, and do not think it healthful to eat at odd times. But if you need food, go and get it, and I will return to the soft grass where I slept last night and take another nap."

The next day the Griffin came again to the little square before the church, and remained there until evening, steadfastly regarding the stone griffin over the door. The Minor Canon came once or twice to look at him, and the Griffin seemed very glad to see him; but the young clergyman could not stay as he had done before, for he had many duties to perform. Nobody went to the church, but the people came to the Minor Canon's house, and anxiously asked him how long the Griffin was going to stay.

"I do not know," he answered, "but I think he will soon be satisfied with regarding his stone likeness, and then he will go away."

But the Griffin did not go away. Morning after morning he came to the church, but after a time he did not stay there all day. He seemed to have taken a great fancy to the Minor Canon, and followed him about as he pursued his various avocations. He would wait for him at the side door of the church, for the Minor Canon held services every day, morning and evening, though nobody came now. "If any one should come," he said to himself, "I must be found at my post." When the young man came out, the Griffin would accompany him in his visits to the sick and the poor, and would often look into the windows of the schoolhouse where the Minor Canon was teaching his unruly scholars. All the other schools were closed, but the parents of the Minor Canon's scholars forced them to go to school, because they were so bad they could not endure them all day at home,— griffin or no griffin. But it must be said they generally behaved very well when that great monster sat up on his tail and looked in at the schoolroom window.

When it was perceived that the Griffin showed no signs of going away, all the people who were able to do so left the town. The canons and the higher officers of the church had fled away during the first day of the Griffin's visit, leaving behind only the Minor Canon and some of the men who opened the doors and swept the church. All the citizens who could afford it shut up their houses and travelled to distant parts, and only the working people and the poor were left behind. After some days these ventured to go about and attend to their business, for if they did not work they would starve. They were getting a little used to seeing the Griffin, and having been told that he did not eat between equinoxes, they did not feel so much afraid of him as before. Day by day the Griffin became more and more attached to the Minor Canon. He kept near him a great part of the time, and often spent the night in front of the little house where the young clergyman lived alone. This strange companionship was often burdensome to the Minor Canon; but, on the other hand, he could not deny that he derived a great deal of benefit and instruction from it. The Griffin had lived for hundreds of years, and had seen much; and he told the Minor Canon many wonderful things.

"It is like reading an old book," said the young clergyman to himself; "but how many books I would have had to read before I would have found out what the Griffin has told me about the earth, the air, the water, about minerals, and metals, and growing things, and all the wonders of the world!"

Thus the summer went on, and drew toward its close. And now the people of the town began to be very much troubled again.

"It will not be long," they said, "before the autumnal equinox is here, and then that monster will want to eat. He will be dreadfully hungry, for he has taken so much exercise since his last meal. He will devour our children. Without doubt, he will eat them all. What is to be done?"

To this question no one could give an answer, but all agreed that the Griffin must not be allowed to remain until the approaching equinox. After talking over the matter a great deal, a crowd of the people went to the Minor Canon, at a time when the Griffin was not with him.

"It is all your fault," they said, "that that monster is among us. You brought him here, and you ought to see that he goes away. It is only on your account that he stays here at all, for, although he visits his image every day, he is with you the greater part of the time. If you were not here, he would not stay. It is your duty to go away and then he will follow you, and we shall be free from the dreadful danger which hangs over us."

"Go away!" cried the Minor Canon, greatly grieved at being spoken to in such a way. "Where shall I go? If I go to some other town, shall I not take this trouble there? Have I a right to do that?"

"No," said the people, "you must not go to any other town. There is no town far enough away. You must go to the dreadful wilds where the Griffin lives; and then he will follow you and stay there."

They did not say whether or not they expected the Minor Canon to stay there also, and he did not ask them any thing about it. He bowed his head, and went into his house, to think. The more he thought, the more clear it became to his mind that it was his duty to go away, and thus free the town from the presence of the Griffin.

That evening he packed a leathern bag full of bread and meat, and early the next morning he set out on his journey to the dreadful wilds. It was a long, weary, and doleful journey, especially after he had gone beyond the habitations of men, but the Minor Canon kept on bravely, and never faltered. The way was longer than he had expected, and his provisions soon grew so scanty that he was obliged to eat but a little every day, but he kept up his courage, and pressed on, and, after many days of toilsome travel, he reached the dreadful wilds.

When the Griffin found that the Minor Canon had left the town he seemed sorry, but showed no disposition to go and look for him. After a few days had passed, he became much annoyed, and asked some of the people where the Minor Canon had gone. But, although the citizens had been anxious that the young clergyman should go to the dreadful wilds, thinking that the Griffin would immediately follow him, they were now afraid to mention the Minor Canon's destination, for the monster seemed angry already, and, if he should suspect their trick, he would doubtless become very much enraged. So every one said he did not know, and the Griffin wandered about disconsolate. One morning he looked into the Minor Canon's schoolhouse, which was always empty now, and thought that it was a shame that every thing should suffer on account of the young man's absence.

"It does not matter so much about the church," he said, "for nobody went there; but it is a pity about the school. I think I will teach it myself until he returns."

It was the hour for opening the school, and the Griffin went inside and pulled the rope which rang the schoolbell. Some of the children who heard the bell ran in to see what was the matter, supposing it to be a joke of one of their companions; but when they saw the Griffin they stood astonished, and scared.

"Go tell the other scholars," said the monster, "that school is about to open, and that if they are not all here in ten minutes, I shall come after them." In seven minutes every scholar was in place.

Never was seen such an orderly school. Not a boy or girl moved, or uttered a whisper. The Griffin climbed into the master's seat, his wide wings spread on each side of him, because he could not lean back in his chair while they stuck out behind, and his great tail coiled around, in front of the desk, the barbed end sticking up, ready to tap any boy or girl who might misbehave. The Griffin now addressed the scholars, telling them that he intended to teach them while their master was away. In speaking he endeavored to imitate, as far as possible, the mild and gentle tones of the Minor Canon, but it must be admitted that in this he was not very successful. He had paid a good deal of attention to the studies of the school, and he determined not to attempt to teach them anything new, but to review them in what they had been studying; so he called up the various classes, and questioned them upon their previous lessons. The children racked their brains to remember what they had learned. They were so afraid of the Griffin's displeasure that they recited as they had never recited before. One of the boys far down in his class answered so well that the Griffin was astonished.

"I should think you would be at the head," said he. "I am sure you have never been in the habit of reciting so well. Why is this?"

"Because I did not choose to take the trouble," said the boy, trembling in his boots. He felt obliged to speak the truth, for all the children thought that the great eyes of the Griffin could see right through them, and that he would know when they told a falsehood.

"You ought to be ashamed of yourself," said the Griffin. "Go down to the very tail of the class, and if you are not at the head in two days, I shall know the reason why."

The next afternoon the boy was number one.

It was astonishing how much these children now learned of what they had been studying. It was as if they had been educated over again. The Griffin used no severity toward them, but there was a look about him which made them unwilling to go to bed until they were sure they knew their lessons for the next day.

The Griffin now thought that he ought to visit the sick and the poor; and he began to go about the town for this purpose. The effect upon the sick was miraculous. All, except those who were very ill indeed, jumped from their beds when they heard he was coming, and declared themselves quite well. To those who could not get up, he gave herbs and roots, which none of them had ever before thought of as medicines, but which the Griffin had seen used in various parts of the world; and most of them recovered. But, for all that, they afterward said that no matter what happened to them, they hoped that they should never again have such a doctor coming to their bedsides, feeling their pulses and looking at their tongues.

As for the poor, they seemed to have utterly disappeared. All those who had depended upon charity for their daily bread were now at work in some way or other; many of them offering to do odd jobs for their neighbors just for the sake of their meals,—a thing which before had been seldom heard of in the town. The Griffin could find no one who needed his assistance.

The summer had now passed, and the autumnal equinox was rapidly approaching. The citizens were in a state of great alarm and anxiety. The Griffin showed no signs of going away, but seemed to have settled himself permanently among them. In a short time, the day for his semi-annual meal would arrive, and then what would happen? The monster would certainly be very hungry, and would devour all their children.

Now they greatly regretted and lamented that they had sent away the Minor Canon; he was the only one on whom they could have depended in this trouble, for he could talk freely with the Griffin, and so find out what could be done. But it would not do to be inactive. Some step must be taken immediately. A meeting of the citizens was called, and two old men were appointed to go and talk to the Griffin. They were instructed to offer to prepare a splendid dinner for him on equinox day,—one which would entirely satisfy his hunger. They would offer him the fattest mutton, the most tender beef, fish, and game of various sorts, and any thing of the kind that he might fancy. If none of these suited, they were to mention that there was an orphan asylum in the next town.

"Any thing would be better," said the citizens, "than to have our dear children devoured."

The old men went to the Griffin, but their propositions were not received with favor.

"From what I have seen of the people of this town," said the monster, "I do not think I could relish any thing which was prepared by them. They appear to be all cowards, and, therefore, mean and selfish. As for eating one of them, old or young, I could not think of it for a moment. In fact, there was only one creature in the whole place for whom I could have had any appetite, and that is the Minor Canon, who has gone away. He was brave, and good, and honest, and I think I should have relished him."

"Ah!" said one of the old men very politely, "in that case I wish we had not sent him to the dreadful wilds!"

"What!" cried the Griffin. "What do you mean? Explain instantly what you are talking about!"

The old man, terribly frightened at what he had said, was obliged to tell how the Minor Canon had been sent away by the people, in the hope that the Griffin might be induced to follow him.

When the monster heard this, he became furiously angry. He dashed away from the old men and, spreading his wings, flew backward and forward over the town. He was so much excited that his tail became red-hot, and glowed like a meteor against the evening sky. When at last he settled down in the little field where he usually rested, and thrust his tail into the brook, the steam arose like a cloud, and the water of the stream ran hot through the town. The citizens were greatly frightened, and bitterly blamed the old man for telling about the Minor Canon.

"It is plain," they said, "that the Griffin intended at last to go and look for him, and we should have been saved. Now who can tell what misery you have brought upon us."

The Griffin did not remain long in the little field. As soon as his tail was cool he flew to the town-hall and rang the bell. The citizens knew that they were expected to come there, and although they were afraid to go, they were still more afraid to stay away; and they crowded into the hall. The Griffin was on the platform at one end, flapping his wings and walking up and down, and the end of his tail was still so warm that it slightly scorched the boards as he dragged it after him.

When everybody who was able to come was there the Griffin stood still and addressed the meeting.

"I have had a contemptible opinion of you," he said, "ever since I discovered what cowards you are, but I had no idea that you were so ungrateful, selfish, and cruel as I now find you to be. Here was your Minor Canon, who labored day and night for your good, and thought of nothing else but how he might benefit you and make you happy; and as soon as you imagine yourselves threatened with a danger,—for well I know you are dreadfully afraid of me,—you send him off, caring not whether he returns or perishes, hoping thereby to save yourselves. Now, I had conceived a great liking for that young man, and had intended, in a day or two, to go and look him up. But I have changed my mind about him. I shall go and find him, but I shall send him back here to live among you, and I intend that he shall enjoy the reward of his labor and his sacrifices. Go, some of you, to the officers of the church, who so cowardly ran away when I first came here, and tell them never to return to this town under penalty of death. And if, when your Minor Canon comes back to you, you do not bow yourselves before him, put him in the highest place among you, and serve and honor him all his life, beware of my terrible vengeance! There were only two good things in this town: the Minor Canon and the stone image of myself over your church-door. One of these you have sent away, and the other I shall carry away myself."

With these words he dismissed the meeting, and it was time, for the end of his tail had become so hot that there was danger of its setting fire to the building.

The next morning, the Griffin came to the church, and tearing the stone image of himself from its fastenings over the great door, he grasped it with his powerful fore-legs and flew up into the air. Then, after hovering over the town for a moment, he gave his tail an angry shake and took up his flight to the dreadful wilds. When he reached this desolate region, he set the stone Griffin upon a ledge of a rock which rose in front of the dismal cave he called his home. There the image occupied a position somewhat similar to that it had had over the church-door; and the Griffin, panting with the exertion of carrying such an enormous load to so great a distance, lay down upon the ground, and regarded it with much satisfaction. When he felt somewhat rested he went to look for the Minor Canon. He found the young man, weak and half-starved, lying under the shadow of a rock. After picking him up and carrying him to his cave, the Griffin flew away to a distant marsh, where he procured some roots and herbs which he well knew were strengthening and beneficial to man, though he had never tasted them himself. After eating these the Minor Canon was greatly revived, and sat up and listened while the Griffin told him what had happened in the town.

"Do you know," said the monster, when he had finished, "that I have had, and still have, a great liking for you?"

"I am very glad to hear it," said the Minor Canon, with his usual politeness.

"I am not at all sure that you would be," said the Griffin, "if you thoroughly understood the state of the case, but we will not consider that now. If some things were different, other things would be otherwise. I have been so enraged by discovering the manner in which you have been treated that I have determined that you shall at last enjoy the rewards and honors to which you are entitled. Lie down and have a good sleep, and then I will take you back to the town."

As he heard these words, a look of trouble came over the young man's face. "You need not give yourself any anxiety," said the Griffin, "about my return to the town. I shall not remain there. Now that I have that admirable likeness of myself in front of my cave, where I can sit at my leisure, and gaze upon its noble features and magnificent proportions, I have no wish to see that abode of cowardly and selfish people."

The Minor Canon, relieved from his fears, lay back, and dropped into a doze; and when he was sound asleep the Griffin took him up, and carried him back to the town. He arrived just before daybreak, and putting the young man gently on the grass in the little field where he himself used to rest, the monster, without having been seen by any of the people, flew back to his home.

When the Minor Canon made his appearance in the morning among the citizens, the enthusiasm and cordiality with which he was received were truly wonderful. He was taken to a house which had been occupied by one of the vanished high officers of the place, and every one was anxious to do all that could be done for his health and comfort. The people crowded into the church when he held services, so that the three old women who used to be his week-day congregation could not get to the best seats, which they had always been in the habit of taking; and the parents of the bad children determined to reform them at home, in order that he might be spared the trouble of keeping up his former school. The Minor Canon was appointed to the highest office of the old church, and before he died, he became a bishop.

During the first years after his return from the dreadful wilds, the people of the town looked up to him as a man to whom they were bound to do honor and reverence; but they often, also, looked up to the sky to see if there were any signs of the Griffin coming back. However, in the course of time, they learned to honor and reverence their former Minor Canon without the fear of being punished if they did not do so.

But they need never have been afraid of the Griffin. The autumnal equinox day came round, and the monster ate nothing. If he could not have the Minor Canon, he did not care for any thing. So, lying down, with his eyes fixed upon the great stone griffin, he gradually declined, and died. It was a good thing for some people of the town that they did not know this.

If you should ever visit the old town, you would still see the little griffins on the sides of the church; but the great stone griffin that was over the door is gone.

NOTE: [1] Written in 1887. This story is used by permission of and special arrangement with *Charles Scribner's Sons*, publishers.

# BIOGRAPHY

Frank Richard Stockton, one of America's foremost story-tellers and humorists, was born in Philadelphia in 1834. His father was a Presbyterian minister who devoutly wished that his son might study medicine. This wish was shattered early, for the son showed symptoms of being a writer while yet in the Central High School of Philadelphia. In competition with many of his schoolmates for a prize offered for the best story, young Stockton won easily.

After finishing his high school course, he adopted the profession of wood-engraver. Although he earned his living for several years by carving wood, he never lost his desire to write, and practised, at every spare moment, his favorite avocation. It was this careful and patient training during his apprenticeship that finally made him the expert story-teller that he is. It is very interesting to any one who cares for the acquirement of an excellent style to note how all the authors contained in this text have had to work with almost a superhuman force to reach the heights of successful short-story writing.

His first important publication, *Kate*, appeared in the *Southern Literary Messenger* in 1859. He then joined the staff of the *Philadelphia Morning Post*, where he did regular newspaper work and contributed to the *Riverside Magazine* and *Hearth and Home*. In 1872 his *Stephen Skarridge's Christmas* appeared in *Scribner's Monthly*. Dr. J.G. Holland, editor of *Scribner's*, was so impressed with the story that he made Mr. Stockton an assistant editor and persuaded him to move to New York. In 1873 he joined the staff of the *St. Nicholas Magazine*. His publication of the *Rudder Grange* series in *Scribner's Monthly* in 1878 made him famous. In 1882 he resigned all editorial work and spent his entire time in literary composition.

Mr. Stockton possessed a frail body and very little physical endurance. In spite of this physical handicap he was very vivacious and gay. He was a genial and companionable man, loved by all who knew him. He was very modest, even to the point of shyness, exceptionally sincere, and quaintly humorous. He established homes in New Jersey and West Virginia, where he spent the greater part of his time from 1882 until his death in 1902.

# BIOGRAPHICAL REFERENCES

*Famous Authors* (107-122), B.F. Harkness.
*American Authors* (59-73), F.W. Halsey.
"Character Sketch," *Book-Buyer*, 24:355-357.
"Home at Claymont," *Current Literature*, 30:221.
"Sketch," *Outlook*, 70: 1000-1001,
"Stockton and his Work," *Atlantic Monthly*, 87:136-138.

# CRITICISMS

The writings of Frank R. Stockton are excellent representatives of the man himself. How closely allied writer and writings are is very well stated by Hamilton W. Mabie in the *Book-Buyer* for June, 1902, "His talk had much of the quality of his writing; it was full of quaint conceits, whimsicalities, impossible suggestions offered with perfect gravity. He was always perfectly natural; he never attempted to live up to his part; in talk, at least, he never forced the note. His attitude toward himself was slightly tinged with humor, and he knew how to foil easily and pleasantly too great a pressure of praise."

His tales are extravagantly impossible but extremely realistic in effect, filled with humorous situations and singular plots, and peopled with eccentric characters that afford amusement on every page. His most successful writing is done when he explains contrivances upon which his story depends. He is an original and inventive expert juggler who moves with careless ease to the most effective ends. His characters are little more than pieces of mechanism that act when he pulls the string. They have little emotion and even in their love-making they show their emotion mostly for the sake of the reader's amusement. His negro characters are exceptions to his general treatment and are true to life. He inveigles the reader into believing the most extravagant incidents by having a reliable witness narrate them.

Stockton never stoops to the burlesque, cynic, or vulgar phases of life to secure amusement. He is grotesque and droll in his manner, and above all always restrained. His literary life is full of sprites and gnomes that frolic before young children and once before mature people. *The Griffin and the Minor Canon* is a beautiful fairy story lifted from childhood's thought and diction into a mature realm. His humor is plain and simple, cool and keenly calculating. A friendly critic has said of one of his stories, "With a gentle, ceaseless murmur of amusement, and a flickering twinkle of smiles, the story moves steadily on in the calm triumph of its assured and unassailable absurdity, to its logical and indisputable impossibility." This observation is very largely true of all his stories.

# GENERAL REFERENCES

*Frank R. Stockton*, A.T.Q. Couch.
"Stockton's Method of Working," *Current Literature*, 32:495.
"Criticism," *Atheneum*, 1:532.
"Estimate," *Harper's Weekly*, 46:555.

# COLLATERAL READINGS

*The Beeman of Orn, and Other Fanciful Tales*, Frank R. Stockton.
*The Lady or the Tiger*, Frank R. Stockton.
*Rudder Grange*, Frank R. Stockton.
*A Tale of Negative Gravity*, Frank R. Stockton.
*The Remarkable Wreck of the Thomas Hyde*, Frank R. Stockton.
*His Wife's Deceased Sister*, Frank R. Stockton.
*Legend of Sleepy Hollow*, Washington Irving.
*Monsieur du Miroir*, Nathaniel Hawthorne.
*At the End of the Passage*, Rudyard Kipling.
*The Vacant Lot*, Mary Wilkins Freeman.
*The Princess Pourquoi*, Margaret Sherwood.
*What Was It? A Mystery*, Fitz-James O'Brien.
*Wandering Willie's Tale*, Walter Scott.

# THE PIECE OF STRING[1]

*By Guy de Maupassant (1850-1893)*
On all the roads about Goderville the peasants and their wives were coming toward the town, for it was market day. The men walked at an easy gait, the whole body thrown forward with every movement of their long, crooked legs, misshapen by hard work, by the bearing down on the plough which at the same time causes the left shoulder to rise and the figure to slant; by the mowing of the grain, which makes one hold his knees apart in order to obtain a firm footing; by all the slow and laborious tasks of the fields. Their starched blue blouses, glossy as if varnished, adorned at the neck and wrists with a bit of white stitchwork, puffed out about their bony chests like balloons on the point of taking flight, from which protrude a head, two arms, and two feet.

Some of them led a cow or a calf at the end of a rope. And their wives, walking behind the beast, lashed it with a branch still covered with leaves, to hasten its pace. They carried on their arms great baskets, from which heads of chickens or of ducks were thrust forth. And they walked with a shorter and quicker step than their men, their stiff, lean figures wrapped in scanty shawls pinned over their flat breasts, their heads enveloped in a white linen cloth close to the hair, with a cap over all.

Then a *char-à-bancs[2]* passed, drawn by a jerky-paced nag, with two men seated side by side shaking like jelly, and a woman behind, who clung to the side of the vehicle to lessen the rough jolting.

On the square at Goderville there was a crowd, a medley of men and beasts. The horns of the cattle, the high hats, with a long, hairy nap, of the wealthy peasants, and the head dresses of the peasant women, appeared on the surface of the throng. And the sharp, shrill, high-pitched voices formed an incessant, uncivilized uproar, over which soared at times a roar of laughter from the powerful chest of a sturdy yokel, or the prolonged bellow of a cow fastened to the wall of a house.

There was an all-pervading smell of the stable, of milk, of the dunghill, of hay, and of perspiration—that acrid, disgusting odor of man and beast peculiar to country people.

Master Hauchecorne, of Bréauté, had just arrived at Goderville, and was walking toward the square, when he saw a bit of string on the ground. Master Hauchecorne, economical like every true Norman, thought that it was well to pick up everything that might be of use; and he stooped painfully, for he suffered with rheumatism. He took the piece of slender cord from the ground, and was about to roll it up carefully, when he saw Master Malandain, the harness-maker, standing in his doorway and looking at him. They had formerly had trouble on the subject of a halter, and had remained at odds, being both inclined to bear malice. Master Hauchecorne felt a sort of shame at being seen thus by his enemy, fumbling in the mud for a bit of string. He hurriedly concealed his treasure in his blouse, then in his breeches pocket; then he pretended to look on the ground for something else, which he did not find; and finally he went on toward the market, his head thrust forward, bent double by his pains.

He lost himself at once in the slow-moving, shouting crowd, kept in a state of excitement by the interminable bargaining. The peasants felt of the cows, went away, returned, sorely perplexed, always afraid of being cheated, never daring to make up their minds, watching the vendor's eye, striving incessantly to detect the tricks of the man and the defect in the beast.

The women, having placed their great baskets at their feet, took out their fowls, which lay on the ground, their legs tied together, with frightened eyes and scarlet combs.

They listened to offers, adhered to their prices, short of speech and impassive of face; or else, suddenly deciding to accept the lower price offered, they would call out to the customer as he walked slowly away:— "All right, Mast' Anthime. You can have it."

Then, little by little, the square became empty, and when the Angelus[3] struck midday those who lived too far away to go home betook themselves to the various inns.

At Jourdain's the common room was full of customers, as the great yard was full of vehicles of every sort—carts, cabriolets,[4] *char-à-bancs*, tilburys,[5] unnamable carriages, shapeless, patched, with, their shafts reaching heavenward like arms, or with their noses in the ground and their tails in the air.

The vast fireplace, full of clear flame, cast an intense heat against the backs of the row on the right of the table. Three spits were revolving, laden with chickens, pigeons, and legs of mutton; and a delectable odor of roast meat, and of gravy dripping from the browned skin, came forth from the hearth, stirred the guests to merriment, and made their mouths water.

All the aristocracy of the plough ate there, at Mast' Jourdain's, the innkeeper and horse trader—a shrewd rascal who had money.

The dishes passed and were soon emptied, like the jugs of yellow cider. Every one told of his affairs, his sales and his purchases. They inquired about the crops. The weather was good for green stuffs, but a little wet for wheat.

Suddenly a drum rolled in the yard, in front of the house. In an instant everybody was on his feet, save a few indifferent ones; and they all ran to the door and windows with their mouths still full and napkins in hand.

Having finished his long tattoo, the public crier shouted in a jerky voice, making his pauses in the wrong places:—

"The people of Goderville, and all those present at the market are informed that between—nine and ten o'clock this morning on the Beuzeville—road, a black leather wallet was lost, containing five hundred—francs, and business papers. The finder is requested to carry it to—the mayor's at once, or to Master Fortuné Huelbrèque of Manneville. A reward of twenty francs will be paid."

Then he went away. They heard once more in the distance the muffled roll of the drum and the indistinct voice of the crier.

Then they began to talk about the incident, reckoning Master Houlbrèque's chance of finding or not finding his wallet.

And the meal went on.

They were finishing their coffee when the corporal of gendarmes appeared in the doorway.

He inquired:—

"Is Master Hauchecorne of Bréauté here?"

Master Hauchecorne, who was seated at the farther end of the table, answered:—

"Here I am."

And the corporal added:—

"Master Hauchecorne, will you be kind enough to go to the mayor's office with me? Monsieur the mayor would like to speak to you."

The peasant, surprised and disturbed, drank his *petit verre[6]* at one swallow, rose, and even more bent than in the morning, for the first steps after each rest were particularly painful, he started off, repeating:—

"Here I am, here I am."

And he followed the brigadier.

The mayor was waiting for him, seated in his arm-chair. He was the local notary, a stout, solemn-faced man, given to pompous speeches.

"Master Hauchecorne," he said, "you were seen this morning, on the Beuzeville road, to pick up the wallet lost by Master Huelbrèque of Manneville."

The rustic, dumfounded, stared at the mayor, already alarmed by this suspicion which had fallen upon him, although he failed to understand it.

"I, I—I picked up that wallet?"

"Yes, you."

"On my word of honor, I didn't even so much as see it."

"You were seen."

"They saw me, me? Who was it saw me?"

"Monsieur Malandain, the harness-maker."

Thereupon the old man remembered and understood; and flushing with anger, he cried:—

"Ah! he saw me, did he, that sneak? He saw me pick up this string, look, m'sieu' mayor."

And fumbling in the depths of his pocket, he produced the little piece of cord.

But the mayor was incredulous and shook his head.

"You won't make me believe, Master Hauchecorne, that Monsieur Malandain, who is a man deserving of credit, mistook this string for a wallet."

The peasant, in a rage, raised his hand, spit to one side to pledge his honor, and said:—

"It's God's own truth, the sacred truth, all the same, m'sieu' mayor. I say it again, by my soul and my salvation."

"After picking it up," rejoined the mayor, "you hunted a long while in the mud, to see if some piece of money hadn't fallen out."

The good man was suffocated with wrath and fear.

"If any one can tell—if any one can tell lies like that to ruin an honest man! If any one can say—"

To no purpose did he protest; he was not believed.

He was confronted with Monsieur Malandain, who repeated and maintained his declaration. They insulted each other for a whole hour. At his own request, Master Hauchecorne was searched. They found nothing on him. At last the mayor, being sorely perplexed, discharged him, but warned him that he proposed to inform the prosecuting attorney's office and to ask for orders.

The news had spread. On leaving the mayor's office, the old man was surrounded and questioned with serious or bantering curiosity, in which, however, there was no trace of indignation. And he began to tell the story of the string. They did not believe him. They laughed.

He went his way, stopping his acquaintances, repeating again and again his story and his protestations, showing his pockets turned inside out, to prove that he had nothing.

They said to him:—

"You old rogue, *va!*"

And he lost his temper, lashing himself into a rage, feverish with excitement, desperate because he was not believed, at a loss what to do, and still telling his story. Night came. He must needs go home. He started with three neighbors, to whom he pointed out the place where he had picked up the bit of string: and all the way he talked of his misadventure.

During the evening he made a circuit of the village of Bréauté, in order to tell everybody about it. He found none but incredulous listeners.

He was ill over it all night.

The next afternoon, about one o'clock, Marius Paumelle, a farmhand employed by Master Breton, a farmer of Ymauville, restored the wallet and its contents to Master Huelbrèque of Manneville.

The man claimed that he had found it on the road; but, being unable to read, had carried it home and given it to his employer.

The news soon became known in the neighborhood; Master Hauchecorne was informed of it. He started out again at once, and began to tell his story, now made complete by the dénouement. He was triumphant.

"What made me feel bad," he said, "wasn't so much the thing itself, you understand, but the lying. There's nothing hurts you so much as being blamed for lying."

All day long he talked of his adventure; he told it on the roads to people who passed; at the wine-shop to people who were drinking; and after church on the following Sunday. He even stopped strangers to tell them about it. His mind was at rest now, and yet something embarrassed him, although he could not say just what it was. People seemed to laugh while they listened to him. They did not seem convinced. He felt as if remarks were made behind his back.

On Tuesday of the next week, he went to market at Goderville, impelled solely by the longing to tell his story.

Malandain, standing in his doorway, began to laugh when he saw him coming. Why?

He accosted a farmer from Criquetot, who did not let him finish, but poked him in the pit of his stomach, and shouted in his face: "Go on, you old fox!" Then he turned on his heel.

Master Hauchecorne was speechless, and more and more disturbed. Why did he call him "old fox"?

When he was seated at the table, in Jourdain's Inn, he set about explaining the affair once more.

A horse-trader from Montvilliers called out to him:—

"Nonsense, nonsense, you old dodger! I know all about your string!"

"But they've found the wallet!" faltered Hauchecorne.

"None of that, old boy; there's one who finds it, and there's one who carries it back. I don't know just how you did it, but I understand you."

The peasant was fairly stunned. He understood at last. He was accused of having sent the wallet back by a confederate, an accomplice.

He tried to protest. The whole table began to laugh.

He could not finish his dinner, but left the inn amid a chorus of jeers.

He returned home, shamefaced and indignant, suffocated by wrath, by confusion, and all the more cast down because, with his Norman cunning, he was quite capable of doing the thing with which he was charged, and even of boasting of it as a shrewd trick. He had a confused idea that his innocence was impossible to establish, his craftiness being so well known. And he was cut to the heart by the injustice of the suspicion.

Thereupon he began once more to tell of the adventure, making the story longer each day, adding each time new arguments, more forcible protestations, more solemn oaths, which he devised and prepared in his hours of solitude, his mind being wholly engrossed by the story of the string. The more complicated his defence and the more subtle his reasoning, the less he was believed.

"Those are a liar's reasons," people said behind his back.

He realized it: he gnawed his nails, and exhausted himself in vain efforts. He grew perceptibly thinner.

Now the jokers asked him to tell the story of "The Piece of String" for their amusement, as a soldier who has seen service is asked to tell about his battles. His mind, attacked at its source, grew feebler.

Late in December he took to his bed.

In the first days of January he died, and in his delirium, of the death agony, he protested his innocence, repeating:

"A little piece of string—a little piece of string—see, here it is, m'sieu' mayor."

# NOTES

[1] *The Piece of String* was written in 1884. Reprinted from *Little French Masterpieces*, by permission of the publishers, *G.P. Putnam's Sons*.
[2] 34:5 char-à-bancs. A pleasure car.
[3] 35:26 Angelus. A bell tolled at morning, noon, and night, according to the Roman Catholic Church custom, to indicate the time of the service of song and recitation in memory of the Virgin Mary. The name is taken from the first word of the recitation.
[4] 35:30 cabriolet. A cab. Originally a light, one-horse pleasure carriage with two seats.
[5] 35:30 tilbury. An old form of gig, seating two persons.
[6] 37:20 petit verre. Little glass.

# BIOGRAPHY

Henri René Albert Guy de Maupassant, French novelist, dramatist, and short-story writer, was born in 1850. Until he was thirteen years old he had no teacher except his mother, who personally superintended the training of her two sons. Life for the two boys, during these early years, was free and happy, Guy was a strong and robust Norman, overflowing with animal spirits and exuberant with the joy of youthful life.
When thirteen years of age Maupassant attended the seminary at Yvetot, where he found school life irksome and a most distasteful contrast to his former free life. Later he became a student in the Lycée in Rouen. His experience as a student here was very pleasant, and he easily acquired his degree. In 1870 he was appointed to a clerkship in the Navy, and a little later to a more lucrative position in the Department of Public Instruction. His work in these two positions suffered very materially because of his negligence and daily practice in writing verses and essays for Flaubert, the most careful literary technicist in the history of literature, to criticize. For seven years Maupassant served this severe task-master, always writing, receiving criticisms, and publishing nothing.
Immediately after the publication of his first story Maupassant was hailed as a finished master artist. From 1880 to 1890 he published six novels, sixteen volumes of short-stories, three volumes of travels, and many newspaper articles. This gigantic task was performed only because of his

regular habits and splendid physique. He wrote regularly every morning from seven o'clock until noon, and at night always wrote out notes on the impressions from his experiences of the day.

Maupassant was a natural artist deeply in love with the technique of his work. He did not write for money, although he believed that a writer should have plenty of this world's possessions, nor did he write for art's sake. In fact he avoided talking on the subject of writing and to all appearances seemed to despise his profession. He wrote because the restless, immitigable force within him compelled him to work like a slave. He thought little of morals, or religion, but was enamored with physical life and its insolvable problems. He was, above everything else, a truthful man. Sometimes his subjects are unclean and he treats them as such, but, if his subject is clean, his treatment is undefiled.

In 1887 the shadows of insanity began to creep athwart his life. Even in 1884 he seemed to feel a premonition of his coming catastrophe when he wrote: "I am afraid of the walls, of the furniture, of the familiar objects which seem to me to assume a kind of animal life. Above all, I fear the horrible confusion of my thought, of my reason escaping, entangled and scattered by an invisible and mysterious anguish." The dreaded disease developed until, in 1890, he had to suspend his writing. In 1892 he became wholly insane and had to be committed to an insane asylum where he died in a padded cell one year later.

## BIOGRAPHICAL REFERENCES

*The New International Encyclopaedia.*
*Encyclopaedia Britannica.*
*Bookman*, 25:290-294_.

# CRITICISMS

Maupassant's short-stories are generally conceded to be the best in French literature. He handles his materials with great care, and his descriptions of scenes and characters are unequalled. In his first writings he seems impassive to the point of frigidity. He is a recorder who sets down exactly the life before him. This is one of the lessons he learned from Flaubert. He was not interested in what a character thought or felt, but he noted and fondled every action of his characters.

He loved life, despite the lack of solutions. At times his fondness for mere physical life leads him to the brutal stage. In his story, *On the Water*, he gives a confession of a purely sensual man: "How gladly, at times, I would think no more, feel no more, live the life of a brute, in a warm, bright country, in a yellow country, without crude and brutal verdure, in one of those Eastern countries in which one falls asleep without concern, is active and has no cares, loves and has no distress, and is scarcely aware that one is going on living!"

Maupassant was a keen observer, possessed an excellent but not lofty imagination, and never asserted a philosophy of life. His writings are all interesting, terse, precise, and truthful, but lack the glow that comes with a sympathetic and spiritual outlook on life. Zola says of him: ".... a Latin of good, clear, solid head, a maker of beautiful sentences shining like gold...." He chooses a single incident, a few characteristics and then moulds them into a compact story. Nine-tenths of his stories deal with selfishness and hypocrisy.

Tolstoi wrote: "Maupassant possessed genius, that gift of attention revealing in the objects and facts of life properties not perceived by others; he possessed a beautiful form of expression, uttering clearly, simply, and with charm what he wished to say; and he possessed also the merit of sincerity, without which a work of art produces no effect; that is he did not merely pretend to love or hate, but did indeed love or hate what he described."

# GENERAL REFERENCES

*Inquiries and Opinions*, Brander Matthews.
"A Criticism," *Outlook*, 88:973-976.
"Greatest Short Story Writer that Ever Lived," *Current Literature*, 42:636-638.

# COLLATERAL READINGS

*Happiness* (Odd Number), Guy de Maupassant.
*The Wolf*, Guy de Maupassant.
*La Mère Sauvage*, Guy de Maupassant.
*The Confession*, Guy de Maupassant.
*On the Journey*, Guy de Maupassant.
*The Beggar*, Guy de Maupassant.
*A Ghost*, Guy de Maupassant.
*Little Soldier*, Guy de Maupassant.
*The Wreck*, Guy de Maupassant.
*The Necklace*, Guy de Maupassant.
*A Note of Scarlet*, Ruth Stuart.
*Expiation*, Octave Thanet.
*Fagan*, Rowland Thomas.
*La Grande Bretêche* ("Jessup and Canby"), Honoré de Balzac.

# THE MAN WHO WAS[1]

*By Rudyard Kipling (1865-   )*

Let it be clearly understood that the Russian is a delightful person till he tucks his shirt in. As an Oriental he is charming. It is only when he insists upon being treated as the most easterly of Western peoples, instead of the most westerly of Easterns, that he becomes a racial anomaly[2] extremely difficult to handle. The host never knows which side of his nature is going to turn up next.

Dirkovitch was a Russian—a Russian of the Russians, as he said—who appeared to get his bread by serving the czar as an officer in a Cossack regiment, and corresponding for a Russian newspaper with a name that was never twice the same. He was a handsome young Oriental, with a taste for wandering through unexplored portions of the earth, and he arrived in India from nowhere in particular. At least no living man could ascertain whether it was by way of Balkh, Budukhshan, Chitral, Beloochistan, Nepaul, or anywhere else. The Indian government, being in an unusually affable mood, gave orders that he was to be civilly treated, and shown everything that was to be seen; so he drifted, talking bad English and worse French, from one city to another till he forgathered with her Majesty's White Hussars[3] in the city of Peshawur,[4] which stands at the mouth of that narrow sword-cut in the hills that men call the Khyber Pass. He was undoubtedly an officer, and he was decorated, after the manner of the Russians, with little enameled crosses, and he could talk, and (though this has nothing to do with his merits) he had been given up as a hopeless task or case by the Black Tyrones[5], who, individually and collectively, with hot whisky and honey, mulled brandy and mixed spirits of all kinds, had striven in all hospitality to make him drunk. And when the Black Tyrones, who are exclusively Irish, fail to disturb the peace of head of a foreigner, that foreigner is certain to be a superior man. This was the argument of the Black Tyrones, but they were ever an unruly and self-opinionated regiment, and they allowed junior subalterns of four years' service to choose their wines. The spirits were always purchased by the colonel and a committee of majors. And a regiment that would so behave may be respected but cannot be loved.

The White Hussars were as conscientious in choosing their wine as in charging the enemy. There was a brandy that had been purchased by a cultured colonel a few years after the battle of Waterloo. It has been maturing ever since, and it was a marvelous brandy at the purchasing. The memory of that liquor would cause men to weep as they lay dying in the teak forests of upper Burmah[6] or the slime of the Irrawaddy[7]. And there was a port which was notable; and there was a champagne of an obscure brand, which always came to mess without any labels, because the White Hussars wished none to know where the source of supply might be found. The officer on whose head the champagne choosing lay was forbidden the use of tobacco for six weeks previous to sampling.

This particularity of detail is necessary to emphasize the fact that that champagne, that port, and above all, that brandy—the green and yellow and white liqueurs did not count—was placed at the absolute disposition of Dirkovitch, and he enjoyed himself hugely—even more than among the Black Tyrones.

But he remained distressingly European through it all. The White Hussars were—"My dear true friends," "Fellow-soldiers glorious," and "Brothers inseparable." He would unburden himself by the hour on the glorious future that awaited the combined arms of England and Russia when their hearts and their territories should run side by side, and the great mission of civilizing Asia should begin. That was unsatisfactory, because Asia is not going to be civilized after the methods of the West. There is too much Asia, and she is too old. You cannot reform a lady of many lovers, and Asia has been insatiable in her flirtations aforetime. She will never attend Sunday school, or learn to vote save with swords for tickets.

Dirkovitch knew this as well as any one else, but it suited him to talk special-correspondently and to make himself as genial as he could. Now and then he volunteered a little, a very little, information about his own Sotnia[8] of Cossacks, left apparently to look after themselves somewhere at the back of beyond. He had done rough work in Central Asia, and had seen rather more help-yourself fighting than most men of his years. But he was careful never to betray his superiority, and more than careful to praise on all occasions the appearance, drill, uniform, and organization of her Majesty's White Hussars. And, indeed, they were a regiment to be admired. When Mrs. Durgan, widow of the late Sir John Durgan, arrived in their station, and after a short time had been proposed to by every single man at mess, she put the public sentiment very neatly when she explained that they were all so nice that unless she could marry them all, including the colonel and some majors who were already married, she was not going to content herself with one of them. Wherefore she wedded a little man in a rifle regiment—being by nature contradictious—and the White Hussars were going to wear crape on their arms, but compromised by attending the wedding in full force, and lining the aisle with unutterable reproach. She had jilted them all—from Basset-Holmer, the senior captain, to Little Mildred, the last subaltern, and he could have given her four thousand a year and a title. He was a viscount, and on his arrival the mess had said he had better go into the Guards, because they were all sons of large grocers and small clothiers in the Hussars, but Mildred begged very hard to be allowed to stay, and behaved so prettily that he was forgiven, and became a man, which is much more important than being any sort of viscount.

The only persons who did not share the general regard for the White Hussars were a few thousand gentlemen of Jewish extraction who lived across the border, and answered to the name of Pathan. They had only met the regiment officially, and for something less than twenty minutes, but the interview, which was complicated with many casualties, had filled them with prejudice. They even called the White Hussars "children of the devil," and sons of persons whom it would be perfectly impossible to meet in decent society. Yet they were not above making their aversion fill their money belts. The regiment possessed carbines, beautiful Martini-Henri carbines, that would cob a bullet into an enemy's camp at one thousand yards, and were even handier than the long rifle. Therefore they were coveted all along the border, and since demand inevitably breeds supply, they were supplied at the risk of life and limb for exactly their weight in coined silver—seven and one half pounds of rupees[9], or sixteen pounds and a few shillings each, reckoning the rupee at par. They were stolen at night by snaky-haired thieves that crawled on their stomachs under the nose of the sentries; they disappeared mysteriously from armracks; and in the hot weather, when all the doors and windows were open, they vanished like puffs of their own smoke. The border people desired them first for their own family vendettas[10] and then for contingencies. But in the long cold nights of the Northern Indian winter they were stolen most extensively. The traffic of murder was liveliest among the hills at that season, and prices ruled high. The regimental guards were first doubled and then trebled. A trooper does not much care if he loses a weapon—government must make it good—but he deeply resents the loss of his sleep. The regiment grew very angry, and one night-thief who managed to limp away bears the visible marks of their anger upon him to this hour. That incident stopped the burglaries for a time, and the guards were reduced accordingly, and the regiment devoted itself to polo with unexpected results, for it beat by two goals to one that very terrible polo corps the Lushkar Light Horse, though the latter had four ponies apiece for a short hour's fight, as well as a native officer who played like a lambent flame across the ground.

Then they gave a dinner to celebrate the event. The Lushkar team came, and Dirkovitch came, in the fullest full uniform of Cossack officer, which is as full as a dressing-gown, and was introduced to the Lushkars, and opened his eyes as he regarded them. They were lighter men than the Hussars, and they carried themselves with the swing that is the peculiar right of the Punjab[11] frontier force and all irregular horse. Like everything else in the service, it has to be learned; but unlike many things, it is never forgotten, and remains on the body till death.

The great beam-roofed mess room of the White Hussars was a sight to be remembered. All the mess plate was on the long table—the same table that had served up the bodies of five dead officers in a forgotten fight long and long ago—the dingy, battered standards faced the door of entrance, clumps of winter roses lay between the silver candlesticks, the portraits of eminent officers deceased looked down on their successors from between the heads of sambhur[12], nilghai[13], maikhor, and, pride of all the mess, two grinning snow-leopards that had cost Basset-Holmer four months' leave that he might have spent in England instead of on the road to Thibet, and the daily risk of his life on ledge, snowslide, and glassy grass slope.

The servants, in spotless white muslin and the crest of their regiments on the brow of their turbans, waited behind their masters, who were clad in the scarlet and gold of the White Hussars and the cream and silver of the Lushkar Light Horse. Dirkovitch's dull green uniform was the only dark spot at the board, but his big onyx eyes made up for it. He was fraternizing effusively with the captain of the Lushkar team, who was wondering how many of Dirkovitch's Cossacks his own long, lathy down-countrymen could account for in a fair charge. But one does not speak of these things openly.

The talk rose higher and higher, and the regimental band played between the courses, as is the immemorial custom, till all tongues ceased for a moment with the removal of the dinner slips and the First Toast of Obligation, when the colonel, rising, said, "Mr. Vice, the Queen," and Little Mildred from the bottom of the table answered, "The Queen, God bless her!" and the big spurs clanked as the big men heaved themselves up and drank the Queen, upon whose pay they were falsely supposed to pay their mess bills. That sacrament of the mess never grows old, and never ceases to bring a lump into the throat of the listener wherever he be, by land or by sea. Dirkovitch rose with his "brothers glorious," but he could not understand. No one but an officer can understand what the toast means; and the bulk have more sentiment than comprehension. It all comes to the same in the end, as the enemy said when he was wriggling on a lance point. Immediately after the little silence that follows on the ceremony there entered the native officer who had played for the Lushkar team. He could not of course eat with the alien, but he came in at dessert, all six feet of him, with the blue-and-silver turban atop, and the big black top-boots below. The mess rose joyously as he thrust forward the hilt of his saber, in token of fealty, for the colonel of the White Hussars to touch, and dropped into a vacant chair amid shouts of "*Rung ho*! Hira Singh!" (which being translated means "Go in and win!"). "Did I whack you over the knee, old man?" "Ressaidar Sahib, what the devil made you play that kicking pig of a pony in the last ten minutes?" "Shabash, Ressaidar Sahib!" Then the voice of the colonel, "The health of Ressaidar Hira Singh!"

After the shouting had died away, Hira Singh rose to reply, for he was the cadet of a royal house, the son of a king's son, and knew what was due on these occasions. Thus he spoke in the vernacular:—

"Colonel Sahib and officers of this regiment, much honor have you done me. This will I remember. We came down from afar to play you; but we were beaten." ("No fault of yours, Ressaidar Sahib. Played on our own ground, y' know. Your ponies were cramped from the railway. Don't apologize.") "Therefore perhaps we will come again if it be so ordained." ("Hear! Hear, hear, indeed! Bravo! Hsh!") "Then we will play you afresh" ("Happy to meet you"), "till there are left no feet upon our ponies. Thus far for sport." He dropped one hand on his sword hilt and his eye wandered to Dirkovitch lolling back in his chair. "But if by the will of God there arises any other game which is not the polo game, then be assured, Colonel Sahib and officers, that we shall play it out side by side, though *they*"—again his eye sought Dirkovitch—"though *they*, I say, have fifty ponies to our one horse." And with a deep-mouthed *Rung ho*! that rang like a musket butt on flagstones, he sat down amid shoutings.

Dirkovitch, who had devoted himself steadily to the brandy—the terrible brandy aforementioned—did not understand, nor did the expurgated[14] translations offered to him at all convey the point. Decidedly the native officer's was the speech of the evening, and the clamor might have continued to the dawn had it not been broken by the noise of a shot without that sent every man feeling at his defenseless left side. It is notable that Dirkovitch "reached back," after the American fashion—a gesture that set the captain of the Lushkar team wondering how Cossack officers were armed at mess. Then there was a scuffle, and a yell of pain.

"Carbine stealing again!" said the adjutant, calmly sinking back in his chair. "This comes of reducing the guards. I hope the sentries have killed him."

The feet of armed men pounded on the veranda flags, and it sounded as though something was being dragged.

"Why don't they put him in the cells till the morning?" said the colonel, testily. "See if they've damaged him, sergeant."

The mess-sergeant fled out into the darkness, and returned with two troopers and a corporal, all very much perplexed.

"Caught a man stealin' carbines, sir," said the corporal.

"Leastways 'e was crawling toward the barricks, sir, past the main-road sentries; an' the sentry 'e says, sir—"

The limp heap of rags upheld by the three men groaned. Never was seen so destitute and demoralized an Afghan. He was turbanless, shoeless, caked with dirt, and all but dead with rough handling. Hira Singh started slightly at the sound of the man's pain. Dirkovitch took another liqueur glass of brandy.

"*What* does the sentry say?" said the colonel.

"Sez he speaks English, sir," said the corporal.

"So you brought him into mess instead of handing him over to the sergeant! If he spoke all the tongues of the Pentecost you've no business—"

Again the bundle groaned and muttered. Little Mildred had risen from his place to inspect. He jumped back as though he had been shot.

"Perhaps it would be better, sir, to send the men away," said he to the colonel, for he was a much-privileged subaltern. He put his arms round the rag-bound horror as he spoke, and dropped him into a chair. It may not have been explained that the littleness of Mildred lay in his being six feet four, and big in proportion. The corporal, seeing that an officer was disposed to look after the capture, and that the colonel's eye was beginning to blaze, promptly removed himself and his men. The mess was left alone with the carbine thief, who laid his head on the table and wept bitterly, hopelessly, and inconsolably, as little children weep.

Hira Singh leaped to his feet with a long-drawn vernacular oath "Colonel Sahib," said he, "that man is no Afghan, for they weep '*Ai! Ai!*' Nor is he of Hindustan, for they weep,'*Oh! Ho!*' He weeps after the fashion of the white men, who say '*Ow! Ow!*'"

"Now where the dickens did you get that knowledge, Hira Singh?" said the captain of the Lushkar team.

"Hear him!" said Hira Singh, simply, pointing at the crumpled figure that wept as though it would never cease.

"He said, 'My God!'" said Little Mildred, "I heard him say it."

The colonel and the mess room looked at the man in silence. It is a horrible thing to hear a man cry. A woman can sob from the top of her palate, or her lips, or anywhere else, but a man cries from his diaphragm, and it rends him to pieces. Also, the exhibition causes the throat of the on-looker to close at the top.

"Poor devil!" said the colonel, coughing tremendously, "We ought to send him to hospital. He's been manhandled."

Now the adjutant loved his rifles. They were to him as his grandchildren—the men standing in the first place. He grunted rebelliously: "I can understand an Afghan stealing, because he's made that way. But I can't understand his crying. That makes it worse."

The brandy must have affected Dirkovitch, for he lay back in his chair and stared at the ceiling. There was nothing special in the ceiling beyond a shadow as of a huge black coffin. Owing to some peculiarity in the construction of the mess room this shadow was always thrown when the candles were lighted. It never disturbed the digestion of the White Hussars. They were, in rather proud of it.

"Is he going to cry all night?" said the colonel, "or are we supposed to sit up with Little Mildred's guest until he feels better?"

The man in the chair threw up his head and stared at the mess. Outside, the wheels of the first of those bidden to the festivities crunched the roadway.

"Oh, my God!" said the man in the chair, and every soul in the mess rose to his feet. Then the Lushkar captain did a deed for which he ought to have been given the Victoria Cross—distinguished gallantry in a fight against overwhelming curiosity. He picked up his team with his eyes as the hostess picks up the ladies at the opportune moment, and pausing only by the colonel's chair to say, "This isn't *our* affair, you know, sir," led the team into the veranda and the gardens. Hira Singh was the last, and he looked at Dirkovitch as he moved. But Dirkovitch had departed into a brandy paradise of his own. His lips moved without sound, and he was studying the coffin on the ceiling.

"White—white all over," said Basset-Holmer, the adjutant. "What a pernicious renegade[15] he must be! I wonder where he came from?"

The colonel shook the man gently by the arm, and "Who are you?" said he.

There was no answer. The man stared round the mess room and smiled in the colonel's face. Little Mildred, who was always more of a woman than a man till "Boot and saddle" was sounded, repeated the question in a voice that would have drawn confidences from a geyser. The man only smiled. Dirkovitch, at the far end of the table, slid gently from his chair to the floor, No son of Adam, in this present imperfect world, can mix the Hussars' champagne with the Hussars' brandy by five and eight glasses of each without remembering the pit whence he has been digged and descending thither. The band began to play the tune with which the White Hussars, from the date of their formation, preface all their functions. They would sooner be disbanded than abandon that tune. It is a part of their system. The man straightened himself in his chair and drummed on the table with his fingers.

"I don't see why we should entertain lunatics," said the colonel; "call a guard and send him off to the cells. We'll look into the business in the morning. Give him a glass of wine first, though."

Little Mildred filled a sherry glass with the brandy and thrust it over to the man. He drank, and the tune rose louder, and he straightened himself yet more. Then he put out his long-taloned hands to a piece of plate opposite and fingered it lovingly. There was a mystery connected with that piece of plate in the shape of a spring, which converted what was a seven-branched candlestick, three springs each side and one on the middle, into a sort of wheel-spoke candelabrum[16]. He found the spring, pressed it, and laughed weakly. He rose from his chair and inspected a picture on the wall, then moved on to another picture, the mess watching him without a word. When he came to the mantelpiece he shook his head and seemed distressed. A piece of plate representing a mounted hussar in full uniform caught his eye. He pointed to it, and then to the mantelpiece, with inquiry in his eyes.

"What is it—oh, what is it?" said Little Mildred. Then, as a mother might speak to a child, "That is a horse—yes, a horse."

Very slowly came the answer, in a thick, passionless guttural: "Yes, I—have seen. But—where is *the* horse?"

You could have heard the hearts of the mess beating as the men drew back to give the stranger full room in his wanderings. There was no question of calling the guard.

Again he spoke, very slowly, "Where is *our* horse?"

There is no saying what happened after that. There is but one horse in the White Hussars, and his portrait hangs outside the door of the mess room. He is the piebald drum-horse the king of the regimental band, that served the regiment for seven-and-thirty years, and in the end was shot for old age. Half the mess tore the thing down from its place and thrust it into the man's hands. He placed it above the mantelpiece; it clattered on the ledge, as his poor hands dropped it, and he staggered toward the bottom of the table, falling into Mildred's chair. The band began to play the "River of Years" waltz, and the laughter from the gardens came into the tobacco-scented mess room. But nobody, even the youngest, was thinking of waltzes. They all spoke to one another something after this fashion: "The drum-horse hasn't hung over the mantelpiece since '67." "How does he know?" "Mildred, go and speak to him again." "Colonel, what are you going to do?" "Oh, dry up, and give the poor devil a chance to pull himself together!" "It isn't possible, anyhow. The man's a lunatic."

Little Mildred stood at the colonel's side talking into his ear. "Will you be good enough to take your seats, please, gentlemen?" he said, and the mess dropped into the chairs.

Only Dirkovitch's seat, next to Little Mildred's, was blank, and Little Mildred himself had found Hira Singh's place. The wide-eyed mess sergeant filled the glasses in dead silence. Once more the colonel rose, but his hand shook, and the port spilled on the table as he looked straight at the man in Little Mildred's chair and said, hoarsely, "Mr. Vice, the Queen." There was a little pause, but the man sprang to his feet and answered, without hesitation, "The Queen, God bless her!" and as he emptied the thin glass he snapped the shank between his fingers.

Long and long ago, when the Empress of India was a young woman, and there were no unclean ideals in the land, it was the custom in a few messes to drink the Queen's toast in broken glass, to the huge delight of the mess contractors. The custom is now dead, because there is nothing to break anything for, except now and again the word of a government, and that has been broken already.

"That settles it," said the colonel, with a gasp. "He's not a sergeant. What in the world is he?"

The entire mess echoed the word, and the volley of questions would have scared any man. Small wonder that the ragged, filthy invader could only smile and shake his head.

From under the table, calm and smiling urbanely[17], rose Dirkovitch, who had been roused from healthful slumber by feet upon his body. By the side of the man he rose, and the man shrieked and groveled at his feet. It was a horrible sight, coming so swiftly upon the pride and glory of the toast that had brought the strayed wits together.

Dirkovitch made no offer to raise him, but Little Mildred heaved him up in an instant. It is not good that a gentleman who can answer to the Queen's toast should lie at the feet of a subaltern of Cossacks.

The hasty action tore the wretch's upper clothing nearly to the waist, and his body was seamed with dry black scars. There is only one weapon in the world that cuts in parallel lines, and it is neither the cane nor the cat. Dirkovitch saw the marks, and the pupils of his eyes dilated—also, his face changed. He said something that sounded like "Shto ve takete"; and the man, fawning, answered, "Chetyre."

"What's that?" said everybody together.

"His number. That is number four, you know." Dirkovitch spoke very thickly.

"What has a Queen's officer to do with a qualified number?" said the colonel, and there rose an unpleasant growl round the table.

"How can I tell?" said the affable Oriental, with a sweet smile. "He is a—how you have it?—escape—runaway, from over there."

He nodded toward the darkness of the night.

"Speak to him, if he'll answer you, and speak to him gently," said Little Mildred, settling the man in a chair. It seemed most improper to all present that Dirkovitch. should sip brandy as he talked in purring, spitting Russian to the creature who answered so feebly and with such evident dread. But since Dirkovitch appeared to understand, no man said a word. They breathed heavily, leaning forward, in the long gaps of the conversation. The next time that they have no engagements on hand the White Hussars intend to go to St. Petersburg and learn Russian.

"He does not know how many years ago," said Dirkovitch, facing the mess, "but he says it was very long ago, in a war, I think that there was an accident. He says he was of this glorious and distinguished regiment in the war."

"The rolls! The rolls! Holmer, get the rolls!" said Little Mildred, and the adjutant dashed off bareheaded to the orderly room where the rolls of the regiment were kept. He returned just in time to hear Dirkovitch conclude, "Therefore I am most sorry to say there was an accident, which would have been, reparable if he had apologized to our colonel, whom he had insulted."

Another growl, which the colonel tried to beat down. The mess was in no mood to weigh insults to Russian colonels just then.

"He does not remember, but I think that there was an accident, and so he was not exchanged among the prisoners, but he was sent to another place—how do you say?—the country. *So*, he says, he came here. He does not know how he came. Eh? He *was* at Chepany[18]"—the man caught the word, nodded, and shivered—"at Zhigansk[19] and Irkutsk[20]. I cannot understand how he escaped. He says, too, that he was in the forests for many years, but how many years he has forgotten—that with many things. It was an accident; done because he did not apologise to our colonel. Ah!" Instead of echoing Dirkovitch's sigh of regret, it is sad to record that the White Hussars livelily exhibited unchristian delight and other emotions, hardly restrained by their sense of hospitality. Holmer flung the frayed and yellow regimental rolls on the table, and the men flung themselves atop of these.

"Steady! Fifty-six—fifty-five—fifty-four," said Holmer. "Here we are. 'Lieutenant Austin Limmason—*missing*.' That was before Sebastopol[21]. What an infernal shame! Insulted one of their colonels, and was quietly shipped off. Thirty years of his life wiped out."

"But he never apologized. Said he'd see him——first," chorussed the mess.

"Poor devil! I suppose he never had the chance afterward. How did he come here?" said the colonel.

The dingy heap in the chair could give no answer.

"Do you know who you are?"

It laughed weakly.

"Do you know that you are Limmason—Lieutenant Limmason, of the White Hussars?"

Swift as a shot came the answer, in a slightly surprised tone, "Yes, I'm Limmason, of course." The light died out in his eyes, and he collapsed afresh, watching every motion of Dirkovitch with terror. A flight from Siberia may fix a few elementary facts in the mind, but it does not lead to continuity of thought. The man could not explain how, like a homing pigeon, he had found his way to his own old mess again. Of what he had suffered or seen he knew nothing. He cringed before Dirkovitch as instinctively as he had pressed the spring of the candlestick, sought the picture of the drum-horse, and answered to the Queen's toast. The rest was a blank that the dreaded Russian tongue could only in part remove. His head bowed on his breast, and he giggled and cowered alternately.

The devil that lived in the brandy prompted Dirkovitch at this extremely inopportune moment to make a speech. He rose, swaying slightly, gripped the table edge, while his eyes glowed like opals, and began:—"Fellow-soldiers glorious—true friends and hospitables. It was an accident, and deplorable—most deplorable." Here he smiled sweetly all round the mess. "But you will think of this little, little thing. So little, is it not? The czar!

Posh! I slap my fingers—I snap my fingers at him. Do I believe in him? No! But the Slav who has done nothing, *him* I believe. Seventy—how much?—millions that have done nothing—not one thing. Napoleon was an episode." He banged a hand on the table. "Hear you, old peoples, we have done nothing in the world—out here. All our work is to do: and it shall be done, old peoples. Get away!" He waved his hand imperiously, and pointed to the man. "You see him. He is not good to see. He was just one little—oh, so little—accident, that no one remembered. Now he is *That*. So will you be, brother-soldiers so brave—so will you be. But you will never come back. You will all go where he has gone, or"—he pointed to the great coffin shadow on the ceiling, and muttering, "Seventy millions—get away, you old people," fell asleep.

"Sweet, and to the point," said Little Mildred. "What's the use of getting wroth? Let's make the poor devil comfortable."

But that was a matter suddenly and swiftly taken from the loving hands of the White Hussars. The lieutenant had returned only to go away again three days later, when the wail of the "Dead March" and the tramp of the squadrons told the wondering station, that saw no gap in the table, an officer of the regiment had resigned his new-found commission.

And Dirkovitch—bland, supple, and always genial—went away too by a night train. Little Mildred and another saw him off, for he was the guest of the mess, and even had he smitten the colonel with the open hand the law of the mess allowed no relaxation of hospitality.

"Good-by, Dirkovitch, and a pleasant journey," said Little Mildred.

"*Au revoir[22]* my true friends," said the Russian.

"Indeed! But we thought you were going home?"

"Yes; but I will come again. My friends, is that road shut?" He pointed to where the north star burned over the Khyber Pass.

"By Jove! I forgot. Of course. Happy to meet you, old man, any time you like. Got everything you want,—cheroots, ice, bedding? That's all right. Well, *au revoir*, Dirkovitch."

"Um," said the other man, as the tail-lights of the train grew small. "Of—all—the—unmitigated[23]—"

Little Mildred answered nothing, but watched the north star, and hummed a selection from a recent burlesque that had much delighted the White Hussars. It ran:—

"I'm sorry for Mister Bluebeard,
I'm sorry to cause him pain;

But a terrible spree there's sure to be
When he comes back again."

# NOTES

[1] *The Man Who Was* was written in 1889.
[2] 46:6 anomaly. Deviation from type.
[3] 47:1 Hussars. Light-horse troopers armed with sabre and carbine.
[4] 47:1 Peshawur. City in British India.
[5] 47:7 Tyrones. From a county in Ireland by this name.
[6] 47:26 Burmah. In southeastern Asia. Part of the British Empire.
[7] 47:27 Irrawaddy. Chief river of Burma.
[8] 48:27 Sotnia. Company of the Cossacks.
[9] 50:14 rupee. Indian coin worth about forty-eight cents.
[10] 50:21 vendettas. Private blood-feuds.
[11] 51:14 Punjab. Country of five rivers, tributaries of the Indus.
[12] 81:26 Sambhur. A rusine deer found in India.
[13] 51:26 nilghai. Antelope with hind legs shorter than its fore-legs.
[14] 54:9 expurgated. Purified.
[15] 57:23 renegade. One who deserts his faith.
[16] 58:26 candelabrum. Stand supporting several lamps.
[17] 61:3 urbanely. Politely.
[18] 63:2 Chepany. Town in Siberia.
[19] 63:4 Zhigansk. Town in Siberia.
[20] 63:4 Irkutsk. Province and city in Siberia.
[21] 63:17 Sebastopol. Seaport in Russia.
[22] 65:26 Au revoir. Till we meet again.
[23] 66:6 unmitigated. As bad as can be.

# BIOGRAPHICAL REFERENCES

*Essays on Modern Novelists*, William Lyon Phelps.
*A Kipling Primer*, Knowles.
*Rudyard Kipling*, Richard Le Galliene.
"Kipling to French Eyes," *Bookman*, 26: 584.
"Life of Kipling," _Encyclopaedia Britannica.
"Life of Kipling," *The Universal Encyclopedia.*

# BIOGRAPHY

Rudyard Kipling, the most vigorous, versatile, and highly endowed of the present-day writers of fiction, was born in Bombay, India, December 30, 1865. His place of birth and extensive travelling make him more Anglo-Saxon than British. His father was for many years connected with the schools of art at Bombay and Lahore in India. His mother, Alice MacDonald, was the daughter of a Methodist clergyman.

Kipling was brought to England when he was five years old to be educated. While in college at Westward Ho he edited the *College Chronicle*. For this paper he contributed regularly, poetry and stories. After his school days and on his return to India, he served on the editorial staff of the Lahore *Civil and Military Gazette* from 1882 to 1887, and was assistant editor of the *Pioneer* at Allahabad from 1887 to 1889.

Kipling has travelled extensively. He is at home in India, China, Japan, Africa, Australia, England, and America. The odd part about his realistic observations, however, is that his notes, whether written about California or India, are often repudiated by the people whom he has visited. After visiting England and the United States in a vain effort to find a publisher for his writings, he returned to India and published in the *Pioneer* his *American Notes*, which were immediately reproduced in book form in New York in 1891.

He married Miss Balestier of New York in 1892. They settled at Brattleboro, Vermont, immediately after their marriage and lived there until 1896. Kipling revisited the United States in 1899. While on this trip he suffered a severe attack of pneumonia which brought out a demonstration of interest from the American people that clearly showed their appreciation of him as a man and a writer.

# CRITICISMS

Kipling is journalistic in all his writings. Oftentimes his material is very thin, flippant, and sensational, but he always is interesting, for he possesses the expert reporter's unerring judgment for choosing the essentials of his situation, character, or description, that catch and hold the reader's attention. In his earlier writings, like *Plain Tales from the Hills* or *The Jungle Books*, the radical racial differences between his characters and readers, and the background of primitive, mysterious India caught the reading world and instantly established Kipling's fame.

His technique is brilliant, his wit keen, and his energy of the bold and dashing military type. This audacious energy leads him very often into sprawling situations, a worship of imperialism, and reckless statements concerning moral and spiritual laws. Unlike Bret Harte, who was in many respects one of Kipling's ideals, he leaves his bad and coarse characters disreputable to the end. This is due in a large measure to the lack of warmth and light in his writings. In contradiction to this type of his works his *William the Conqueror* and *An Habitation Enforced* are filled with a gentle-human sympathy that causes us to forget and forgive any vulgarity he may have used in his more primitive and coarse characters. Even Kipling partisans must sometimes wish that Kipling's vision were not so dimmed by the British flag and that he might forget for a time the British soldier he loves so ardently.

His writings since 1899 are much more mechanical than his earlier works. He seems, at times, to resort to the orator's superficial tricks in his attempts to attract readers. The *Athenaeum*, a friendly organ, says of his later work: "In his new part—the missionary of Empire—Mr. Kipling is living the strenuous life. He has frankly abandoned story telling, and is using his complete and powerful armory in the interests of patriotic zeal."

Whatever may be the final judgment of the world concerning Kipling's claim to literary genius, the young student may rest assured that there is no one in England who can compare with this strenuous and versatile writer. He is original and powerful, interesting and realistic. He is a lover of the men who earn their bread by the sweat of their faces and a despiser of "flannelled fools." He lacks the day-dreams of Stevenson and preaches from every housetop the gospel of virile, acting morality. Many of his readers have criticised adversely his spiritual teachings, because of the furious energy with which he denounces an apathetic religion and eulogizes the person who works with all his might, day after day, for the highest he knows and never fears the day of death and judgment.

# GENERAL REFERENCES

*The Book of the Short Story*, Alexander Jessup.
*The Short Story in English*, Henry Seidel Canby.
*Bibliography of Kipling's Works*, Eugene P, Saxton.
"Contradictory Elements in Rudyard Kipling," *Current Literature*, 44: 274.
"Where Kipling Stands," *Bookman*, 29: 120-122.
"Are there two Kiplings?" *Cosmopolitan*, 31: 653-660.
"Literary Style of Kipling," *Lippincott*, 73: 99-103.

# COLLATERAL READINGS

*The Man Who Would be King*, Rudyard Kipling.
*William the Conqueror*, Rudyard Kipling.
*Phantom Rickshaw*, Rudyard Kipling.
*The Finest Story in the World*, Rudyard Kipling.
*Under the Deodars*, Rudyard Kipling.
*An Habitation Enforced*, Rudyard Kipling.
*Plain Tales from the Hills*, Rudyard Kipling.
*The Light that Failed*, Rudyard Kipling.
*Wee Willie Winkie*, Rudyard Kipling.
*Baa Baa Black Sheep*, Rudyard Kipling.
*Captains Courageous*, Rudyard Kipling.
*The Jungle Books*, Rudyard Kipling.
*They*, Rudyard Kipling.
*The Brushwood Boy*, Rudyard Kipling.
*Christ in Flanders*, Honoré de Balzac.
*The Old Gentleman of the Black Stock*, Thomas Nelson Page.
*A New England Nun*, Mary Wilkins Freeman.
*Outcasts of Poker Flat*, Bret Harte.
*The Siege of Berlin*, Alphonse Dadoed.
*The Prisoner of Assiout*, Grant Allen.

*A Terribly Strange Bed*, Wilkie Collins.
*The Prisoners*, Guy de Maupassant.
*Mr. Isaacs*, F. Marion Crawford.
*Where Love Is, There God Is Also*, Leo Tolstoi.

# THE FALL OF THE HOUSE OF USHER [1]

*By Edgar Allan Poe (1809-1849)*

Son coeur est un luth suspendu;
Sitôt qu'on le touche il résonne.
—De Béranger.[2]

During the whole of a dull, dark, and soundless day in the autumn of the year, when the clouds hung oppressively low in the heavens, I had been passing alone, on horseback, through a singularly dreary tract of country; and at length found myself, as the shades of the evening drew on, within view of the melancholy House of Usher. I know not how it was; but, with the first glimpse of the building, a sense of insufferable gloom pervaded my spirit. I say insufferable; for the feeling was unrelieved by any of that half-pleasurable, because poetic, sentiment, with which the mind usually receives even the sternest natural images of the desolate or terrible. I looked upon the scene before me—upon the mere house, and the simple landscape features of the domain—upon the bleak walls—upon the vacant eye-like windows—a few rank sedges—and upon a few white trunks of decayed trees—with an utter depression of soul which I can compare to no earthly sensation more properly than to the after-dream of the reveller upon opium—the bitter lapse into every-day life—the hideous dropping off of the veil. There was an iciness, a sinking, a sickening of the heart—an unredeemed dreariness of thought which no goading of the imagination could torture into aught of the sublime. What was it—I paused to think— what was it that so unnerved me in the contemplation of the House of Usher? It was a mystery all insoluble; nor could I grapple with the shadowy fancies that crowded upon me as I pondered. I was forced to fall back upon the unsatisfactory conclusion that while, beyond doubt, there *are* combinations of very simple natural objects which have the power of thus affecting us, still the analysis of this power lies among considerations beyond our depth. It was possible, I reflected, that a mere different arrangement of the particulars of the scene, of the details of the picture, would be sufficient to modify, or perhaps to annihilate its capacity for sorrowful impression; and, acting upon this idea, I reined my horse to the precipitous brink of a black and lurid tarn[3] that lay in unruffled lustre by the dwelling, and gazed down—but with a shudder even more thrilling than before—upon the remodelled and inverted images of the gray sedge, and the ghastly tree stems, and the vacant and eye-like windows.

Nevertheless, in this mansion of gloom I now proposed to myself a sojourn of some weeks. Its proprietor, Roderick Usher, had been one of my boon companions in boyhood; but many years had elapsed since our last meeting. A letter, however, had lately reached me in a distant part of the country—a letter from him—which, in its wildly importunate nature, had admitted of no other than a personal reply. The Ms. gave evidence of nervous agitation. The writer spoke of acute bodily illness, of a mental disorder which oppressed him, and of an earnest desire to see me, as his best, and indeed his only, personal friend, with a view of attempting, by the cheerfulness of my society, some alleviation of his malady. It was the manner in which all this, and much more, was said—it was the apparent *heart* that went with his request—which allowed me no room for hesitation; and I accordingly obeyed forthwith what I still considered a very singular summons.

Although, as boys, we had been even intimate associates, yet I really knew little of my friend. His reserve had been always excessive and habitual. I was aware, however, that his very ancient family had been noted, time out of mind, for a peculiar sensibility of temperament, displaying itself, through long ages, in many works of exalted art, and manifested, of late, in repeated deeds of munificent, yet unobtrusive, charity, as well as in a passionate devotion to the intricacies, perhaps even more than to the orthodox and easily recognizable beauties, of musical science. I had learned, too, the very remarkable fact that the stem of the Usher race, all time-honored as it was, had put forth, at no period, any enduring branch; in other words, that the entire family lay in the direct line of descent, and had always, with very trifling and very temporary variation, so lain. It was this deficiency, I considered, while running over in thought the perfect keeping of the character of the premises with the accredited character of the people, and while speculating upon the possible influence which the one, in the long lapse of centuries, might have exercised upon the other— it was this deficiency, perhaps, of collateral issue, and the consequent undeviating transmission, from sire to son, of the patrimony with the name, which had, at length, so identified the two as to merge the original title of the estate in the quaint and equivocal appellation of the *House of Usher*— an appellation which seemed to include, in the minds of the peasantry who used it, both the family and the family mansion.

I have said that the sole effect of my somewhat childish experiment of looking down within the tarn had been to deepen the first singular impression. There can be no doubt that the consciousness of the rapid increase of my superstition—for why should I not so term it?—served mainly to accelerate the increase itself. Such, I have long known, is the paradoxical law of all sentiments having terror as a basis. And it might have been for this reason only, that, when I again uplifted my eyes to the house itself, from its image in the pool, there grew in my mind a strange fancy—a fancy so ridiculous, indeed, that I but mention it to show the vivid force of the sensations which oppressed me. I had so worked upon my imagination as really to believe that about the whole mansion and domain there hung an atmosphere peculiar to themselves and their immediate vicinity—an atmosphere which had no affinity with the air of heaven, but which had reeked up from the decayed trees, and the gray wall, and the silent tarn—a pestilent and mystic vapor, dull, sluggish, faintly discernible, and leaden-hued.

Shaking off from my spirit what *must* have been a dream, I scanned more narrowly the real aspect of the building. Its principal feature seemed to be that of an excessive antiquity. The discoloration of ages had been great. Minute fungi overspread the whole exterior, hanging in a fine, tangled web-work from the eaves. Yet all this was apart from any extraordinary dilapidation. No portion of the masonry had fallen; and there appeared to be a wild inconsistency between its still perfect adaptation of parts, and the crumbling condition of the individual stones. In this there was much that reminded me of the specious totality of old woodwork which has rotted for years in some neglected vault, with no disturbance from the breath of the external air. Beyond this indication of extensive decay, however, the fabric gave little token of instability. Perhaps the eye of a scrutinizing observer might have discovered a barely perceptible fissure, which, extending from the roof of the building in front, made its way down the wall in a zigzag direction, until it became lost in the sullen waters of the tarn.

Noticing these things, I rode over a short causeway to the house. A servant in waiting took my horse, and I entered the Gothic archway of the hall. A valet, of stealthy step, thence conducted me, in silence, through many dark and intricate passages in my progress to the *studio* of his master. Much that I encountered on the way contributed, I know not how, to heighten the vague sentiments of which I have already spoken. While the objects around me—while the carvings of the ceilings, the sombre tapestries of the walls, the ebon blackness of the floors, and the phantasmagoric armorial trophies which rattled as I strode, were but matters to which, or to such as which, I had been accustomed from my infancy—while I hesitated not to acknowledge how familiar was all this—I still wondered to find how unfamiliar were the fancies which ordinary images were stirring up. On one of the staircases I met the physician of the family. His countenance, I thought, wore a mingled expression of low cunning and perplexity. He accosted me with trepidation and passed on. The valet now threw open a door and ushered me into the presence of his master.

The room in which I found myself was very large and lofty. The windows were long, narrow, and pointed, and at so vast a distance from the black oaken floor as to be altogether inaccessible from within. Feeble gleams of encrimsoned light made their way through the trellised panes, and served to render sufficiently distinct the more prominent objects around; the eye, however, struggled in vain to reach the remoter angles of the chamber, or the recesses of the vaulted and fretted ceiling. Dark draperies hung upon the walls. The general furniture was profuse, comfortless, antique, and tattered. Many books and musical instruments lay scattered about, but failed to give any vitality to the scene. I felt that I breathed an atmosphere of sorrow. An air of stern, deep, and irredeemable gloom hung over and pervaded all.

Upon my entrance, Usher arose from a sofa on which he had been lying at full length, and greeted me with, a vivacious warmth which had much in it, I at first thought, of an overdone cordiality—of the constrained effort of the *ennuyé*[4] man of the world. A glance, however, at his countenance convinced me of his perfect sincerity. We sat down; and for some moments, while he spoke not. I gazed upon him with a feeling half of pity, half of awe. Surely, man had never before so terribly altered, in so brief a period, as had Roderick Usher! It was with difficulty that I could bring myself to admit the identity of the wan being before me with the companion of my early boyhood. Yet the character of his face had been at all times remarkable. A cadaverousness of complexion; an eye large, liquid, and luminous beyond comparison; lips somewhat thin and very pallid, but of a surpassingly beautiful curve; a nose of a delicate Hebrew model, but with a breadth of nostril unusual in similar formations; a finely moulded chin, speaking, in its want of prominence, of a want of moral energy; hair of a more than web-like softness and tenuity; these features, with an inordinate expansion above the regions of the temple, made up altogether a countenance not easily to be forgotten. And now in the mere exaggeration of the prevailing character of these features, and of the expression they were wont to convey, lay so much of change that I doubted to whom I spoke. The now ghastly pallor of the skin, and the now miraculous lustre of the eye, above all things startled, and even awed me.

The silken hair, too, had been suffered to grow all unheeded, and as, in its wild gossamer texture, it floated rather than fell about the face, I could not, even with effort, connect its arabesque expression with any idea of simple humanity.

In the manner of my friend I was at once struck with an incoherence—an inconsistency; and I soon found this to arise from a series of feeble and futile struggles to overcome an habitual trepidancy, an excessive nervous agitation. For something of this nature I had indeed been prepared, no less by his letter than by reminiscences of certain boyish traits, and by conclusions deduced from his peculiar physical conformation and temperament. His action was alternately vivacious and sullen. His voice varied rapidly from a tremulous indecision (when the animal spirits seemed utterly in abeyance) to that species of energetic concision—that abrupt, weighty, unhurried, and hollow-sounding enunciation—that leaden, self-balanced, and perfectly modulated guttural utterance, which may be observed in the lost drunkard, or the irreclaimable eater of opium, during the periods of his most intense excitement.

It was thus that he spoke of the object of my visit, of his earnest desire to see me, and of the solace he expected me to afford him. He entered, at some length, into what he conceived to be the nature of his malady. It was, he said, a constitutional and a family evil, and one for which he despaired to find a remedy—a mere nervous affection, he immediately added, which would undoubtedly soon pass off. It displayed itself in a host of unnatural sensations. Some of these, as he detailed them, interested and bewildered me; although, perhaps, the terms and the general manner of the narration had their weight. He suffered much from a morbid acuteness of the senses. The most insipid food was alone endurable; he could wear only garments of certain texture; the odors of all flowers were oppressive; his eyes were tortured by even a faint light; and there were but peculiar sounds, and these from stringed instruments, which did not inspire him with horror.

To an anomalous species of terror I found him a bounden[5] slave. "I shall perish," said he, "I *must* perish, in this deplorable folly. Thus, thus, and not otherwise, shall I be lost. I dread the events of the future, not in themselves, but in their results. I shudder at the thought of any, even the most trivial, incident, which may operate upon this intolerable agitation of soul. I have, indeed, no abhorrence of danger, except in its absolute effect—in terror. In this unnerved—in this pitiable condition—I feel that the period will sooner or later arrive when I must abandon life and reason together, in some struggle with the grim phantasm, FEAR."

I learned, moreover, at intervals, and through broken and equivocal hints, another singular feature of his mental condition. He was enchained by certain superstitious impressions in regard to the dwelling which he tenanted, and whence, for many years, he had never ventured forth—in regard to an influence whose supposititious force was conveyed in terms too shadowy here to be restated—an influence which some peculiarities in the mere form and substance of his family mansion, had, by dint of long sufferance, he said, obtained over his spirit—an effect which the *physique* of the gray walls and turrets, and of the dim tarn into which they all looked down, had, at length, brought about upon the *morale* of his existence.

He admitted, however, although with hesitation, that much of the peculiar gloom which thus afflicted him could be traced to a more natural and far more palpable origin—to the severe and long-continued illness—indeed to the evidently approaching dissolution—of a tenderly beloved sister, his sole companion for long years, his last and only relative on earth. "Her decease," he said, with a bitterness which I can never forget, "would leave him (him the hopeless and the frail) the last of the ancient race of the Ushers." While he spoke, the lady Madeline (for so was she called) passed slowly through a remote portion of the apartment, and, without having noticed my presence, disappeared. I regarded her with an utter astonishment not unmingled with dread[6]; and yet I found it impossible to account for such feelings. A sensation of stupor oppressed me, as my eyes followed her retreating steps. When a door, at length, closed upon her, my glance sought instinctively and eagerly the countenance of the brother; but he had buried his face in his hands, and I could only perceive that a far more than ordinary wanness had overspread the emaciated fingers through which trickled many passionate tears.

The disease of the lady Madeline had long baffled the skill of her physicians. A settled apathy, a gradual wasting away of the person, and frequent although transient affections of a partially cataleptical character, were the unusual diagnosis. Hitherto she had steadily borne up against the pressure of her malady, and had not betaken herself finally to bed; but on the closing in of the evening of my arrival at the house, she succumbed (as her brother told me at night with inexpressible agitation) to the prostrating power of the destroyer; and I learned that the glimpse I had obtained of her person would thus probably be the last I should obtain—that the lady, at least while living, would be seen by me no more.

For several days ensuing her name was unmentioned by either Usher or myself; and during this period I was busied in earnest endeavors to alleviate the melancholy of my friend. We painted and read together; or I listened, as if in a dream, to the wild improvisations[7] of his speaking guitar. And thus, as a closer and still closer intimacy admitted me more unreservedly into the recesses of his spirit, the more bitterly did I perceive the futility of all attempt at cheering a mind from which darkness, as if an inherent positive quality, poured forth upon all objects of the moral and physical universe, in one unceasing radiation of gloom.

I shall ever bear about me a memory of the many solemn hours I thus spent alone with the master of the House of Usher. Yet I should fail in any attempt to convey an idea of the exact character of the studies, or of the occupations in which he involved me, or led me the way. An excited and highly distempered ideality threw a sulphurous luster over all. His long, improvised dirges will ring forever in my ears. Among other things, I hold painfully in mind a certain singular perversion and amplification of the wild air of the last waltz of von Weber[8]. From the paintings over which his elaborate fancy brooded, and which grew, touch by touch, into vaguenesses at which I shuddered the more thrillingly because I shuddered knowing not why,—from these paintings (vivid as their images now are before, me) I would in vain endeavor to educe more than a small portion which should lie within the compass of merely written words. By the utter simplicity, by the nakedness of his designs, he arrested and overawed attention. If ever mortal painted an idea, that mortal was Roderick Usher. For me, at least, in the circumstances then surrounding me, there arose out of the pure abstractions which the hypochondriac contrived to throw, upon his canvas, an intensity of intolerable awe, no shadow of which felt I ever yet in the contemplation of the certainly glowing yet too concrete reveries of Fuseli.[9]

One of the phantasmagoric conceptions of my friend, partaking not so rigidly of the spirit of abstraction may be shadowed forth, although feebly, in words. A small picture presented the interior of an immensely long and rectangular vault or tunnel, with low walls, smooth, white, and without interruption or device. Certain accessory points of the design served well to convey the idea that this excavation lay at an exceeding depth below the surface of the earth. No outlet was observed in any portion of its vast extent, and no torch or other artificial source of light was discernible; yet a flood of intense rays rolled throughout, and bathed the whole in a ghastly and inappropriate splendor.

I have just spoken of that morbid condition of the auditory nerve which rendered all music intolerable to the sufferer, with the exception of certain effects of stringed, instruments. It was, perhaps, the narrow limits to which he thus confined himself upon the guitar, which gave birth, in great measure, to the fantastic character of his performances. But the fervid *facility* of his *impromptus* could not be so accounted for. They must have been, and were, in the notes, as well as in the words of his wild fantasias (for he not unfrequently accompanied himself with rimed verbal improvisations), the result of that intense mental collectedness and concentration to which I have previously alluded as observable only in particular moments of the highest artificial excitement. The words of one of these rhapsodies I have easily remembered. I was, perhaps, the more forcibly impressed with it, as he gave it, because, in the under or mystic current of its meaning, I fancied that I perceived, and for the first time, a full consciousness on the part of Usher, of the tottering of his lofty reason upon her throne. The verses, which were entitled "The Haunted Palace,"[10] ran very nearly, if not accurately, thus:—

# I

In the greenest of our valleys,
By good angels tenanted,
Once a fair and stately palace—
Radiant palace—reared its head.
In the monarch Thought's dominion—
It stood there!
Never seraph spread a pinion
Over fabric half so fair.

# II

Banners yellow, glorious, golden,
On its roof did float and flow;
(This—all this—was in the olden
Time long ago)
And every gentle air that dallied,
In that sweet day,
Along the ramparts plumed and pallid,
A wingèd odor went away.

# III

Wanderers in that happy valley
Through two luminous windows saw
Spirits moving musically
To a lute's well-tunèd law,
Round about a throne, where sitting
(Porphyrogene!)[11]
In state his glory well befitting,
The ruler of the realm was seen.

# IV

And all with pearl and ruby glowing
Was the fair palace door,
Through which came flowing, flowing, flowing,
And sparkling evermore,
A troop of Echoes whose sweet duty
Was but to sing,
In voices of surpassing beauty,
The wit and wisdom of their king.

# V

But evil things, in robes of sorrow,
Assailed the monarch's high estate
(Ah, let us mourn, for never morrow
Shall dawn upon him, desolate!);
And, round about his home, the glory
That blushed and bloomed
Is but a dim-remembered story
Of the old time entombed.

# VI

And travelers now within that valley,
Through the red-litten windows, see
Vast forms that move fantastically

To a discordant melody;
While, like a rapid ghastly river,
Through the pale door,
A hideous throng rush out forever,
And laugh—but smile no more.

I well remember that suggestions arising from this ballad led us into a train of thought wherein there became manifest an opinion of Usher's which I mention not so much on account of its novelty (for other men[12] have thought thus) as on account of the pertinacity with which he maintained it. This opinion, in its general form, was that of the sentience of all vegetable things. But, in his disordered fancy, the idea had assumed a more daring character, and trespassed, under certain conditions, upon the kingdom of inorganization. I lack words to express the full extent or the earnest *abandon* of his persuasion. The belief, however, was connected (as I have previously hinted) with the gray stones of the home of his forefathers. The conditions of the sentience had been here, he imagined, fulfilled in the method of collocation of these stones—in the order of their arrangement, as well as in that of the many *fungi* which overspread them, and of the decayed trees which stood around—above all, in the long-undisturbed endurance of this arrangement, and in its reduplication in the still waters of the tarn. Its evidence—the evidence of the sentience—was to be seen, he said (and I here started as he spoke), in the gradual yet certain condensation of an atmosphere of their own about the waters and the walls. The result was discoverable, he added, in that silent, yet importunate and terrible influence which for centuries had molded the destinies of his family, and which made *him* what I now saw him—what he was. Such opinions need no comment, and I will make none.

Our books—the books which, for years, had formed no small portion of the mental existence of the invalid—were, as might be supposed, in strict keeping with this character of phantasm. We pored together over such works as the *Ververt et Chartreuse*[13] of Gresset; the *Belphegor*[14] of Machiavelli; the *Heaven and Hell*[15] of Swedenborg; the *Subterranean Voyage of Nicholas Klimm*[16] by Holberg; the *Chiromancy*[17] of Robert Flud, of Jean D'Indaginé, and of De la Chambre[18]; the *Journey into the Blue Distance* of Tieck[19]; and the *City of the Sun*[20] of Campanella. One favorite volume was a small octavo edition of the *Directorium Inquisitorium*[21] by the Dominican Eymeric de Cironne; and there were passages in *Pomponius Mela*,[22] about the old African Satyrs and

Oegipans,[23] over which Usher would sit dreaming for hours. His chief delight, however, was found in the perusal of an exceedingly rare and curious book in quarto Gothic—the manual of a forgotten church—the *Vigiliae Mortuorum secundum Chorum Ecclesiae Maguntinae*.[24]

I could not help thinking of the wild ritual of this work, and of its probable influence upon the hypochondriac, when, one evening, having informed me abruptly that the lady Madeline was no more, he stated his intention of preserving her corpse for a fortnight (previously to its final interment) in one of the numerous vaults within the main walls of the building. The worldly reason, however, assigned for this singular proceeding, was one which I did not feel at liberty to dispute. The brother had been led to his resolution, so he told me, by consideration of the unusual character of the malady of the deceased, of certain obtrusive and eager inquiries on the part of her medical men, and of the remote and exposed situation of the burial ground of the family, I will not deny that when I called to mind the sinister countenance of the person whom I met upon the staircase, on the day of my arrival at the house, I had no desire to oppose what I regarded as at best but a harmless, and by no means an unnatural precaution.

At the request of Usher, I personally aided him in the arrangements for the temporary entombment. The body having been encoffined, we two alone bore it to its rest. The vault in which we placed it (and which had been so long unopened that our torches, half smothered in its oppressive atmosphere, gave us little opportunity for investigation) was small, damp, and entirely without means of admission for light; lying, at great depth, immediately beneath that portion of the building in which was my own sleeping apartment. It had been used, apparently, in remote feudal times, for the worst purposes of a donjon-keep, and in later days, as a place of deposit for powder, or some other highly combustible substance, as a portion of its floor, and the whole interior of a long archway through which we reached it, were carefully sheathed with copper. The door, of massive iron, had been also similarly protected. Its immense weight caused an unusually sharp grating sound as it moved upon its hinges.

Having deposited our mournful burden upon tressels within this region of horror, we partially turned aside the yet unscrewed lid of the coffin, and looked upon the face of the tenant. A striking similitude between the brother and sister now first arrested my attention; and Usher, divining, perhaps, my thoughts, murmured out some few words from which I learned that the deceased and himself had been twins, and that sympathies of a scarcely intelligible nature had always existed between them. Our glances, however, rested not long upon the dead—for we could not regard her unawed. The disease which had thus entombed the lady in the maturity of youth, had left, as usual in all maladies of a strictly cataleptical character, the mockery of a faint blush upon the bosom and the face, and that suspiciously lingering smile upon the lip which is so terrible in death. We replaced and screwed down the lid, and having secured the door of iron, made our way, with toil, into the scarcely less gloomy apartments of the upper portion of the house.

And now, some days of bitter grief having elapsed, an observable change came over the features of the mental disorder of my friend. His ordinary manner had vanished. His ordinary occupations were neglected or forgotten. He roamed from chamber to chamber with hurried, unequal, and objectless step. The pallor of his countenance had assumed, if possible, a more ghastly line—but the luminousness of his eye had utterly gone out. The once occasional huskiness of his tone was heard no more; and a tremulous quaver, as if of extreme terror, habitually characterized his utterance. There were times, indeed, when I thought his unceasingly agitated mind was laboring with some oppressive secret, to divulge which he struggled for the necessary courage. At times, again, I was obliged to resolve all into the mere inexplicable vagaries of madness; for I beheld him gazing upon vacancy for long hours, in an attitude of the profoundest attention, as if listening to some imaginary sound. It was no wonder that his condition terrified—that it infected me. I felt creeping upon me, by slow yet certain degrees, the wild influence of his own fantastic yet impressive superstitions.

It was, especially, upon retiring to bed late in the night of the seventh or eighth day after the placing of the lady Madeline within the donjon, that I experienced the full power of such feelings. Sleep came not near my couch, while the hours waned and waned away, I struggled to reason off the nervousness which had dominion over me. I endeavored to believe that much, if not all of what I felt, was due to the bewildering influence of the gloomy furniture of the room—of the dark and tattered draperies, which, tortured into motion by the breath of a rising tempest, swayed fitfully to and fro upon the walls, and rustled uneasily about the decorations of the bed. But my efforts were fruitless. An irrepressible tremor gradually pervaded my frame; and, at length, there sat upon my very heart an incubus of utterly causeless alarm. Shaking this off with a gasp and a struggle, I uplifted myself upon the pillows, and peering earnestly within the intense darkness of the chamber, hearkened—I know not why, except that an instinctive spirit prompted me—to certain low and indefinite sounds which came, through the pauses of the storm, at long intervals, I knew not whence. Overpowered by an intense sentiment of horror, unaccountable yet unendurable, I threw on my clothes with haste (for I felt that I should sleep no more during the night), and endeavored to arouse myself from the pitiable condition into which I had fallen, by pacing rapidly to and fro through the apartment.

I had taken but few turns in this manner, when a light step on an adjoining staircase arrested my attention. I presently recognized it as that of Usher. In an instant afterward he rapped, with a gentle touch, at my door, and entered, bearing a lamp. His countenance was, as usual, cadaverously wan—but, moreover, there was a species of mad hilarity in his eyes—and evidently restrained hysteria in his whole demeanor. His air appalled me—but anything was preferable to the solitude which I had so long endured, and I even welcomed his presence as a relief.

"And you have not seen it?" he said abruptly, after having stared about him for some moments in silence—"you have not then seen it?—but stay! you shall." Thus speaking, and having carefully shaded his lamp, he hurried to one of the casements, and threw it freely open to the storm.

The impetuous fury of the entering gust nearly lifted us from our feet. It was, indeed, a tempestuous yet sternly beautiful night, and one wildly singular in its terror and its beauty. A whirlwind had apparently collected its force in our vicinity; for there were frequent and violent alterations in the direction of the wind; and the exceeding density of the clouds (which hung so low as to press upon the turrets of the house) did not prevent our perceiving the lifelike velocity with which they flew careering from all points against each other, without passing away into the distance. I say that even their exceeding density did not prevent our perceiving this—yet we had no glimpse of the moon or stars—nor was there any flashing forth of the lightning. But the under surfaces of the huge masses of agitated vapor, as well as all terrestrial objects immediately around us, were glowing in the unnatural light of a faintly luminous and distinctly visible gaseous exhalation which hung about and enshrouded the mansion.

"You must not—you shall not behold this!" said I, shudderingly, to Usher, as I led him, with a gentle violence, from the window to a seat. "These appearances, which bewilder you, are merely electrical phenomena not uncommon—or it may be that they have their ghastly origin in the rank miasma of the tarn. Let us close this casement—the air is chilling and dangerous to your frame. Here is one of your favorite romances. I will read and you shall listen; and so we will pass away this terrible night together." The antique volume which I had taken up was the *Mad Trist* of Sir Launcelot Canning[25]; but I had called it a favorite of Usher's more in sad jest than in earnest; for, in truth, there is little in its uncouth and unimaginative prolixity which could have had interest for the lofty and spiritual ideality of my friend. It was, however, the only book immediately at hand; and I indulged a vague hope that the excitement which now agitated the hypochondriac, might find relief (for the history of mental disorder is full of similar anomalies) even in the extremeness of the folly which I should read. Could I have judged, indeed, by the wild, overstrained air of vivacity with which he hearkened, or apparently hearkened, to the words of the tale, I might well have congratulated myself upon the success of my design.

I had arrived at that well-known portion of the story where Ethelred, the hero of the "Trist," having sought in vain for peaceable admission into the dwelling of the hermit, proceeds to make good an entrance by force. Here, it will be remembered, the words of the narrative run thus:—

"And Ethelred, who was by nature of a doughty heart, and who was now mighty withal, on account of the powerfulness of the wine which he had drunken, waited no longer to hold parley with the hermit, who, in sooth, was of an obstinate and maliceful turn; but, feeling the rain upon his shoulders, and fearing the rising of the tempest, uplifted his mace outright, and, with blows, made quickly room in the plankings of the door for his gauntleted hand; and now pulling therewith sturdily, he so cracked, and ripped, and tore all asunder, that the noise of the dry and hollow-sounding wood alarummed[26] and reverberated throughout the forest."

At the termination of this sentence I started, and for a moment paused; for it appeared to me (although I at once concluded that my excited fancy had deceived me)—it appeared to me that, from some very remote portion of the mansion, there came, indistinctly, to my ears what might have been, in its exact similarity of character, the echo (but a stifled and dull one certainly) of the very cracking and ripping sound which Sir Launcelot had so particularly described. It was, beyond doubt, the coincidence alone which had arrested my attention; for, amid the rattling of the sashes of the casements, and the ordinary commingled noises of the still increasing storm, the sound, in itself, had nothing, surely, which should have interested or disturbed, me. I continued the story:—

"But the good champion Ethelred, now entering within the door, was sore enraged and amazed to perceive no signal of the maliceful hermit; but, in the stead thereof, a dragon of a scaly and prodigious demeanor, and of a fiery tongue, which sate in guard before a palace of gold, with a floor of silver; and upon the wall there hung a shield of shining brass with this legend enwritten:—

Who entereth herein, a conqueror hath been;
Who slayeth the dragon, the shield he shall win.

"And Ethelred uplifted his mace, and struck upon the head of the dragon, which fell before him, and gave up his pesty breath, with a shriek so horrid and harsh, and withal so piercing, that Ethelred had fain[27] to close his ears with his hands against the dreadful noise of it, the like whereof was never before heard."

Here again I paused abruptly, and now with a feeling of wild amazement—for there could be no doubt whatever that, in this instance, I did actually hear (although from what direction it proceeded I found it impossible to say) a low and apparently distant, but harsh, protracted, and most unusual screaming or grating sound—the exact counterpart of what my fancy had already conjured up for the dragon's unnatural shriek as described by the romancer.

Oppressed, as I certainly was, upon the occurrence of this second and most extraordinary coincidence, by a thousand conflicting sensations, in which wonder and extreme terror were predominant, I still retained sufficient presence of mind to avoid exciting, by any observation, the sensitive nervousness of my companion. I was by no means certain that he had noticed the sounds in question; although, assuredly, a strange alteration had, during the last few minutes, taken place in his demeanor. From a position fronting my own, he had gradually brought round his chair, so as to sit with his face to the door of the chamber; and thus I could but partially perceive his features, although I saw that his lips trembled as if he were murmuring inaudibly. His head had dropped upon his breast—yet I knew that he was not asleep, from the wide and rigid opening of the eye as I caught a glance of it in profile. The motion of his body, too, was at variance with this idea—for he rocked from side to side with a gentle yet constant and uniform sway. Having rapidly taken notice of all this, I resumed the narrative of Sir Launcelot, which thus proceeded:—

"And now the champion, having escaped from the terrible fury of the dragon, bethinking himself of the brazen shield, and of the breaking up of the enchantment which was upon it, removed the carcass from out of the way before him, and approached valorously over the silver pavement of the castle to where the shield was upon the wall; which in sooth tarried not for his full coming, but fell down at his feet upon the silver floor, with a mighty, great and terrible ringing sound."

No sooner had these syllables passed my lips, than—as if a shield of brass had indeed, at the moment, fallen heavily upon a floor of silver—I became aware of a distinct, hollow, metallic and clangorous, yet apparently muffled reverberation. Completely unnerved, I leaped to my feet; but the measured rocking movement of Usher was undisturbed. I rushed to the chair in which he sat. His eyes were bent fixedly before him, and throughout his whole countenance there reigned a stony rigidity. But, as I placed my hand upon his shoulder, there came a strong shudder over his whole person; a sickly smile quivered about his lips; and I saw that he spoke in a low, hurried, and gibbering murmur, as if unconscious of my presence. Bending closely over him, I at length drank in the hideous import of his words.

"Not hear it?—yes, I hear it, and *have* heard it. Long—long—long—many minutes, many hours, many days, have I heard it—yet I dared not—oh, pity me, miserable wretch that I am!—I dared not—I *dared* not speak! *We have put her living in the tomb!* Said I not that my senses were acute? I *now* tell you that I heard her first feeble movements in the hollow coffin. I heard them—many, many days ago—yet I dared not—*I dared not speak!* And now—to-night—Ethelred—ha! ha!—-the breaking of the hermit's door, and the death-cry of the dragon, and the clangor of the shield!—-say, rather, the rending of her coffin, and the grating of the iron hinges of her prison, and her struggles within the coppered archway of the vault! Oh, whither shall I fly? Will she not be here anon? Is she not hurrying to upbraid me for my haste? Have I not heard her footstep on the stair? Do I not distinguish that heavy and horrible beating of her heart? Madman!"—here he sprang furiously to his feet, and shrieked out his syllables, as if in the effort he were giving up his soul—"*Madman! I tell you that she now stands without the door!*"

As if in the superhuman energy of his utterance there had been found the potency of a spell—the huge antique panels to which the speaker pointed threw slowly back, upon the instant, their ponderous and ebony jaws. It was the work of the rushing gust—but then without those doors there *did* stand the lofty and enshrouded figure of the lady Madeline of Usher. There was blood upon her white robes, and the evidence of some bitter struggle upon every portion of her emaciated frame. For a moment she remained trembling and reeling to and fro upon the threshold—then, with a low, moaning cry, fell heavily inward upon the person of her brother, and in her violent and now final death-agonies, bore him to the floor a corpse, and a victim to the terrors he had anticipated.

From that chamber, and from that mansion, I fled aghast. The storm was still abroad in all its wrath as I found myself crossing the old causeway. Suddenly there shot along the path a wild light, and I turned to see whence a gleam so unusual could have issued; for the vast house and its shadows were alone behind me. The radiance was that of the full, setting, and blood-red moon, which now shone vividly through that once barely discernible fissure, of which I have before spoken as extending from the roof of the building, in a zigzag direction, to the base. While I gazed, this fissure rapidly widened—there came a fierce breath of the whirlwind—the entire orb of the satellite burst at once upon my sight—my brain reeled as I saw the mighty walls rushing asunder—there was a long tumultuous shouting sound like the voice of a thousand waters—and the deep and dank tarn at my feet closed sullenly and silently over the fragments of the "*House of Usher*."

# NOTES

[1] *The Fall of the House of Usher* was written in 1839 and published at the end of the same year in his Tales of the Grotesque and of the Arabesque.

[2] 70: Motto de Béranger. Popular French lyric poet (1780-1857). "His heart is a suspended lute; as soon as it is touched it resounds."

[3] 71:23 tarn. A small mountain lake.

[4] 76:7 ennuyé. Mentally wearied or bored.

[5] 78:11 bounden. An archaic word.

[6] 79:19 Dread. Reading of the first edition, "Her figure, her air, her features,—all, in their very minutest development, were those—were identically (I can use no other sufficient term), were identically those of the Roderick Usher who sat beside me. A feeling of stupor," etc.

[7] 80:16 Improvisations. Extemporaneous composition of poetry or music.

[8] 81:4 von Weber. The celebrated German composer (1786-1826).

[9] 81:20 Fuseli. An artist and professor of painting at the Royal Academy in London (1741-1825).

[10] 82:24 "The Haunted Palace." First published in the *Baltimore Museum* for April, 1839.

[11] 83:18 Porphyrogene. Of royal birth.

[12] 84:16 for other men. Watson, Dr. Percival, and especially the Bishop of Llandaff. See "Chemical Essays," Vol. V.

[13] 85:16 Ververt et Chartreuse. Two poems by Jean Baptiste Cresset (1709-1777).

[Footnote 14] 85:17 Belphegor. Satire on Marriage by Machiavelli (1469-1527).

[15] 85:17 Heaven and Hell. Extracts from "Arcana Coelestia" by Swedenborg (1688-1772).

[16] 85:18 Subterranean Voyage of Nicholas Klimm. A celebrated poem by Ludwig Holberg (1684-1754).

[17] 85:19 Chiromancy. Palmistry applied to the future. Poe refers rather to physiognomy. The book was written by the English mystic, Robert Fludd (1574-1637).

[18] 85:19 Jean d'Indaginé and De la Chambre. Two continental writers of the sixteenth and seventeenth centuries respectively.

[19] 85:21 Tieck. A great German romanticist (1773-1853).

[20] 85:21 City of the Sun. A sketch of an ideal state by Campanella (1568-1639).

[21] 85:23 Directorium Inquisitorium. A detailed account of the methods of the Inquisition by Cironne, inquisitor-general for Castile, in 1356.

[22] 85:24 Pomponius Mela. Spanish geographer in the first century A.D. Author of "De Chorographia," the earliest extant account of the geography of the ancient world.

[23] 85:25 Oegipans. An epithet applied to Pan.

[24] 85:30 Vigiliae Mortuorum. No such book is known.

[25] 90:30 Mad Trist. No such book is known.

[26] 91:29 alarummed. Alarmed.

[27] 92:25 had fain. In the sense of was glad.

# BIOGRAPHY

Edgar Allan Poe was born in Boston, January 19, 1809. His parents, who were actors, died before their son was three years old. Mr. Allan, a wealthy Richmond merchant, adopted the child and gave him a splendid home. How scantily Poe appreciated and improved the advantages of this kindness he himself confesses in a letter to Lowell in 1844. "I have been too deeply conscious of the mutability and evanescence of temporal things to give any continuous effort to anything—to be consistent in anything. My life has been *whim*—impulse—passion—a longing for solitude—a scorn of all things present in an earnest desire for the future." He was a dreamer who had a fair chance to be happy, but he flung the opportunity away. He was a spoiled child who remained ignorant of life even unto his death.

He entered the University of Virginia in 1826, where his conduct was so bad that he was, after a year, removed from the college. This action broke the strong friendship Mr. Allan had long held for his adopted son. Poe, urged by a hot temper or possibly by a remorse for his actions, ran away and enlisted in the regular army. In 1829 Mr. Allan became partially reconciled with Poe, and again came to his assistance. In 1830 Poe entered West Point, but was there only a short time when he was dismissed for wilful neglect of duty.

Following this dismissal Poe went to Baltimore, where he did hack work for newspapers. This was the beginning of a process of writing that has brought him high rank and an imperishable honor. His narrative is clear, compressed, and powerful, and throughout his writings choice symbols abound. He was fond of themes of death, insanity, and terror. The wonder of it all is that this struggling, poverty-stricken craftsman, irregular in his habits of living, using only negative life and shadowy abstractions, should, from out his disordered fancies, weave stories and poems of such undying beauty and force.

Poe married his thirteen-year-old cousin, Virginia Clemm. Her health was always delicate and her death confirmed Poe's tendency toward dissipation. His life was filled with dire poverty and a hard struggle for a livelihood. His home relations were happy. The last years of his life were spent at Fordham, a suburb of New York. He died in a Baltimore hospital, October 7, 1849.

# BIOGRAPHICAL REFERENCES

*Introduction to American Literature*, Brander Matthews.
*Studies in American Literature*, Charles Noble.
*Introduction to American Literature*, F.V.N. Painter.
*Life of Poe*, Richard Henry Stoddard.
*Edgar Allan Poe*, G.E. Woodberry.
*Makers of English Fiction*, W.J. Dawson.
"Art of Poe, *Independent*, 66: 157-8. January 21, 1909.
"Dual Personality," *Current Literature*, 43: 287-8.

# CRITICISMS

Some critics have maintained that Poe is our only original genius in American Literature. Lowell wrote in his *Fable for Critics*:—
"There comes Poe with his raven, like Barnaby Rudge, Three-fifths of him genius, and two-fifths sheer fudge."
Whatever judgments the various critics may give of Poe and his writings, they must all agree that he is original. He is a clever writer in a limited field. His writings have a glow and burnish that have their origin in his fondness for sensations, color, and vividness of details. He loves mystery and terror,—not the fancies and fears of a child, but overwrought nerves. His material is unreal, and remote from ordinary life. His characters are abnormal, and the world they live in is exceptional. He is inventive, original in arranging his material, and shallow but keen in his thinking.
He believed that art and life have little in common, and in his writings seemed to be unmoved by friendship, loyalty, patriotism, courage, self-sacrifice or any of the great positive attributes of life that make living worth while. His writings lack the human touch, tenderness, and the buoyancy of sympathy. He is an artist who does his work with a clear-cut, hard finish. His choice of words, vivid pictures, and clearly evolved plots make his writings excellent studies for any one who wishes to develop literary appreciation and to learn to write.

# GENERAL REFERENCES

*Studies and Appreciations*, L.E. Gates.
*American Prose Masters*, William Crary Brownwell.
*The Short Story in English*, Henry Seidel Canby.
*Edgar Poe*, R.H. Button.
*Inquiries and Opinions*, Brander Matthews.
"Life of Edgar Allan Poe," *Nation*, 89: 100-110.
"Weird Genius," *Cosmopolitan*, 46:243-252.

# COLLATERAL READINGS

*Ligeia*, Edgar Allan Poe.
*The Cask of Amontillado*, Edgar Allan Poe.
*The Assignation*, Edgar Allan Poe.
*Ms. Pound in Bottle*, Edgar Allan Poe.
*The Black Cat*, Edgar Allan Poe.
*Berenice*, Edgar Allan Poe.
*The Tell-Tale Heart*, Edgar Allan Poe.
*The White Old Maid*, Nathaniel Hawthorne.
*Moonlight* ("Odd Number"), Guy de Maupassant.
*A Journey*, Edith Wharton.
*The Brushwood Boy*, Rudyard Kipling.
*At the Pit's Mouth*, Rudyard Kipling.

# THE GOLD-BUG[1]

*By Edgar Allan Poe (1809-1849)*
What ho! what ho! this fellow is dancing mad!
He hath been bitten by the Tarantula.
                    *—All in the Wrong.*[2]

Many years ago I contracted an intimacy with a Mr. William Legrand. He was of an ancient Huguenot[3] family, and had once been wealthy; but a series of misfortunes had reduced him to want. To avoid the mortification consequent upon his disasters, he left New Orleans, the city of his forefathers, and took up his residence at Sullivan's Island, near Charleston, South Carolina.

This island is a very singular one. It consists of little else than the sea sand, and is about three miles long. Its breadth at no point exceeds a quarter of a mile. It is separated from the mainland by a scarcely perceptible creek, oozing its way through a wilderness of reeds and slime, a favorite resort of the marsh-hen. The vegetation, as might be supposed, is scant, or at least dwarfish. No trees of any magnitude are to be seen. Near the western extremity, where Fort Moultrie[4] stands, and where are some miserable frame buildings, tenanted, during summer, by the fugitives from Charleston dust and fever, may be found, indeed, the bristly palmetto; but the whole island, with the exception of this western point, and a line of hard, white beach on the seacoast, is covered with a dense undergrowth of the sweet myrtle, so much prized by the horticulturists of England. The shrub here often attains the height of fifteen or twenty feet, and forms an almost impenetrable coppice, burthening the air with its fragrance.

In the utmost recesses of this coppice, not far from the eastern or more remote end of the island, Legrand had built himself a small hut, which he occupied when I first, by mere accident, made his acquaintance. This soon ripened into friendship, for there was much in the recluse to excite interest and esteem. I found him well educated, with unusual powers of mind, but infected with misanthropy, and subject to perverse moods of alternate enthusiasm and melancholy. He had with him many books, but rarely employed them. His chief amusements were gunning and fishing, or sauntering along the beach and through the myrtles, in quest of shells or entomological specimens—his collection of the latter might have been envied by a Swammerdam.[5] In these excursions he was usually accompanied by an old negro, called Jupiter, who had been manumitted[6] before the reverses of the family, but who could be induced, neither by threats nor by promises, to abandon what he considered his right of attendance upon the footsteps of his young "Massa Will." It is not improbable that the relatives of Legrand, conceiving him to be somewhat unsettled in intellect, had contrived to instil this obstinacy into Jupiter, with a view to the supervision and guardianship of the wanderer.

The winters in the latitude of Sullivan's Island are seldom very severe, and in the fall of the year it is a rare event indeed when a fire is considered necessary. About the middle of October, 18—, there occurred, however, a day of remarkable chilliness. Just before sunset I scrambled my way through the evergreens to the hut of my friend, whom I had not visited for several weeks—my residence being at that time in Charleston, a distance of nine miles from the island, while the facilities of passage and re-passage were very far behind those of the present day. Upon reaching the hut I rapped, as was my custom, and getting no reply, sought for the key where I knew it was secreted, unlocked the door, and went in. A fine fire was blazing upon the hearth. It was a novelty, and by no means an ungrateful one. I threw off an over-coat, took an armchair by the crackling logs, and awaited patiently the arrival of my hosts.

Soon after dark they arrived, and gave me a most cordial welcome. Jupiter, grinning from ear to ear, bustled about to prepare some marsh-hens for supper. Legrand was in one of his fits—how else shall I term them?—of enthusiasm. He had found an unknown bivalve, forming a new genus, and, more than this, he had hunted down and secured, with Jupiter's assistance, a *scarabaeus*[7] which he believed to be totally new, but in respect to which he wished to have my opinion on the morrow.

"And why not to-night?" I asked, rubbing my hands over the blaze, and wishing the whole tribe of *scarabaei* at the devil.

"Ah, if I had only known you were here!" said Legrand, "but it's so long since I saw you; and how could I foresee that you would pay me a visit this very night of all others? As I was coming home I met Lieutenant G——, from the fort, and, very foolishly, I lent him the bug; so it will be impossible for you to see it until the morning. Stay here to-night, and I will send Jup down for it at sunrise. It is the loveliest thing in creation!"

"What!—sunrise?"

"Nonsense! no!—the bug. It is of a brilliant gold color—about the size of a large hickory-nut—with two jet-black spots near one extremity of the back, and another, somewhat longer, at the other. The *antennae[8]* are—"

"Dey ain't *no* tin in him, Massa Will, I keep a tellin' on you," here interrupted Jupiter; "de bug is a goolebug, solid, ebery bit of him, inside and all, 'sep him wing—neber feel half so hebby a bug in my life."

"Well, suppose it is, Jup," replied Legrand, somewhat more earnestly, it seemed to me, than the case demanded; "is that any reason for your letting the birds burn? The color"—here he turned to me—"is really almost enough to warrant Jupiter's idea. You never saw a more brilliant metallic lustre than the scales emit—but of this you cannot judge till to-morrow. In the meantime I can give you some idea of the shape." Saying this, he seated himself at a small table, on which were a pen and ink, but no paper. He looked for some in a drawer, but found none.

"Never mind," said he at length, "this will answer;" and he drew from his waistcoat pocket a scrap of what I took to be very dirty foolscap, and made upon it a rough drawing with the pen. While he did this I retained my seat by the fire, for I was still chilly. When the design was complete, he handed it to me without rising. As I received, it, a loud growl was heard, succeeded by a scratching at the door. Jupiter opened it, and a large Newfoundland, belonging to Legrand, rushed in, leaped upon my shoulders, and loaded me with caresses; for I had shown him much attention during previous visits. When his gambols were over, I looked at the paper, and, to speak the truth, found myself not a little puzzled at what my friend had depicted.

"Well!" I said, after contemplating it for some minutes, "this *is* a strange *scarabaeus*, I must confess: new to me: never saw anything like it before— unless it was a skull, or a death's-head—which, it more nearly resembles than, anything else that has come under *my* observation."

"A death's-head!" echoed Legrand. "Oh—yes—well, it has something of that appearance upon paper, no doubt. The two upper black spots look like eyes, eh? and the longer one at the bottom like a mouth—and then the shape of the whole is oval."

"Perhaps so," said I; "but, Legrand, I fear you are no artist. I must wait until I see the beetle itself, if I am to form any idea of its personal appearance."

"Well, I don't know," said he, a little nettled, "I draw tolerably—*should* do it at least—have had good masters, and flatter myself that I am not quite a blockhead."

"But, my dear fellow, you are joking then," said I; "this is a very passable *skull*—indeed, I may say that it is a very *excellent* skull, according to the vulgar notions about such specimens of physiology—and your *scarabaeus* must be the queerest *scarabaeus* in the world if it resembles it. Why, we may get up a very thrilling bit of superstition upon this hint. I presume, you will call the bug *scarabaeus caput hominis*,[9] or something of that kind—there are many similar titles in the natural histories. But where are the *antennae* you spoke of?"

"The *antennae*!" said Legrand, who seemed to be getting unaccountably warm upon the subject; "I am sure you must see the *antennae*. I made them as distinct as they are in the original insect, and I presume that is sufficient."

"Well, well," I said, "perhaps you have—still I don't see them;" and I handed him the paper without additional remark, not wishing to ruffle his temper; but I was much surprised at the turn affairs had taken; his ill-humor puzzled me—and, as for the drawing of the beetle, there were positively *no antennae* visible, and the whole *did* bear a very close resemblance to the ordinary cuts of a death's-head.

He received the paper very peevishly, and was about to crumple it, apparently to throw it in the fire, when a casual glance at the design seemed suddenly to rivet his attention. In an instant his face grew violently red—in another as excessively pale. For some minutes he continued to scrutinize the drawing minutely where he sat. At length he arose, took a candle from the table, and proceeded to seat himself upon a sea-chest in the farthest corner of the room. Here again he made an anxious examination of the paper, turning it in all directions. He said nothing, however, and his conduct greatly astonished me; yet I thought it prudent not to exacerbate the growing moodiness of his temper by any comment. Presently he took from, his coat pocket a wallet, placed the paper carefully in it, and deposited both in a writing-desk, which he locked. He now grew more composed in his demeanor; but his original air of enthusiasm had quite disappeared. Yet he seemed not so much sulky as abstracted. As the evening wore away he became more and more absorbed in reverie, from which no sallies of mine could arouse him. It had been my intention to pass the night at the hut, as I had frequently done before, but, seeing my host in this mood, I deemed it proper to take leave. He did not press me to remain, but, as I departed, he shook my hand with even more than his usual cordiality.

It was about a month after this (and during the interval I had seen nothing of Legrand) when I received a visit, at Charleston, from his man Jupiter. I had never seen the good old negro look so dispirited, and I feared that some serious disaster had befallen my friend.

"Well, Jup," said I, "what is the matter now?—how is your master?"

"Why, to speak de troof, massa, him not so berry well as mought be."

"Not well! I am truly sorry to hear it. What does he complain of?"

"Dar! dat's it!—him nebber 'plain of notin'—but him berry sick for all dat."

"*Very* sick, Jupiter!—why didn't you say so at once? Is he confined to bed?"

"No, dat he ain't!—he ain't 'find nowhar—dat's just whar de shoe pinch—my mind is got to be berry hebby 'bout poor Massa Will."

"Jupiter, I should like to understand what it is you are talking about. You say your master is sick. Hasn't he told you what ails him?"

"Why, massa, 'tain't worf while for to git mad 'bout de matter—Massa Will say noffin' at all ain't de matter wid him—but den what make him go about looking dis here way, wid he head down and he soldiers up, and as white as a gose? And den he keep a syphon all de time—"

"Keeps a what, Jupiter?"

"Keeps a syphon wid de figgurs on de slate—de queerest figgurs I ebber did see. Ise gittin' to be skeered I tell you. Hab for to keep mighty tight eye pon him noovers.[10] Todder day he gib me slip fore de sun up, and was gone de whole ob de blessed day. I had a big stick ready cut for to gib him d——d good beating when he did come—but Ise sich a fool dat I hadn't de heart after all—he look so berry poorly."

"Eh?—what? Ah, yes!—upon the whole, I think you had better not be too severe with the poor fellow—don't flog him, Jupiter, he can't very well stand it—but can you form an idea of what has occasioned this illness, or rather this change of conduct? Has anything unpleasant happened since I saw you?"

"No, massa, dey ain't bin noffin' onpleasant *since* den—'twas *'fore* den, I'm feared—'twas de berry day you was dare.'"

"How? what do you mean?"

"Why, massa, I mean de bug—dare now."

"The *what?*"

"De bug—I'm berry sartain dat Massa Will bin bit somewhere 'bout de head by dat goole-bug."

"And what cause have you, Jupiter, for such a supposition?"

"Claws enuff, massa, and mouff, too. I nebber did see sich a d——d bug—he kick and he bite ebery ting what cum near him. Massa Will cotch him fuss, but had for to let him go 'gin mighty quick, I tell you—den was de time he must ha' got de bite. I didn't like de look ob de bug mouff, myself, nohow, so I wouldn't take hold ob him wid my finger, but I cotch him wid a piece ob paper dat I found. I wrap him up in de paper and stuff piece ob it in he mouff—dat was de way."

"And you think, then, that your master was really bitten by the beetle, and that the bite made him sick?" "I don't t'ink noffin' 'bout it—I nose it. What make him dream 'bout de goole so much, if 'tain't cause he bit by de goole-bug? Ise heerd 'bout dem goole-bugs 'fore dis."

"But how do you know he dreams about gold?"

"How I know? why, 'cause he talk about it in he sleep—dat's how I nose."

"Well, Jup, perhaps you are right; but to what fortunate circumstances am I to attribute the honor of a visit from you to-day?"

"What de matter, massa?"

"Did you bring any message from Mr. Legrand?"

"No, massa, I bring dis here 'pissel;" and here Jupiter handed me a note, which ran thus:

My dear ————:

Why have I not seen you for so long a time? I hope you have not been so foolish as to take offence at any little *brusquerie*[11] of mine; but no, that is improbable.

Since I saw you I have had great cause for anxiety. I have something to tell you, yet scarcely know how to tell it, or whether I should tell it at all.

I have not been quite well for some days past, and poor old Jup annoys me, almost beyond endurance, by his well-meant attentions. Would you believe it?—he had prepared a huge stick, the other day, with which to chastise me for giving him the slip, and spending the day, *solus*, among the hills on the mainland. I verily believe that my ill looks alone saved me a flogging.

I have made no addition to my cabinet since we met.

If you can, in any way, make it convenient, come over with Jupiter. *Do* come. I wish to see you *to-night*, upon business of importance. I assure you that it is of the *highest* importance.

Ever yours,

William Legrand.

There was something in the tone of this note which gave me great uneasiness. Its whole style differed materially from that of Legrand. What could he be dreaming of? What new crotchet possessed his excitable brain? What "business of the highest importance" could *he* possibly have to transact? Jupiter's account of him boded no good. I dreaded lest the continued pressure of misfortune had, at length, fairly unsettled the reason of my friend. Without a moment's hesitation, therefore, I prepared to accompany the negro.

Upon reaching the wharf, I noticed a scythe and three spades, all apparently new, lying in the bottom of the boat in which we were to embark.

"What is the meaning of all this, Jup?" I inquired.

"Him syfe, massa, and spade."

"Very true; but what are they doing here?"

"Him de syfe and de spade what Massa Will 'sis' 'pon my buying for him in de town, and de debbil's own lot of money I had to gib for 'em."

"But what, in the name of all that is mysterious, is your 'Massa Will' going to do with scythes and spades?"

"Dat's more dan *I* know, and debbil take me if I don't b'lieve 'tis more dan he know, too. But it's all come ob de bug."

Finding that no satisfaction was to be obtained of Jupiter, whose whole intellect seemed to be absorbed by "de bug," I now stepped into the boat and made sail. With a fair and strong breeze we soon ran into the little cove to the northward of Fort Moultrie, and a walk of some two miles brought us to the hut. It was about three in the afternoon when we arrived. Legrand had been awaiting us in eager expectation. He grasped my hand with a nervous *empressement*[12] which alarmed me and strengthened the suspicions already entertained. His countenance was pale even to ghastliness, and his deep-set eyes glared with unnatural lustre. After some inquiries respecting his health, I asked him, not knowing what better to say, if he had yet obtained the *scarabaeus* from Lieutenant G——.

"Oh, yes," he replied, coloring violently, "I got it from him the next morning. Nothing could tempt me to part with that *scarabaeus*. Do you know that Jupiter is quite right about it!"

"In what way?" I asked, with a sad foreboding at heart.

"In supposing it to be a bug of *real gold*." He said this with an air of profound seriousness, and I felt inexpressibly shocked.

"This bug is to make my fortune," he continued, with a triumphant smile, and reinstate me in my family possessions. Is it any wonder, then, that I prize it? Since Fortune has thought fit to bestow it upon me, I have only to use it properly and I shall arrive at the gold of which it is the index. Jupiter, bring me that *scarabaeus*!"

"What! de bug, massa? I'd rudder not go fer trubble dat bug—you mus' git him for your own self." Hereupon Legrand arose, with a grave and stately air, and brought me the beetle from a glass case in which it was enclosed. It was a beautiful *scarabaeus*, and, at that time, unknown to naturalists— of course a great prize in a scientific point of view. There were two round black spots near one extremity of the back, and a long one near the other. The scales were exceedingly hard and glossy, with all the appearance of burnished gold. The weight of the insect was very remarkable, and, taking all things into consideration, I could hardly blame Jupiter for his opinion respecting it; but what to make of Legrand's agreement with that opinion, I could not, for the life of me, tell.

"I sent for you," said he, in a grandiloquent tone when I had completed my examination of the beetle, "I sent for you, that I might have your counsel and assistance in furthering the views of Fate and of the bug"—

"My dear Legrand," I cried, interrupting him, "you are certainly unwell, and had better use some little precautions. You shall go to bed, and I will remain with you a few days, until you get over this. You are feverish and"—

"Feel my pulse," said he.

I felt it, and, to say the truth, found not the slightest indication of fever.

"But you may be ill and yet have no fever. Allow me this once to prescribe for you. In the first place, go to bed. In the next"—

"You are mistaken," he interposed; "I am as well as I can expect to be under the excitement which I suffer. If you really wish me well, you will relieve this excitement."

"And how is this to be done?"

"Very easily, Jupiter and myself are going upon an expedition into the hills, upon the mainland, and, in this expedition, we shall need the aid of some person in whom we can confide. You are the only one we can trust. Whether we succeed or fail, the excitement which you now perceive in me will be equally allayed."

"I am anxious to oblige you in any way," I replied; "but do you mean to say that this infernal beetle has any connection with your expedition into the hills?"

"It has."

"Then, Legrand, I can become a party to no such absurd proceeding."

"I am sorry—very sorry—for we shall have to try it by ourselves."

"Try it by yourselves! The man is surely mad!—but stay!—how long do you propose to be absent?"

"Probably all night. We shall start immediately, and be back, at all events, by sunrise."

"And will you promise me upon your honor, that when this freak of yours is over, and the bug business (good God!) settled to your satisfaction, you will then return home and follow my advice implicitly, as that of your physician?"

"Yes; I promise; and now let us be off, for we have no time to lose."

With a heavy heart I accompanied my friend. We started about four o'clock—Legrand, Jupiter, the dog, and myself. Jupiter had with him the scythe and spades, the whole of which he insisted upon carrying, more through fear, it seemed to me, of trusting either of the implements within reach of his master, than from any excess of industry or complaisance. His demeanor was dogged in the extreme, and "dat d——d bug" were the sole words which escaped his lips during the journey. For my own part, I had charge of a couple of dark lanterns, while Legrand contented himself with the *scarabaeus*, which he carried attached to the end of a bit of whipcord, twirling it to and fro, with the air of a conjurer, as he went. When I observed this last plain evidence of my friend's aberration of mind, I could scarcely refrain from tears. I thought it best, however, to humor his fancy, at least for the present, or until I could adopt some more energetic measures with a chance of success. In the meantime I endeavored, but all in vain, to sound him in regard to the object of the expedition. Having succeeded in inducing me to accompany him, he seemed unwilling to hold conversation upon any topic of minor importance, and to all my questions vouchsafed no other reply than "We shall see!"

We crossed the creek at the head of the island by means of a skiff, and, ascending the high grounds on the shore of the mainland, proceeded in a northwesterly direction, through a tract of country excessively wild and desolate, where no trace of a human footstep was to be seen. Legrand led the way with decision, pausing only for an instant, here and there, to consult what appeared is to be certain landmarks of his own contrivance upon a former occasion.

In this manner we journeyed for about two hours, and the sun was just setting when we entered a region infinitely more dreary than any yet seen. It was a species of table-land, near the summit of an almost inaccessible hill, densely wooded from base to pinnacle, and interspersed with huge crags that appeared to lie loosely upon the soil, and in many cases were prevented from precipitating themselves into the valleys below, merely by the support of the trees against which they reclined. Deep ravines, in various directions, gave an air of still sterner solemnity to the scene.

The natural platform to which we had clambered was thickly overgrown with brambles, through which we soon discovered that it would have been impossible to force our way but for the scythe; and Jupiter, by direction of his master, proceeded to clear for us a path to the foot of an enormously tall tulip-tree, which stood, with some eight or ten oaks, upon the level, and far surpassed them all, and all other trees which I had ever seen, in the beauty of its foliage and form, in the wide spread of its branches, and in the general majesty of its appearance. When we reached this tree, Legrand turned to Jupiter, and asked him if he thought he could climb it. The old man seemed a little staggered by the question, and for some moments made no reply. At length he approached the huge trunk, walked slowly around it, and examined it with minute attention. When he had completed his scrutiny, he merely said:

"Yes, massa, Jup climb any tree he ebber see in he life."

"Then up with you as soon as possible, for it will soon be too dark to see what we are about."

"How far mus' go up, massa?" inquired Jupiter.

"Get up the main trunk first, and then I will tell you which way to go—and here—stop! take this beetle with you."

"De bug, Massa Will! de goole-bug!" cried the negro, drawing back in dismay, "what for mus' tote de bug way up de tree?—d——n if I do!"

"If you are afraid, Jup, a great big negro like you, to take hold of a harmless little dead beetle, why, you can carry it up by this string; but if you do not take it up with you in some way, I shall be under the necessity of breaking your head with this shovel."

"'What de matter, now, massa?" said Jup, evidently shamed into compliance; "always want fur to raise fuss wid old nigger. Was only funnin' anyhow. *Me* feered de bug! what I keer for de bug?" Here he took cautiously hold of the extreme end of the string, and, maintaining the insect as far from his person as circumstances would permit, prepared to ascend the tree.

In youth the tulip-tree, or *Liriodendron tulipifera,* the most magnificent of American foresters, has a trunk peculiarly smooth, and often rises to a great height without lateral branches; but, in its riper age, the bark becomes gnarled and uneven, while many short limbs make their appearance on the stem. Thus the difficulty of ascension, in the present case, lay more in semblance than in reality. Embracing the huge cylinder as closely as possible with his arms and knees, seizing with his hands some projections, and resting his naked toes upon others, Jupiter, after one or two narrow escapes from falling, at length wriggled himself into the first great fork, and seemed to consider the whole business as virtually accomplished. The *risk* of the achievement was, in fact, now over, although the climber was some sixty or seventy feet from the ground.

"Which way mus' go now, Massa Will?" he asked.

"Keep up the largest branch, the one on this side," said Legrand. The negro obeyed him promptly, and apparently with but little trouble; ascending higher and higher, until no glimpse of his squat figure could be obtained through the dense foliage which enveloped it. Presently his voice was heard in a sort of halloo.

"How much fudder I's got for go?"

"How high up are you?" asked Legrand.

"Ebber so fur," replied the negro; "can see de sky fru de top ob de tree."

"Never mind the sky, but attend to what I say. Look down the trunk and count the limbs below you on this side. How many limbs have you passed?"

"One, two, three, four, fibe—I done pass fibe big limb, massa, 'pon dis side."

"Then go one limb higher."

In a few minutes the voice was heard again, announcing that the seventh limb was attained.

"Now, Jup," cried Legrand, evidently much excited, "I want you to work your way out upon that limb as far as you can. If you see anything strange, let me know."

By this time what little doubt I might have entertained of my poor friend's insanity was put finally at rest. I had no alternative but to conclude him stricken with lunacy, and I became seriously anxious about getting him home. While I was pondering upon what was best to be done, Jupiter's voice was again heard.

"Mos' feerd for to ventur' 'pon dis limb berry far—'tis dead limb putty much all de way."

"Did you say it was a *dead* limb, Jupiter?" cried Legrand, in a quavering voice.

"Yes, massa, him dead as de door-nail—done up for sartain—done departed dis here life."

"What in the name of heaven shall I do?" asked Legrand, seemingly in the greatest distress.

"Do!" said I, glad of an opportunity to interpose a word, "why, come home and go to bed. Come now!—that's a fine fellow. It's getting late, and, besides, you remember your promise."

"Jupiter," cried he, without heeding me in the least, "do you hear me?"

"Yes, Massa Will, hear you ebber so plain,"

"Try the wood well, then, with your knife, and see if you think it *very* rotten."

"Him rotten, massa, sure nuff," replied the negro in a few moments, "but not so berry rotten as mought be, Mought ventur' out leetle way 'pon de limb by myself, dat's true."

"By yourself! What do you mean?"

"Why, I mean de bug. 'Tis *berry* hebby bug. S'pose I drop him down fust, and den de limb won't break wid just de weight of one nigger."

"You infernal scoundrel!" cried Legrand, apparently much relieved, "what do you mean by telling me such nonsense as that? As sure as you drop that beetle, I'll break your neck. Look here, Jupiter, do you hear me?"

"Yes, massa, needn' hollo at poor nigger dat style."

"Well!—now listen! if you will venture out on the limb as far as you think safe, and not let go the beetle, I'll make you a present of a silver dollar as soon as you get down."

"I'm gwine, Massa Will—deed I is," replied the negro very promptly— "mos' out to de eend now."

"*Out to the end*!" here fairly screamed Legrand; "do you say you are out to the end of that limb?"

"Soon be to de eend, massa—o-o-o-o-oh! Lor-gol-a-marcy! what *is* dis here 'pon de tree?"

"Well," cried Legrand, highly delighted, "what is it?"

"Why, 'taint noffin' but a skull—somebody bin lef' him head up de tree, and de crows done gobble ebery bit ob de meat off."

"A skull, you say! Very well; how is it fastened to the limb? What holds it on?"

"Shure 'nuff, massa; mus' look. Why, dis berry curous sarcumstance, 'pon my word—dare's a great big nail in do skull, what fastens ob it on to de tree."

"Well now, Jupiter, do exactly as I tell you—do you hear?"

"Yes, massa."

"Pay attention, then!—find the left eye of the skull."

"Hum! hoo! dat's good! why, dare ain't no eye lef' at all."

"Curse your stupidity! do you know your right hand from your left?"

"Yes, I nose dat—nose all 'bout dat—'tis my lef' hand what I chops de wood wid."

"To be sure! you are left-handed; and your left eye is on the same side as your left hand. Now, I suppose you can find the left eye of the skull, or the place where the left eye has been. Have you found it?"

Here was a long pause. At length the negro asked:

"Is de lef' eye ob de skull 'pon de same side as de lef' hand ob de skull, too?—'cause the skull ain't got not a bit ob a hand at all—nebber mind! I got de lef' eye now—here de lef' eye! what mus' do wid it?"

"Let the beetle drop through it, as far as the string will reach, but be careful and not let go your hold of the string."

"All dat done, Massa Will; mighty easy ting for to put de bug fru de hole; look out for him dar below!"

During this colloquy no portion of Jupiter's person could be seen; but the beetle, which he had suffered to descend, was now visible at the end of the string, and glistened, like a globe of burnished gold, in the last rays of the setting sun, some of which still faintly illumined the eminence upon which we stood. The *scarabaeus* hung quite clear of any branches, and if allowed to fall, would have fallen at our feet. Legrand immediately took the scythe, and cleared with it a circular space, three or four yards in diameter, just beneath the insect, and, having accomplished this, ordered Jupiter to let go the string and come down from the tree.

Driving a peg, with great nicety, into the ground, at the precise spot where the beetle fell, my friend now produced from his pocket a tape-measure. Fastening one end of this at that point of the trunk of the tree which was nearest the peg, he unrolled it till it reached the peg, and thence farther unrolled it, in the direction already established by the two points of the tree and the peg, for the distance of fifty feet—Jupiter clearing away the brambles with the scythe. At the spot thus attained a second peg was driven, and about this, as a centre, a rude circle, about four feet in diameter, described. Taking now a spade himself, and giving one to Jupiter and one to me, Legrand begged us to set about digging as quickly as possible.

To speak the truth, I had no especial relish for such amusement at any time, and, at that particular moment, would most willingly have declined it; for the night was coming on, and I felt much fatigued with the exercise already taken; but I saw no mode of escape, and was fearful of disturbing my poor friend's equanimity by a refusal. Could I have depended, indeed, upon Jupiter's aid, I would have had no hesitation in attempting to get the lunatic home by force; but I was too well assured of the old negro's disposition, to hope that he would assist me, under any circumstances, in a personal contest with his master. I made no doubt that the latter had been infected with some of the innumerable Southern superstitions about money buried, and that his fantasy had received confirmation by the finding of the *scarabaeus*, or, perhaps, by Jupiter's obstinacy in maintaining it to be "a bug of real gold." A mind disposed to lunacy would readily be led away by such suggestions—especially if chiming in with favorite preconceived ideas—and then I called to mind the poor fellow's speech about the beetle's being "the index of his fortune." Upon the whole, I was sadly vexed and puzzled, but, at length, I concluded to make a virtue of necessity—to dig with a good will, and thus the sooner to convince the visionary, by ocular demonstration, of the fallacy of the opinions he entertained.

The lanterns having been lit, we all fell to work with a zeal worthy a more rational cause; and, as the glare fell upon our persons and implements, I could not help thinking how picturesque a group we composed, and how strange and suspicious our labors must have appeared to any interloper who, by chance, might have stumbled upon our whereabouts.

We dug very steadily for two hours. Little was said; and our chief embarrassment lay in the yelping of the dog, who took exceeding interest in our proceedings. He at length became so obstreperous, that we grew fearful of his giving the alarm to some stragglers in the vicinity—or, rather, this was the apprehension of Legrand; for myself, I should have rejoiced at any interruption which might have enabled me to get the wanderer home. The noise was, at length, very effectually silenced by Jupiter, who, getting out of the hole with a dogged air of deliberation, tied the brute's mouth up with one of his suspenders, and then returned, with a grave chuckle, to his task.

When the time mentioned had expired, we had reached a depth of five feet, and yet no signs of any treasure became manifest. A general pause ensued, and I began to hope that the farce was at an end. Legrand, however, although evidently much disconcerted, wiped his brow thoughtfully and recommenced. We had excavated the entire circle of four feet diameter, and now we slightly enlarged the limit, and went to the farther depth of two feet. Still nothing appeared. The gold seeker, whom I sincerely pitied, at length clambered from the pit, with the bitterest disappointment imprinted upon every feature, and proceeded, slowly and reluctantly, to put on his coat, which he had thrown off at the beginning of his labor. In the meantime I made no remark. Jupiter, at a signal from his master, began to gather up his tools. This done, and the dog having been unmuzzled, we turned in profound silence towards home.

We had taken, perhaps, a dozen steps in this direction, when, with a loud oath, Legrand strode up to Jupiter and seized him by the collar. The astonished negro opened his eyes and mouth to the fullest extent, let fall the spades, and fell upon his knees.

"You scoundrel," said Legrand, hissing out the syllables from between his clenched teeth, "you infernal black villain! speak, I tell you! answer me this instant, without prevarication! which—which is your left eye?"

"Oh, my golly, Massa Will! ain't dis here my lef' eye for sartain?" roared the terrified Jupiter, placing his hand upon his *right* organ of vision, and holding it there with a desperate pertinacity, as if in immediate dread of his master's attempt at a gouge.

"I thought so! I knew it! hurrah!" vociferated Legrand, letting the negro go, and executing a series of curvets and caracoles[13], much to the astonishment of his valet, who, arising from his knees, looked mutely from his master to myself, and then from myself to his master.

"Come! we must go back," said the latter; "the game's not up yet;" and he again led the way to the tulip-tree.

"Jupiter," said he, when he reached its foot, "come here! was the skull nailed to the limb with the face outwards, or with the face to the limb?"

"De face was out, massa, so dat de crows could get at de eyes good, widout any trouble."

"Well, then, was it this eye or that through which you dropped the beetle?"—here Legrand touched each of Jupiter's eyes.

"'Twas dis eye, massa—de lef' eye—jis as you tell me," and here it was his right eye that the negro indicated.

"That will do—we must try it again."

Here my friend, about whose madness I now saw or fancied that I saw, certain indications of method, removed the peg which marked the spot where the beetle fell, to a spot about three inches to the westward of its former position, Taking now the tape-measure from the nearest point of the trunk to the peg, as before, and continuing the extension in a straight line to the distance of fifty feet, a spot was indicated, removed by several yards from the point at which we had been digging.

Around the new position a circle, somewhat larger than in the former instance, was now described, and we again set to work with the spades, I was dreadfully weary, but scarcely understanding what had occasioned the change in my thoughts, I felt no longer any great aversion from the labor imposed, I had become most unaccountably interested—nay, even excited. Perhaps there was something, amid all the extravagant demeanor of Legrand—some air of forethought, or of deliberation, which impressed me. I dug eagerly, and now and then caught myself actually looking, with something that very much resembled expectation, for the fancied treasure, the vision of which had demented my unfortunate companion. At a period when such vagaries of thought most fully possessed me, and when we had been at work perhaps an hour and a half, we were again interrupted by the violent howlings of the dog. His uneasiness in the first instance had been, evidently, but the result of playfulness or caprice, but he now assumed a bitter and serious tone. Upon Jupiter's again attempting to muzzle him, he made furious resistance, and, leaping into the hole, tore up the mould frantically with his claws. In a few seconds he had uncovered a mass of human bones, forming two complete skeletons, intermingled with several buttons of metal, and what appeared to be the dust of decayed woolen. One or two strokes of a spade upturned the blade of a large Spanish knife, and, as we dug farther, three or four pieces of gold and silver coin came to light. At sight of these the joy of Jupiter could scarcely be restrained, but the countenance of his master wore an air of extreme disappointment. He urged us, however, to continue our exertions, and the words were hardly uttered when I stumbled and fell forward, having caught the toe of my boot in a large ring of iron that lay half buried in the loose earth.

We now worked in earnest, and never did I pass ten minutes of more intense excitement. During this interval we had fairly unearthed an oblong chest of wood which, from its perfect preservation and wonderful hardness, had plainly been subjected to some mineralizing process—perhaps that of the bichloride of mercury. This box was three feet and a half long, three feet broad, and two and a half feet deep. It was firmly secured by bands of wrought iron, riveted, and forming a kind of trellis-work over the whole. On each side of the chest, near the top, were three rings of iron—six in all—by means of which a firm hold could be obtained by six persons. Our utmost united endeavors served only to disturb the coffer very slightly in its bed. We at once saw the impossibility of removing so great a weight. Luckily, the sole fastenings of the lid consisted of two sliding bolts. These we drew back—trembling and panting with anxiety. In an instant, a treasure of incalculable value lay gleaming before us. As the rays of the lanterns fell within the pit, there flashed upwards a glow and a glare, from a confused heap of gold and of jewels, that absolutely dazzled our eyes.

I shall not pretend to describe the feelings with which I gazed. Amazement was, of course, predominant. Legrand appeared exhausted with excitement, and spoke very few words. Jupiter's countenance wore, for some minutes, as deadly a pallor as it is possible, in the nature of things, for any negro's visage to assume. He seemed stupefied——thunder-stricken. Presently he fell upon his knees in the pit, and, burying his naked arms up

to the elbows in gold, let them there remain, as if enjoying the luxury of a bath. At length, with a deep sigh, he exclaimed, as if in a soliloquy:
"And dis all cum ob de goole-bug! de putty goole-bug! de poor little goole-bug, what I 'boosed in dat sabage kind ob style! Ain't you 'shamed ofa yourself, nigger?—answer me dat!"
It became necessary, at last, that I should arouse both master and valet to the expediency of removing the treasure. It was growing late, and it behooved us to make exertion, that we might get everything housed before daylight. It was difficult to say what should be done, and much time was spent in deliberation—so confused were the ideas of all. We, finally, lightened the box by removing two-thirds of its contents, when we were enabled, with some trouble, to raise it from the hole. The articles taken out were deposited among the brambles, and the dog left to guard them, with strict orders from Jupiter neither, upon any pretence, to stir from the spot, nor to open his mouth until our return. We then hurriedly made for home with the chest, reaching the hut in safety, but after excessive toil, at one o'clock in the morning. Worn out as we were, it was not in human nature to do more just now. We rested until two, and had supper, starting for the hills immediately afterwards, armed with three stout sacks, which, by good luck, were upon the premises. A little before four we arrived at the pit, divided the remainder of the booty as equally as might be among us, and, leaving the holes unfilled, again set out for the hut, at which, for the second time, we deposited our golden burdens, just as the first streaks of dawn gleamed from over the treetops in the east.
We were now thoroughly broken down; but the intense excitement of the time denied us repose. After an unquiet slumber of some three or four hours' duration, we arose, as if by preconcert, to make examination of our treasure.
The chest had been full to the brim, and we spent the whole day, and the greater part of the next night, in a scrutiny of its contents. There had been nothing like order or arrangement. Everything had been heaped in promiscuously.
Having assorted all with care, we found ourselves possessed of even vaster wealth than we had at first supposed. In coin there was rather more than four hundred and fifty thousand dollars—estimating the value of the pieces, as accurately as we could, by the tables of the period. There was not a particle of silver. All was gold of antique date and of great variety— French, Spanish, and German money, with a few English guineas, and some counters[14] of which we had never seen specimens before. There

were several very large and heavy coins, so worn that we could make nothing of their inscriptions. There was no American money. The value of the jewels we found more difficulty in estimating. There were diamonds—some of them exceedingly large and fine—a hundred and ten in all, and not one of them small; eighteen rubies of remarkable brilliancy; three hundred and ten emeralds, all very beautiful; and twenty-one sapphires, with an opal. These stones had all been broken from their settings and thrown loose in the chest. The settings themselves, which we picked out from among the other gold, appeared to have been beaten up with hammers, as if to prevent indentification. Besides all this, there was a vast quantity of solid gold ornaments—nearly two hundred massive finger and ear rings; rich chains—thirty of these, if I remember; eighty-three very large and heavy crucifixes; five gold censers of great value; a prodigious golden punch-bowl, ornamented with richly chased vine-leaves and Bacchanalian[15] figures; with two sword handles exquisitely embossed, and many other smaller articles which I cannot recollect. The weight of these valuables exceeded three hundred and fifty pounds avoirdupois; and in this estimate I have not included one hundred and ninety-seven superb gold watches, three of the number being worth each five hundred dollars, if one. Many of them were very old, and as time-keepers valueless, the works having suffered, more or less, from corrosion; but all were richly jewelled and in cases of great worth. We estimated the entire contents of the chest, that night, at a million and a half of dollars; and, upon the subsequent disposal of the trinkets and jewels (a few being retained for our own use), it was found we had greatly undervalued the treasure.

When, at length, we had concluded our examination, and the intense excitement of the time had in some measure subsided, Legrand, who saw that I was dying with impatience for a solution of this most extraordinary riddle, entered into a full detail of all the circumstances connected with it.

"You remember," said he, "the night when I handed you the rough sketch I had made of the *scarabaeus*. You recollect, also, that I became quite vexed at you for insisting that my drawing resembled a death's-head. When you first made this assertion I thought you were jesting; but afterwards I called to mind the peculiar spots on the back of the insect, and admitted to myself that your remark had some, little foundation in fact. Still, the sneer at my graphic powers irritated me—for I am considered a good artist—and, therefore, when you handed me the scrap of parchment, I was about to crumple it up and throw it angrily into the fire."

"The scrap of paper, you mean," said I.

"No; it had much of the appearance of paper, and at first I supposed it to be such, but when I came to draw upon it, I discovered it at once to be a piece of very thin parchment. It was quite dirty, you remember. Well, as I was in the very act of crumpling it up, my glance fell upon the sketch at which you had been looking, and you may imagine my astonishment when I perceived, in fact, the figure of a death's-head just where, it seemed to me, I had made the drawing of the beetle. For a moment I was too much amazed to think with accuracy. I knew that my design was very different in detail from this, although there was a certain similarity in general outline. Presently I took a candle, and seating myself at the other end of the room, proceeded to scrutinize the parchment more closely. Upon turning it over, I saw my own sketch upon, the reverse, just as I had made it. My first idea, now, was mere surprise at the really remarkable similarity of outline—at the singular coincidence involved in the fact that, unknown to me, there should have been a skull upon the other side of the parchment, immediately beneath my figure of the *scarabaeus*, and that this skull, not only in outline, but in size, should so closely resemble my drawing. I say the singularity of this coincidence absolutely stupefied me for a time. This is the usual effect of such coincidences. The mind struggles to establish a connection—a sequence of cause and effect—and being unable to do so, suffers a species of temporary paralysis. But when I recovered from this stupor, there dawned upon me gradually a conviction which startled me even far more than the coincidence. I began distinctly, positively, to remember that there had been *no* drawing upon the parchment when I made my sketch of the *scarabaeus*. I became perfectly certain of this; for I recollected turning up first one side and then the other, in search of the cleanest spot. Had the skull been then there, of course, I could not have failed to notice it. Here was indeed a mystery which I felt it impossible to explain; but, even at that early moment, there seemed to glimmer, faintly, within the most remote and secret chambers of my intellect, a glowworm-like conception of that truth which last night's adventure brought to so magnificent a demonstration. I arose at once, and putting the parchment securely away, dismissed all further reflection until I should be alone.

"When you had gone, and when Jupiter was fast asleep, I betook myself to a more methodical investigation of the affair. In the first place I considered the manner in which the parchment had come into my possession. The spot where we discovered the *scarabaeus* was on the coast of the mainland, about a mile eastward of the island, and but a short distance above high water mark. Upon my taking hold of it, it gave me a sharp bite, which caused me to let it drop. Jupiter, with his accustomed caution, before seizing the insect, which had flown towards him, looked about him for a leaf, or something of that nature, by which to take hold of it. It was at this moment that his eyes, and mine also, fell upon the scrap of parchment, which I then supposed to be paper. It was lying half buried in the sand, a corner sticking up. Near the spot where we found it, I observed the remnants of the hull of what appeared to have been a ship's long-boat. The wreck seemed to have been there for a very great while; for the resemblance to boat timbers could scarcely be traced.

"Well, Jupiter picked up the parchment, wrapped the beetle in it, and gave it to me. Soon afterwards we turned to go home, and on the way met Lieutenant G——. I showed him the insect, and he begged me to let him take it to the fort. Upon my consenting, he thrust it forthwith into his waistcoat pocket, without the parchment in which it had been wrapped, and which I had continued to hold in my hand during his inspection. Perhaps he dreaded my changing my mind, and thought it best to make sure of the prize at once—you know how enthusiastic he is on all subjects connected with Natural History. At the same time, without being conscious of it, I must have deposited the parchment in my own pocket.

"You remember that when I went to the table, for the purpose of making a sketch of the beetle, I found no paper where it was usually kept, I looked in the drawer, and found none there. I searched my pockets, hoping to find an old letter, when my hand fell upon the parchment. I thus detail the precise mode in which it came into my possession; for the circumstances impressed me with peculiar force.

"No doubt you will think me fanciful, but I had already established a kind of *connection*. I had put together two links of a great chain. There was a boat lying upon a seacoast, and not far from the boat was a parchment—*not a paper*—with a skull depicted upon it. You will, of course, ask, 'Where is the connection?' I reply that the skull, or death's-head, is the well-known emblem of the pirate. The flag of the death's-head is hoisted in all engagements.

"I have said that the scrap was parchment, and not paper. Parchment is durable—almost imperishable. Matters of little moment are rarely consigned to parchment, since, for the mere ordinary purposes of drawing or writing, it is not nearly so well adapted as paper. This reflection suggested some meaning—some relevancy—in the death's-head. I did not fail to observe, also, the *form* of the parchment. Although one of its corners had been, by some accident, destroyed, it could be seen that the original form was oblong. It was just such a slip, indeed, as might have been chosen for a memorandum—for a record of something to be long remembered and carefully preserved."

"But," I interposed, "you say that the skull was *not* upon the parchment when you made the drawing of the beetle. How, then, do you trace any connection between the boat and the skull—since this latter, according to your own admission, must have been designed (God only knows how or by whom) at some period subsequent to your sketching the *scarabaeus*?"

"Ah, hereupon turns the whole mystery; although the secret, at this point, I had comparatively little difficulty in solving. My steps were sure, and could afford but a single result. I reasoned, for example, thus: When I drew the *scarabaeus*, there was no skull apparent upon the parchment. When I had completed the drawing I gave it to you, and observed you narrowly until you returned it, *You*, therefore, did not design the skull, and no one else was present to do it. Then it was not done by human agency. And nevertheless it was done.

"At this stage of my reflections I endeavored to remember, and *did* remember, with entire distinctness, every incident which occurred about the period in question. The weather was chilly (oh, rare and happy accident!), and a fire was blazing upon the hearth. I was heated with exercise, and sat near the table. You, however, had drawn a chair close to the chimney. Just as I placed the parchment in your hand, and as you were in the act of inspecting it, Wolf, the Newfoundland, entered, and leaped upon your shoulders. With, your left hand you caressed him and kept him off, while your right, holding the parchment, was permitted to fall listlessly between your knees, and in close proximity to the fire. At one moment I thought the blaze had caught it, and was about to caution you, but before I could speak you had withdrawn it, and were engaged in its examination. When I considered all these particulars, I doubted not for a moment that *heat* had been the agent in bringing to light, upon the parchment, the skull which I saw designed upon it. You are well aware that chemical preparations exist, and have existed time out of mind, by means of which it is possible to write upon either paper or vellum, so that the characters shall become visible only when subjected to the action of fire. Zaffre[16], digested in *aqua regia*[17], and diluted with four times its weight of water, is sometimes employed; a green tint results. The regulus[18] of cobalt, dissolved in spirit of nitre, gives a red. These colors disappear at longer or shorter intervals after the material written upon cools, but again become apparent upon the re-application of heat.

"I now scrutinized the death's-head with care. Its outer edges—the edges of the drawing nearest the edge of the vellum—were far more *distinct* than the others. It was clear that the action of the caloric had been imperfect or unequal. I immediately kindled a fire, and subjected every portion of the parchment to a glowing heat. At first, the only effect was the strengthening of the faint lines in the skull; but, upon persevering in the experiment, there became visible, at the corner of the slip diagonally opposite to the spot in which the death's-head was delineated, the figure of what I at first supposed to be a goat. A closer scrutiny, however, satisfied me that it was intended for a kid."

"Ha! ha!" said I; "to be sure I have no right to laugh at you—a million and a half of money is too serious a matter for mirth—but you are not about to establish a third link in your chain: you will not find any especial connection between your pirates and a goat; pirates, you know, have nothing to do with goats; they appertain to the farming interests."

"But I have said that the figure was *not* that of a goat."

"Well, a kid, then—pretty much the same thing."

"Pretty much, but not altogether," said Legrand.

"You may have heard of one *Captain* Kidd[19]. I at once looked on the figure of the animal as a kind of punning or hieroglyphical signature. I say signature because its position upon the vellum suggested this idea. The death's-head at the corner diagonally opposite had, in the same manner, the air of a stamp, or seal. But I was sorely put out by the absence of all else— of the body to my imagined instrument—of the text for my context."

"I presume you expected to find a letter between the stamp and the signature."

"Something of the kind. The fact is, I felt irresistibly impressed with a presentiment of some vast good fortune impending. I can scarcely say why. Perhaps, after all, it was rather a desire than an actual belief; but do you know that Jupiter's silly words, about the bug being of solid gold, had a remarkable effect upon my fancy? And then the series of accidents and coincidences—these were so *very* extraordinary. Do you observe how mere an accident it was that these events should have occurred upon the *sole* day of all the year in which it has been, or may be, sufficiently cool for fire, and that without the fire, or without the intervention of the dog at the precise moment in which he appeared, I should, never have become aware of the death's-head, and so never the possessor of the treasure?"

"But proceed—I am all impatience."

"Well; you have heard, of course, the many stories current—the thousand vague rumors afloat about money buried, somewhere, upon the Atlantic coast, by Kidd and his associates. These rumors must have had some foundation in fact. And that the rumors have existed so long and so continuously could have resulted, it appeared to me, only from the circumstance of the buried treasure still *remaining* entombed. Had Kidd concealed his plunder for a time, and afterwards reclaimed it, the rumors would scarcely have reached us in their present unvarying form. You will observe that the stories told are all about money-seekers, not about money-finders. Had the pirate recovered his money, there the affair would have dropped. It seemed to me that some accident—say the loss of a memorandum indicating its locality—had deprived him of the means of recovering it, and that this accident had become known to his followers who otherwise might never have heard that treasure had been concealed at all, and who, busying themselves in vain, because unguided attempts to regain it had given first birth, and then universal currency, to the reports which are now so common. Have you ever heard of any important treasure being unearthed along the coast?"

"Never."

"But that Kidd's accumulations were immense is well known. I took it for granted, therefore, that the earth still held them; and you will scarcely be surprised when I tell you that I felt a hope, nearly amounting to certainty, that the parchment so strangely found involved a lost record of the place of deposit."

"But how did you proceed?"

"I held the vellum again to the fire, after increasing the heat; but nothing appeared. I now thought it possible that the coating of dirt might have something to do with the failure; so I carefully rinsed the parchment by pouring warm water over it, and, having done this, I placed it in a tin pan, with the skull downwards, and put the pan upon a furnace of lighted charcoal. In a few minutes, the pan having become thoroughly heated, I removed the slip, and to my inexpressible joy, found it spotted, in several places, with what appeared to be figures arranged in lines. Again I placed it in the pan, and suffered it to remain another minute. Upon taking it off, the whole was just as you see it now."

Here Legrand, having reheated the parchment, submitted it to my inspection, The following characters were rudely traced, in a red tint between the death's-head and the goat:

"53‡‡†305))6*;4826)4‡.);806*;48†8
¶60))85;1‡(;:‡*8†83(88)5*†;46(;88*96
?;8)*‡(;485);5*†2:*‡(;4956*2(5*—4)8
¶8*;4069285);)6†8)4‡‡;1(‡9;48081;8:8‡
1;48†85;4)485†528806*81(‡9;48;(88;4 (‡?34;48)4‡;161;:188;‡?;"
"But," said I, returning him the slip, "I am as much in the dark as ever. Were all the jewels of Golconda[20] awaiting me on my solution of this enigma, I am quite sure that I should be unable to earn them."
"And yet," said Legrand, "the solution is by no means so difficult as you might be led to imagine from the first hasty inspection of the characters. These characters, as any one might readily guess, form a cipher, that is to say, they convey a meaning; but then, from what is known of Kidd, I could not suppose him capable of constructing any of the more abstruse cryptographs[21]. I made up my mind, at once, that this was of a simple species—such, however, as would appear, to the crude intellect of the sailor, absolutely insoluble without the key."
"And you really solved it?"
"Readily; I have solved others of an abstruseness ten thousand times greater. Circumstances, and a certain bias of mind, have led me to take interest in such riddles, and it may well be doubted whether human ingenuity can construct an enigma of the kind which human ingenuity may not, by proper application, resolve. In fact, having once established connected and legible characters, I scarcely gave a thought to the mere difficulty of developing their import.
"In the present case—indeed, in all cases of secret writing—the first question regards the *language* of the cipher; for the principles of solution, so far especially as the more simple ciphers are concerned, depend upon, and are varied by, the genius of the particular idiom. In general, there is no alternative but experiment (directed by probabilities) of every tongue known to him who attempts the solution, until the true one be attained. But, with the cipher now before us, all difficulty was removed by the signature. The pun upon the word 'Kidd' is appreciable in no other language than the English. But for this consideration I should have begun my attempts with the Spanish and French, as the tongues in which a secret of this kind would most naturally have been written by a pirate of the Spanish main[22]. As it was, I assume the cryptograph to be English.
"You observe there are no divisions between the words. Had there been divisions, the task would have been comparatively easy. In such case I would have commenced with a collation and analysis of the shorter words;

and had a word of a single letter occurred, as is most likely (*a* or *I*, for example), I should have considered the solution as assured. But there being no divisions, my first step was to ascertain the predominant letters, as well as the least frequent,

"Counting all, I constructed a table thus;—

    Of the character 8 there are 33.
                ; " 26.
                4 " 19.
                ‡) " 16.
                * " 13.
                5 " 12.
                6 " 11.
                †1 " 8.
                0 " 6.
                92 " 5.
                :3 " 4.
                ? " 3.
                ¶ " 2.
                —. " 1.

"Now, in English, the letter which most frequently occurs is *e*. Afterwards, the succession runs thus: *a o i d h n r s t u y c f g l m w b k p q x z.* E predominates, however, so remarkably that an individual sentence of any length is rarely seen in which it is not the prevailing character.

"Here, then, we have, in the very beginning, the groundwork for something more than a mere guess. The general use which may be made of the table is obvious—but in this particular cipher we shall only very partially require its aid. As our predominant character is 8, we will commence by assuming it as the *e* of the natural alphabet. To verify the supposition, let us observe if the 8 be seen often in couples—for *e* is doubled with great frequency in English—in such words, for example, as 'meet,' 'fleet,' 'speed,' 'seen,' 'been,' 'agree,' etc. In the present instance we see it doubled no less than five times, although the cryptograph is brief.

"Let us assume 8, then, as *e*. Now of all *words* in the language, 'the' is most usual; let us see, therefore, whether there are not repetitions of any three characters, in the same order of collocation, the last of them being 8. If we discover repetitions of such letters, so arranged, they will most probably represent the word 'the.' Upon inspection, we find no less than seven such arrangements, the characters being ;48. We may, therefore, assume that the semicolon represents *t*, that 4 represents *h*, and that 8 represents *e*—the last being now well confirmed. Thus a great step has been taken.

"But, having established a single word, we are enabled to establish a vastly important point; that is to say, several commencements and terminations of other words. Let us refer, for example, to the last instance but one, in which the combination ;48 occurs—not far from the end of the cipher. We know that the semicolon immediately ensuing is the commencement of a word, and, of the six characters succeeding this 'the,' we are cognizant of no less than five. Let us set these characters down, thus, by the letters we know them to represent, leaving a space for the unknown—
t eeth.

"Here we are enabled, at once, to discard the '*th*,' as forming no portion of the word commencing with the first *t*; since by experiment of the entire alphabet for a letter adapted to the vacancy, we perceive that no word can be formed of which this *th* can be a part. We are thus narrowed into
t ee,

and, going through the alphabet, if necessary, as before, we arrive at the word 'tree,' as the sole possible reading. We thus gain another letter, *r*, represented by (, with the words 'the tree" in juxtaposition.

"Looking beyond these words, for a short distance, we again see the combination ;48, and employ it by way of *termination* to what immediately precedes. We have thus this arrangement:
the tree ;4 (‡?34 the,

or, substituting the natural letters, whereknown, it reads thus:
the tree thr‡?3h the.

"Now, if, in place of the unknown characters, we leave blank spaces, or substitute dots, we read thus:
the tree thr…h the,

when the word '*through*' makes itself evident at once. But the discovery gives us three new letters, *o*, *u*, and *g*, represented by ‡ ? and 3.

"Looking now, narrowly, through the cipher for combinations of known, characters, we find, not very far from the beginning, this arrangement.
83(88, or, egree,

which, plainly, is the conclusion of the word 'degree' and gives us another letter, *d*, represented by †.

"Four letters beyond the word 'degree,' we perceive the combination.
;46(;88*.

"Translating the known characters, and representing the unknown by dots, as before, we read thus:

th.rtee,

an arrangement immediately suggestive of the word 'thirteen,' and again furnishing us with two new characters, *i*, and *n*, represented by 6 and *.

"Referring, now, to the beginning of the cryptograph, we find the combination,

53 ‡‡†.

"Translating, as before, we obtain

.good,

which assures us that the first letter is *A*, and that the first two words are 'A good.'

"To avoid confusion, it is now time that we arrange our key, as far as discovered, in a tabular form. It will stand thus:

5 represents a † " d 8 " e 3 " g 4 " h 6 " i * " n ‡ " o ( " r ; " t

"We have, therefore, no less than ten of the most important letters represented, and it will be unnecessary to proceed with the details of the solution. I have said enough to convince you that ciphers of this nature are readily soluble, and to give you some insight into the rationale[23] of their development. But be assured that the specimen before us appertains to the very simplest species of cryptograph. It now only remains to give you the full translation of the characters upon the parchment, as unriddled. Here it is:

"*A good glass in the bishop's hostel in the devil's seat twenty-one degrees and thirteen minutes northeast and by north main branch seventh limb east side shoot from the left eye of the death's-head a bee-line from the tree through the shot fifty feet out.*'"

"But," said I, "the enigma seems still in as bad a condition as ever. How is it possible to extort a meaning from all this jargon about 'devil's seats,' death's-heads,' and 'bishop's hotels'?"

"I confess," replied Legrand, "that the matter still wears a serious aspect, when regarded with a casual glance. My first endeavor was to divide the sentence into the natural divisions intended by the cryptographist."

"You mean to punctuate it?"

"Something of that kind."

"But how was it possible to effect this?"

"I reflected that it had been a *point* with the writer to run his words together without divisions, so as to increase the difficulty of solution. Now, a not over acute man, in pursuing such, an object, would be nearly certain to overdo the matter. When, in the course of his composition, he arrived at a break in his subject which would naturally require a pause, or a point, he would be exceedingly apt to run his characters, at this place, more than usually close together. If you will observe the Ms. in the present instance, you will easily detect five such cases of unusual crowding. Acting on this hint, I made the division thus:

"*A good glass in the bishop's hostel in the devil's seat—twenty-one degrees and thirteen minutes—northeast and by north—main branch seventh limb east side—shoot from the left eye of the death's-head—a bee-line from the tree through the shot fifty feet out.*'"

"Even this division," said I, "leaves me still in the dark."

"It left me also in the dark," replied Legrand, "for a few days, during which I made diligent inquiry, in the neighborhood of Sullivan's Island, for any building, which went by the name of the 'Bishop's Hotel'—for of course I dropped the obsolete word 'hostel.' Gaining no information on the subject, I was on the point of extending my sphere of search, and proceeding in a more systematic manner, when, one morning, it entered into my head, quite suddenly, that this 'Bishop's Hostel' might have some reference to an old family, of the name of Bessop, which, time out of mind, had held possession of an ancient manor-house, about four miles to the northward of the island. I accordingly went over to the plantation, and reinstituted my inquiries among the older negroes of the place. At length one of the most aged of the women said that she had heard of such a place as *Bessop's Castle* and thought that she could guide me to it, but that it was not a castle, nor tavern, but a high rock.

"I offered to pay her well for her trouble, and, after some demur, she consented to accompany me to the spot. We found it without much difficulty, when, dismissing her, I proceeded to examine the place. The 'castle' consisted of an irregular assemblage of cliffs and rocks—one of the latter being quite remarkable for its height as well as for its insulated and artificial appearance, I clambered to its apex, and then felt much at a loss as to what should be next done.

"While I was buried in reflection, my eyes fell upon a narrow ledge in the eastern face of the rock, perhaps a yard below the summit upon which I stood. This ledge projected about eighteen inches, and was not more than a foot wide, while a niche in the cliff just above it gave it a rude resemblance to one of the hollow-backed chairs used by our ancestors. I made no doubt that here was the 'devil's seat' alluded to in the Ms., and now I seemed to grasp the full secret of the riddle.

"The 'good glass,' I knew, could have reference to nothing but a telescope; for the word 'glass' is rarely employed in any other sense by seamen. Now here, I at once saw, was a telescope to be used, and a definite point of view, *admitting no variation*, from which to use it. Nor did I hesitate to believe that the phrase 'twenty-one degrees and thirteen minutes' and 'northeast and by north,' were intended as directions for the levelling of the glass. Greatly excited by these discoveries, I hurried home, procured a telescope, and returned to the rock.

"I let myself down to the ledge, and found that it was impossible to retain a seat upon it except in one particular position. This fact confirmed my preconceived idea. I proceeded to use the glass. Of course the 'twenty-one degrees and thirteen minutes' could allude to nothing but elevation above the visible horizon, since the horizontal direction was clearly indicated by the words 'northeast and by north.' This latter direction I at once established by means of a pocket-compass; then, pointing the glass as nearly at an angle of twenty-one degrees of elevation as I could do it by guess, I moved it cautiously up or down, until my attention was arrested by a circular rift or opening in the foliage of a large tree that over-topped its fellows in the distance. In the centre of this rift I perceived a white spot, but could not, at first, distinguish what it was. Adjusting the focus of the telescope, I again looked, and now made it out to be a human skull.

"On this discovery I was so sanguine as to consider the enigma solved; for the phrase 'main branch, seventh limb, east side' could refer only to the position of the skull on the tree, while 'shoot from the left eye of the death's-head' admitted also of but one interpretation, in regard to a search for buried treasure. I perceived that the design was to drop a bullet from the left eye of the skull, and that a bee-line, or in other words, a straight line, drawn from the nearest point of the trunk through 'the shot' (or the spot where the bullet fell) and thence extended to a distance of fifty feet, would indicate a definite point—and beneath this point I thought it at least *possible* that a deposit of value lay concealed."

"All this." I said, "is exceedingly clear, and, although ingenious, still simple and explicit. When you left the Bishop's Hotel, what then?"

"Why, having carefully taken the bearings of the tree, I turned homewards. The instant that I left the 'devil's seat,' however, the circular rift vanished; nor could I get a glimpse of it afterwards, turn, as I would. What seems to me the chief ingenuity in this whole business is the fact (for repeated experiment has convinced me it *is* a fact) that the circular opening in question is visible from no other attainable point of view than that afforded by the narrow ledge on the face of the rock.

"In this expedition to the 'Bishop's Hotel' I had been attended by Jupiter, who had no doubt observed for some weeks past the abstraction of my demeanor, and took especial care not to leave me alone. But, on the next day, getting up very early, I contrived to give him the slip, and went into the hills in search of the tree. After much toil I found it. When I came home at night my valet proposed to give me a flogging. With the rest of the adventure I believe you are as well acquainted as myself."

"I suppose," said I, "you missed the spot, in the first attempt at digging, through Jupiter's stupidity in letting the bug fall through the right instead of through the left eye of the skull."

"Precisely. This mistake made a difference of about two inches and a half in the 'shot'—that is to say, in the position of the peg nearest the tree—and had the treasure been *beneath* the 'shot,' the error would have been of little moment; but the 'shot,' together with the nearest point of the tree, were merely two points for the establishment of a line of direction; of course the error, however trivial in the beginning, increased as we proceeded with the line, and by the time we had gone fifty feet, threw us quite off the scent. But for my deep-seated convictions that treasure was here somewhere actually buried, we might have had all our labor in vain."

"I presume the fancy of *the skull*—of letting fall a bullet through the skull's eye—was suggested to Kidd by the piratical flag. No doubt he felt a kind of poetical consistency in recovering his money through this ominous insignium[24]."

"Perhaps so; still, I cannot help thinking that common-sense had quite as much to do with the matter as poetical consistency. To be visible from the Devil's seat, it was necessary that the object, if small, should be *white*: and there is nothing like your human skull for retaining and even increasing its whiteness under exposure to all vicissitudes of weather."

"But your grandiloquence, and your conduct in swinging the beetle—how excessively odd! I was sure you were mad. And why did you insist on letting fall the bug, instead of a bullet, from the skull?"

"Why, to be frank, I felt somewhat annoyed by your evident suspicions touching my sanity, and so resolved to punish you quietly, in my own way, by a little bit of sober mystification. For this reason I swung the beetle, and for this reason I let it fall from the tree. An observation of yours about its great weight suggested the latter idea."

"Yes, I perceive; and now there is only one point which puzzles me. What are we to make of the skeletons found in the hole?"

"That is a question I am no more able to answer than yourself. There seems, however, only one plausible way of accounting for them—and yet it is dreadful to believe in such atrocity as my suggestion would imply. It is clear that Kidd—if Kidd indeed secreted this treasure, which I doubt not— it is clear that he must have had assistance in the labor. But this labor concluded, he may have thought it expedient to remove all participants in his secret. Perhaps a couple of blows with a mattock were sufficient, while his coadjutors were busy in the pit; perhaps it required a dozen—who shall tell?"

# NOTES

[1] *The Gold-Bug* was first published in *The Dollar Magazine* in 1843. The story won a prize of one hundred dollars.

[2] 100:3 All in the Wrong. The title of an amusing comedy by Arthur Murphy (1730-1805).

[3] 100:4 Huguenot. French Protestants, many of whom settled in South Carolina.

[4] 100: 18 Fort Moultrie. Erected in. 1776. Defended against the British by Colonel William Moultrie.

[5] 101:23 Swammerdam. A famous Dutch naturalist (1637-1680).

[6] 101:25 manumitted. Freed from slavery.

[7] 102:27 scarabaeus. The Latin for beetle.

[8] 103:15 antennae. The feelers.

[9] 105:8 scarabaeus caput hominis. Man's-head beetle.

[10] 107:20 noovers. Manoeuvres.

[11] 109:10 brusquerie. Lack of cordiality.

[12] 110:26 empressement. Demonstrativeness.

[13] 123:20 curvets and caracoles. Leaping and prancing of a horse.

[14] 128:9 counters. Various coins.

[15] 128:28 Bacchanalian. Revelling like the worshippers of Bacchus, the god of wine.

[16] 134:28 Zaffre. An oxide of cobalt. See dictionary.

[17] 134:28 aqua regia. Royal water—a mixture of nitric and hydrochloric acids.

[18] 134:30 regulus. An old chemical term.

[19] 135: 28 Captain Kidd. A Scottish sea captain who lived in New York in the seventeenth century.

[20] 138:19 Golconda. A town in India noted for its diamond market.

[21] 138:28 cryptographs. Secret forms of writing.

[22] 139:27 Spanish main. The northeastern portion of South America, the Caribbean Sea, and the coast of North America to the Carolinas were harassed by the Spaniards.

[23] 144:6 rationale. Reasonable basis.

[24] 149:19 insignium. Sign.

# COLLATERAL READINGS

*The Murders in the Rue Morgue*, Edgar Allan Poe.
*The Mystery of Marie Rogêt*, Edgar Allan Poe.
*The Purloined Letter*, Edgar Allan Poe.
*The Sign of the Four*, A. Conan Doyle.
*A Scandal in Bohemia*, A. Conan Doyle.
*The Chronicles of Addington*, B. Fletcher Robinson.
*The Mystery of the Steel Disk*, Broughton Brandenburg.
*The Rajah's Diamond*, R.L. Stevenson.
*The Doctor, his Wife, and the Clock*, Anna Katharine Green.
*The Adventures of Sherlock Holmes*, A. Conan Doyle.
*The Hound of the Baskervilles*, A. Conan Doyle.
*A Double-Barrelled Detective Story*, Mark Twain.
*Gallegher*, Richard Harding Davis.

# THE BIRTHMARK[1]

*By Nathaniel Hawthorne (1804-1862).*

In the latter part of the last century there lived a man of science, an eminent proficient in every branch of natural philosophy, who not long before our story opens had made experience of a spiritual affinity more attractive than any chemical one. He had left his laboratory to the care of an assistant, cleared his fine countenance from the furnace-smoke, washed the stain of acids from his fingers, and persuaded a beautiful woman to become his wife. In those days, when the comparatively recent discovery of electricity and other kindred mysteries of Nature seemed to open paths into the region of miracle, it was not unusual for the love of science to rival the love of woman in its depth and absorbing energy. The higher intellect, the imagination, the spirit, and even the heart might all find their congenial aliment in pursuits which, as some of their ardent votaries believed, would ascend from one step of powerful intelligence to another, until the philosopher should lay his hand on the secret of creative force and perhaps make new worlds for himself. We know not whether Aylmer possessed this degree of faith in man's ultimate control over nature. He had devoted himself, however, too unreservedly to scientific studies ever to be weakened from them by any second passion. His love for his young wife might prove the stronger of the two; but it could only be by intertwining itself with his love of science and uniting the strength of the latter to his own.

Such a union accordingly took place, and was attended with truly remarkable consequences and a deeply impressive moral. One day, very soon after their marriage, Aylmer sat gazing at his wife with a trouble in his countenance that grew stronger until he spoke.

"Georgiana," said he, "has it never occurred to you that the mark upon your cheek might be removed?"

"No, indeed," said she, smiling; but, perceiving the seriousness of his manner, she blushed deeply. "To tell you the truth, it has been so often called a charm, that I was simple enough to imagine it might be so."

"Ah, upon another face perhaps it might," replied her husband; "but never on yours. No, dearest Georgiana, you came so nearly perfect from the hand of Nature that this slightest possible defect, which we hesitate whether to term a defect or a beauty, shocks me, as being the visible mark of earthly imperfection."

"Shocks you, my husband!" cried Georgiana, deeply hurt; at first reddening with momentary anger, but then bursting into tears. "Then why did you take me from my mother's side? You cannot love what shocks you!"

To explain this conversation, it must be mentioned that in the centre of Georgiana's left cheek there was a singular mark, deeply interwoven, as it were, with the texture and substance of her face. In the usual state of her complexion—a healthy though delicate bloom—the mark wore a tint of deeper crimson, which imperfectly defined its shape amid the surrounding rosiness. When she blushed it gradually became more indistinct, and finally vanished amid the triumphant rush of blood that bathed the whole cheek with its brilliant glow. But if any shifting emotion caused her to turn pale, there was the mark again, a crimson stain upon the snow, in what Aylmer sometimes deemed an almost fearful distinctness. Its shape bore not a little similarity to the human hand, though of the smallest pygmy size. Georgiana's lovers were wont to say that some fairy at her birth-hour had laid her tiny hand upon the infant's cheek, and left this impress there in token of the magic endowments that were to give her such sway over all hearts. Many a desperate swain would have risked life for the privilege of pressing his lips to the mysterious hand. It must not be concealed, however, that the impression wrought by this fairy sign-manual varied exceedingly according to the difference of temperament in the beholders. Some fastidious persons—but they were exclusively of her own sex—affirmed that the bloody hand, as they chose to call it, quite destroyed the effect of Georgiana's beauty and rendered her countenance even hideous. But it would be as reasonable to say that one of those small blue stains which sometimes occur in the purest statuary marble would convert the Eve of Powers[2] to a monster. Masculine observers, if the birthmark did not heighten their admiration, contented themselves with wishing it away, that the world might possess one living specimen of ideal loveliness without the semblance of a flaw. After his marriage,—for he thought little or nothing of the matter before,—Aylmer discovered that this was the case with himself.

Had she been less beautiful,—if Envy's self could have found aught else to sneer at,—he might have felt his affection heightened by the prettiness of this mimic hand, now vaguely portrayed, now lost, now stealing forth again and glimmering to and fro with every pulse of emotion that throbbed within her heart; but, seeing her otherwise so perfect, he found this one defect grow more and more intolerable with every moment of their united lives. It was the fatal flaw of humanity which Nature, in one shape or another, stamps ineffaceably on all her productions, either to imply that they are temporary and finite, or that their perfection must be wrought by toil and pain. The crimson hand expressed the ineludible gripe in which mortality clutches the highest and purest of earthly mould, degrading them into kindred with the lowest, and even with the very brutes, like whom their visible frames return to dust. In this manner, selecting it as the symbol of his wife's liability to sin, sorrow, decay, and death, Aylmer's sombre imagination was not long in rendering the birthmark a frightful object, causing him more trouble and horror than ever Georgiana's beauty, whether of soul or sense, had given him delight.

At all the seasons which should have been their happiest he invariably, and without intending it, nay, in spite of a purpose to the contrary, reverted to this one disastrous topic. Trifling as it at first appeared, it so connected itself with innumerable trains of thought and modes of feeling that it became the central point of all. With the morning twilight Aylmer opened his eyes upon his wife's face and recognized the symbol of imperfection, and when they sat together at the evening hearth his eyes wandered stealthily to her cheek, and beheld, flickering with the blaze of the wood-fire, the spectral hand that wrote mortality where he would fain have worshipped, Georgiana soon learned to shudder at his gaze. It needed but a glance with the peculiar expression that his face often wore to change the roses of her cheek into a deathlike paleness, amid which the crimson hand was brought strongly out, like a bas-relief of ruby on the whitest marble.

Late one night, when the lights were growing dim so as hardly to betray the stain on the poor wife's cheek, she herself, for the first time, voluntarily took up the subject.

"Do you remember, my dear Aylmer," said she, with a feeble attempt at a smile, "have you any recollection of a dream last night about this odious hand?"

"None! none whatever!" replied Aylmer, starting: but then he added, in a dry, cold tone, affected for the sake of concealing the real depth of his emotion, "I might well dream of it; for, before I fell asleep, it had taken a pretty firm hold of my fancy."

"And you did dream of it?" continued Georgiana, hastily; for she dreaded lest a gush of tears should interrupt what she had to say. "A terrible dream! I wonder that you can forget it. Is it possible to forget this one expression?—'It is in her heart now; we must have it out!' Reflect, my husband; for by all means I would have you recall that dream."

The mind is in a sad state when Sleep, the all-involving, cannot confine her spectres within the dim region of her sway, but suffers them to break forth, affrighting this actual life with secrets that perchance belong to a deeper one. Aylmer now remembered his dream. He had fancied himself with his servant Aminadab attempting an operation for the removal of the birthmark; but the deeper went the knife, the deeper sank the hand, until at length its tiny grasp appeared to have caught hold of Georgiana's heart; whence, however, her husband was inexorably resolved to cut or wrench it away.

When the dream had shaped itself perfectly in his memory, Aylmer sat in his wife's presence with a guilty feeling. Truth often finds its way to the mind close muffled in robes of sleep, and then speaks with uncompromising directness of matters in regard to which we practice an unconscious self-deception during our waking moments. Until now he had not been aware of the tyrannizing influence acquired by one idea over his mind, and of the lengths which he might find in his heart to go for the sake of giving himself peace.

"Aylmer," resumed Georgiana, solemnly, "I know not what may be the cost to both of us to rid me of this fatal birthmark. Perhaps its removal may cause cureless deformity; or it may be the stain goes as deep as life itself. Again; do we know that there is a possibility, on any terms, of unclasping the firm gripe of this little hand which was laid upon me before I came into the world?"

"Dearest Georgiana, I have spent much thought upon the subject," hastily interrupted Aylmer. "I am convinced of the perfect practicability of its removal."

"If there be the remotest possibility of it," continued Georgiana, "let the attempt be made, at whatever risk. Danger is nothing to rue; for life, while this hateful mark makes me the object of your horror and disgust,—life is a burden which I would fling down with joy. Either remove this dreadful hand, or take my wretched life! You have deep science. All the world bears witness of it. You have achieved great wonders. Cannot you remove this little, little mark, which I cover with the tips of two small fingers? Is this beyond your power, for the sake of your own peace, and to save your poor wife from madness?"

"Noblest, dearest, tenderest wife," cried Aylmer, rapturously, "doubt not my power. I have already given this matter the deepest thought,—thought which might almost have enlightened me to create a being less perfect than yourself. Georgiana, you have led me deeper than ever into the heart of science. I feel myself fully competent to render this dear cheek as faultless as its fellow; and then, most beloved, what will be my triumph when I shall have corrected what Nature left imperfect in her fairest work! Even Pygmalion[3], when his sculptured woman assumed life, felt not greater ecstasy than mine will be."

"It is resolved, then," said Georgiana, faintly smiling. "And, Aylmer, spare me not, though you should find the birthmark take refuge in my heart at last."

Her husband tenderly kissed her cheek,—her right cheek,—not that which bore the impress of the crimson hand.

The next day Aylmer apprised his wife of a plan that he had formed whereby he might have opportunity for the intense thought and constant watchfulness which the proposed operation would require, while Georgiana, likewise, would enjoy the perfect repose essential to its success. They were to seclude themselves in the extensive apartments occupied by Aylmer as a laboratory, and where, during his toilsome youth, he had made discoveries in the elemental powers of nature that had roused the admiration of all the learned societies in Europe. Seated calmly in this laboratory, the pale philosopher had investigated the secrets of the highest cloud-region and of the profoundest mines; he had satisfied himself of the causes that kindled and kept alive the fires of the volcano; and had explained the mystery of fountains, and how it is that they gush forth, some so bright and pure, and others with such rich medicinal virtues, from the dark bosom of the earth. Here, too, at an earlier period, he had studied the wonders of the human frame, and attempted to fathom the very process by which Nature assimilates all her precious influences from earth and air, and from the spiritual world, to create and foster man, her masterpiece. The latter pursuit, however, Aylmer had long laid aside in unwilling recognition of the truth—against which all seekers sooner or later stumble—that our great creative Mother, while she amuses us with apparently working in the broadest sunshine, is yet severely careful to keep her own secrets, and, in spite of her pretended openness, shows us nothing but results. She permits us, indeed, to mar, but seldom to mend, and, like a jealous patentee, on no account to make. Now, however, Aylmer resumed these half-forgotten investigations; not, of course, with such hopes or wishes as first suggested them; but because they involved much physiological truth and lay in the path of his proposed scheme for the treatment of Georgiana.

As he led her over the threshold of the laboratory Georgiana was cold and tremulous. Aylmer looked cheerfully into her face, with intent to reassure her, but was so startled with the intense glow of the birthmark upon the whiteness of her cheek that he could not restrain a strong convulsive shudder. His wife fainted.

"Aminadab! Aminadab!" shouted Aylmer, stamping violently on the floor. Forthwith there issued from an inner apartment a man of low stature, but bulky frame, with shaggy hair hanging about his visage, which was grimed with the vapors of the furnace. This personage had been Aylmer's under-worker during his whole scientific career, and was admirably fitted for that office by his great mechanical readiness, and the skill with which, while incapable of comprehending a single principle, he executed all the details of his master's experiments. With his vast strength, his shaggy hair, his smoky aspect, and the indescribable earthiness that incrusted him, he seemed to represent man's physical nature; while Aylmer's slender figure, and pale, intellectual face, were no less apt a type of the spiritual element. "Throw open the door of the boudoir, Aminadab," said Aylmer, "and burn a pastil."

"Yes, master," answered Aminadab, looking intently at the lifeless form of Georgiana; and then he muttered to himself, "If she were my wife, I'd never part with that birthmark."

When Georgiana recovered consciousness she found herself breathing an atmosphere of penetrating fragrance, the gentle potency of which had recalled her from her deathlike faintness. The scene around her looked like enchantment. Aylmer had converted those smoky, dingy, sombre rooms, where he had spent his brightest years in recondite[4] pursuits, into a series of beautiful apartments not unfit to be the secluded abode of a lovely woman. The walls were hung with gorgeous curtains, which imparted the combination of grandeur and grace that no other species of adornment can achieve; and, as they fell from the ceiling to the floor, their rich and ponderous folds, concealing all angles and straight lines, appeared to shut in the scene from infinite space. For aught Georgiana knew, it might be a pavilion among the clouds. And Alymer, excluding the sunshine, which would have interfered with his chemical processes, had supplied its place with perfumed lamps, emitting flames of various hue, but all uniting in a soft, impurpled radiance. He now knelt by his wife's side, watching her earnestly, but without alarm; for he was confident in his science, and felt that he could draw a magic circle round her within which no evil might intrude.

"Where am I? Ah, I remember," said Georgiana, faintly; and she placed her hand over her cheek to hide the terrible mark from her husband's eyes.

"Fear not, dearest!" exclaimed he. "Do not shrink from me! Believe me, Georgiana, I even rejoice in this single imperfection, since it will be such a rapture to remove it."

"O, spare me!" sadly replied his wife. "Pray do not look at it again. I never can forget that convulsive shudder."

In order to soothe Georgiana, and, as it were, to release her mind from the burden of actual things, Aylmer now put in practice some of the light and playful secrets which science had taught him among its profounder lore. Airy figures, absolutely bodiless ideas, and forms of unsubstantial beauty came and danced before her, imprinting their momentary footsteps on beams of light. Though she had some indistinct idea of the method of these optical phenomena, still the illusion was almost perfect enough to warrant the belief that her husband possessed sway over the spiritual world. Then again, when she felt a wish to look forth from her seclusion, immediately, as if her thoughts were answered, the procession of external existence flitted across a screen. The scenery and the figures of actual life were perfectly represented, but with that bewitching yet indescribable difference which always makes a picture, an image, or a shadow so much more attractive than the original. When wearied of this, Aylmer bade her cast her eyes upon a vessel containing a quantity of earth. She did so with little interest at first; but was soon startled to perceive the germ of a plant shooting upward from the soil: Then came the slender stalk; the leaves gradually unfolded themselves; and amid them was a perfect and lovely flower.

"It is magical!" cried Georgiana. "I dare not touch it."

"Nay, pluck it," answered Aylmer,—"pluck it, and inhale its brief perfume while you may. The flower will wither in a few moments and leave nothing save its brown seed-vessels; but thence may be perpetuated a race as ephemeral as itself."

But Georgiana had no sooner touched the flower than the whole plant suffered a blight, its leaves turning coal black as if by the agency of fire.

"There was too powerful a stimulus," said Aylmer, thoughtfully.

To make up for this abortive experiment, he proposed to take her portrait by a scientific process of his own invention. It was to be effected by rays of light striking upon a polished plate of metal. Georgiana assented; but, on looking at the result, was affrighted to find the features of the portrait blurred and indefinable; while the minute figure of a hand appeared where the cheek should have been. Alymer snatched the metallic plate and threw it into a jar of corrosive[5] acid.

Soon, however, he forgot these mortifying failures. In the intervals of study and chemical experiment he came to her flushed and exhausted, but seemed invigorated by her presence, and spoke in glowing language of the resources of his art. He gave a history of the long dynasty of the alchemists, who spent so many ages in quest of the universal solvent by which the golden principle might be elicited from all things vile and base, Aylmer appeared to believe that, by the plainest scientific logic, it was altogether within the limits of possibility to discover this long-sought medium. "But," he added, "a philosopher who should go deep enough to acquire the power would attain too lofty a wisdom to stoop to the exercise of it." Not less singular were his opinions in regard to the elixir vitae[6]. He more than intimated that it was at his option to concoct a liquid that should prolong life for years, perhaps interminably; but that it would produce a discord in nature which all the world, and chiefly the quaffer of the immortal nostrum, would find cause to curse.

"Aylmer, are you in earnest?" asked Georgiana, looking at him with amazement and fear. "It is terrible to possess such power, or even to dream of possessing it."

"O, do not tremble, my love," said her husband. "I would not wrong either you or myself by working such inharmonious effects upon our lives; but I would have you consider how trifling, in comparison, is the skill requisite to remove this little hand."

At the mention of the birthmark, Georgiana, as usual, shrank as if a red-hot iron had touched her cheek.

Again Aylmer applied himself to his labors. She could hear his voice in the distant furnace-room giving directions to Aminadab, whose harsh, uncouth, misshapen tones were audible in response, more like the grunt or growl of a brute than human speech. After hours of absence, Aylmer reappeared and proposed that she should now examine his cabinet of chemical products and natural treasures of the earth. Among the former he showed her a small vial, in which, he remarked, was contained a gentle yet most powerful fragrance, capable of impregnating all the breezes that blow across a kingdom. They were of inestimable value, the contents of that little vial; and, as he said so, he threw some of the perfume into the air and filled the room with piercing and invigorating delight.

"And what is this?" asked Georgiana, pointing to a small crystal globe containing a gold-colored liquid. "It is so beautiful to the eye that I could imagine it the elixir of life."

"In one sense it is," replied Aylmer; "or rather, the elixir of immortality. It is the most precious poison that ever was concocted in this world. By its aid I could apportion the lifetime of any mortal at whom you might point your finger. The strength of the dose would determine whether he were to linger out years, or drop dead in the midst of a breath. No king on his guarded throne could keep his life if I, in my private station, should deem that the welfare of millions justified me in depriving him of it."

"Why do you keep such a terrific drug?" inquired Georgiana, in horror.

"Do not mistrust me, dearest," said her husband, smiling; "its virtuous potency is yet greater than its harmful one. But see! here is a powerful cosmetic. With a few drops of this in a vase of water, freckles may be washed away as easily as the hands are cleansed. A stronger infusion[7] would take the blood out of the cheek, and leave the rosiest beauty a pale ghost."

"Is it with this lotion that you intend to bathe my cheek?" asked Georgiana, anxiously.

"O no," hastily replied her husband; "this is merely superficial. Your case demands a remedy that shall go deeper."

In his interviews with Georgiana, Aylmer generally made minute inquiries as to her sensations, and whether the confinement of the rooms and the temperature of the atmosphere agreed with her. These questions had such a particular drift that Georgiana began to conjecture that she was already subjected to certain physical influences, either breathed in with the fragrant air or taken with her food. She fancied likewise, but it might be altogether fancy, that there was a stirring up of her system,—a strange, indefinite sensation creeping through her veins, and tingling, half painfully, half pleasurably, at her heart. Still, whenever she dared to look into the mirror, there she beheld herself pale as a white rose and with the crimson birthmark stamped upon her cheek. Not even Aylmer now hated it so much as she.

To dispel the tedium of the hours which her husband found it necessary to devote to the processes of combination and analysis, Georgiana turned over the volumes of his scientific library. In many dark old tomes she met with chapters full of romance and poetry. They were the works of the philosophers of the Middle Ages, such as Albertus Magnus[8], Cornelius Agrippa[9], Paracelsus[10], and the famous friar who created the prophetic

Brazen Head. All these antique naturalists stood in advance of their centuries, yet were imbued with some of their credulity, and therefore were believed, and perhaps imagined themselves to have acquired from the investigation of nature a power above nature, and from physics a sway over the spiritual world. Hardly less curious and imaginative were the early volumes of the Transactions of the Royal Society[11], in which the members, knowing little of the limits of natural possibility, were continually recording wonders or proposing methods whereby wonders might be wrought.

But, to Georgiana, the most engrossing volume was a large folio from her husband's own hand, in which he had recorded every experiment of his scientific career, its original aim, the methods adopted for its development, and its final success or failure, with the circumstances to which either event was attributable. The book, in truth; was both the history and emblem of his ardent, ambitious, imaginative, yet practical and laborious life. He handled physical details as if there were nothing beyond them; yet spiritualized them all, and redeemed himself from materialism by his strong and eager aspiration towards the infinite. In his grasp the veriest clod of earth assumed a soul. Georgiana, as she read, reverenced Aylmer and loved him more profoundly than ever, but with a less entire dependence on his judgment than heretofore. Much as he had accomplished, she could not but observe that his most splendid successes were almost invariably failures, if compared with the ideal at which he aimed. His brightest diamonds were the merest pebbles, and felt to be so by himself, in comparison with the inestimable gems which lay hidden beyond his reach. The volume, rich with achievements that had won renown for its author, was yet as melancholy a record as over mortal hand had penned. It was the sad confession and continual exemplification of the shortcomings of the composite man, the spirit burdened with clay and working in matter, and of the despair that assails the higher nature at finding itself so miserably thwarted by the earthly part. Perhaps every man of genius, in whatever sphere, might recognize the image of his own experience in Aylmer's journal.

So deeply did these reflections affect Georgiana that she laid her face upon the open volume and burst into tears. In this situation she was found by her husband.

"It is dangerous to read in a sorcerer's books," said he with a smile, though his countenance was uneasy and displeased. "Georgiana, there are pages in that volume which I can scarcely glance over and keep my senses. Take heed lest it prove as detrimental to you."

"It has made me worship you more than ever." said she.

"Ah, wait for this one success," rejoined he, "then worship me if you will. I shall deem myself hardly unworthy of it. But come. I have sought you for the luxury of your voice. Sing to me, dearest."

So she poured out the liquid music of her voice to quench the thirst of his spirit. He then took his leave with a boyish exuberance of gayety, assuring her that her seclusion would endure but a little longer, and that the result was already certain. Scarcely had he departed when Georgiana felt irresistibly impelled to follow him. She had forgotten to inform Aylmer of a symptom which for two or three hours past had begun to excite her attention. It was a sensation in the fatal birthmark, not painful, but which induced a restlessness throughout her system. Hastening after her husband, she intruded for the first time into the laboratory.

The first thing that struck her eye was the furnace, that hot and feverish worker, with the intense glow of its fire, which by the quantities of soot clustered above it seemed to have been burning for ages. There was a distilling-apparatus in full operation. Around the room were retorts, tubes, cylinders, crucibles, and other apparatus of chemical research. An electrical machine stood ready for immediate use. The atmosphere felt oppressively close, and was tainted with gaseous odors which had been tormented forth by the processes of science. The severe and homely simplicity of the apartment, with its naked walls and brick pavement, looked strange, accustomed as Georgiana had become to the fantastic elegance of her boudoir. But what chiefly, indeed almost solely, drew her attention, was the aspect of Aylmer himself.

He was pale as death, anxious and absorbed, and hung over the furnace as if it depended upon his utmost watchfulness whether the liquid which it was distilling should be the draught of immortal happiness or misery. How different from the sanguine and joyous mien that he had assumed for Georgiana's encouragement!

"Carefully now, Aminadab; carefully, thou human machine; carefully, thou man of clay," muttered Aylmer, more to himself than his assistant. "Now, If there be a thought too much or too little, it is all over."

"Ho! ho!" mumbled Aminadab. "Look, master! look!"

Aylmer raised his eyes hastily, and at first reddened, then grew paler than ever, on beholding Georgiana. He rushed towards her and seized her arm with a gripe that left the print of his fingers upon it.

"Why do you come thither? Have you no trust in your husband?" cried he, impetuously. "Would you throw the blight of that fatal birthmark over my labors? It is not well done. Go, prying woman! go!"

"Nay, Aylmer," said Georgiana with the firmness of which she possessed no stinted endowment, "it is not you that have a right to complain. You mistrust your wife; you have concealed the anxiety with which you watch the development of this experiment. Think not so unworthily of me, my husband. Tell me all the risk we run, and fear not that I shall shrink: for my share in it is far less than your own."

"No, no, Georgiana!" said Aylmer, impatiently; "it must not be."

"I submit," replied she, calmly. "And, Aylmer, I shall quaff whatever draught you bring me; but it will be on the same principle that would induce me to take a dose of poison if offered by your hand."

"My noble wife," said Aylmer, deeply moved, "I knew not the height and depth of your nature until now. Nothing shall be concealed. Know, then, that this crimson hand, superficial as it seems, has clutched its grasp into your being with a strength of which I had no previous conception. I have already administered agents powerful enough to do aught except to change your entire physical system. Only one thing remains to be tried. If that fail us we are ruined."

"Why did you hesitate to tell me this?" asked she.

"Because, Georgiana," said Aylmer, in a low voice, "there is danger."

"Danger? There is but one danger,—that this horrible stigma shall be left upon my cheek!" cried Georgiana. "Remove it, remove it, whatever be the cost, or we shall both go mad!"

"Heaven knows your words are too true," said Aylmer, sadly. "And now, dearest, return to your boudoir. In a little while all will be tested."

He conducted her back and took leave of her with a solemn tenderness which spoke far more than his words how much was now at stake. After his departure Georgiana became rapt in musings. She considered the character of Aylmer, and did it completer justice than at any previous moment. Her heart exulted, while it trembled, at his honorable love,—so pure and lofty that it would accept nothing less than perfection, nor miserably make itself contented with an earthlier nature than he had dreamed of. She felt how much more precious was such a sentiment than that meaner kind which would have borne with the imperfection for her sake, and have been guilty of treason to holy love by degrading its perfect idea to the level of the actual; and with her whole spirit she prayed that, for a single moment, she might satisfy his highest and deepest conception.

Longer than one moment she well knew it could not be; for his spirit was ever on the march, ever ascending, and each instant required something that was beyond the scope of the instant before.

The sound of her husband's footsteps aroused her. He bore a crystal goblet containing a liquor colorless as water, but bright enough to be the draught of immortality. Aylmer was pale; but it seemed rather the consequence of a highly wrought state of mind and tension of spirit than of fear or doubt.

"The concoction of the draught has been perfect," said he, in answer to Georgiana's look. "Unless all my science have deceived me, it cannot fail."

"Save on your account, my dearest Aylmer," observed his wife, "I might wish to put off this birthmark of mortality by relinquishing mortality itself in preference to any other mode. Life is but a sad possession to those who have attained precisely the degree of moral advancement at which I stand. Were I weaker and blinder, it might be happiness. Were I stronger, it might be endured hopefully. But, being what I find myself, methinks I am of all mortals the most fit to die."

"You are fit for heaven without tasting death!" replied her husband. "But why do we speak of dying? The draught cannot fail. Behold its effect upon this plant."

On the window-seat there stood a geranium diseased with yellow blotches, which had overspread all its leaves. Aylmer poured a small quantity of the liquid upon the soil in which it grew. In a little time, when the roots of the plant had taken up the moisture, the unsightly blotches began to be extinguished in a living verdure.

"There needed no proof," said Georgiana, quietly. "Give me the goblet. I joyfully stake all upon your word."

"Drink, then, thou lofty creature!" exclaimed Aylmer, with fervid admiration. "There is no taint of imperfection on thy spirit. Thy sensible frame, too, shall soon be all perfect."

She quaffed the liquid and returned the goblet to his hand.

"It is grateful," said she, with a placid smile. "Methinks it is like water from a heavenly fountain; for it contains I know not what of unobtrusive fragrance and deliciousness. It allays a feverish thirst that had parched me for many days. Now, dearest, let me sleep. My earthly senses are closing over my spirit like the leaves around the heart of a rose at sunset."

She spoke the last words with a gentle reluctance, as if it required almost more energy than she could command to pronounce the faint and lingering syllables. Scarcely had they loitered through her lips ere she was lost in slumber. Aylmer sat by her side, watching her aspect with the emotions proper to a man, the whole value of whose existence was involved in the process now to be tested. Mingled with this mood, however, was the philosophic investigation characteristic of the man of science. Not the minutest symptom escaped him. A heightened flush of the cheek, a slight irregularity of breath, a quiver of the eyelid, a hardly perceptible tremor through the frame,—such were the details which, as the moments passed, he wrote down, in his folio volume. Intense thought had set its stamp upon every previous page of that volume; but the thoughts of years were all concentrated upon the last.

While thus employed, he failed not to gaze often at the fatal hand, and not without a shudder. Yet once, by a strange and unaccountable impulse, he pressed it with his lips. His spirit recoiled, however, in the very act; and Georgiana, out of the midst of her deep sleep, moved uneasily, and murmured, as if in remonstrance. Again Aylmer resumed, his watch. Nor was it without avail. The crimson hand, which at first had been strongly visible upon the marble paleness of Georgiana's cheek, now grew more faintly outlined. She remained not less pale than ever; but the birthmark, with every breath that came and went, lost somewhat of its former distinctness. Its presence had been awful; its departure was more awful still. Watch the stain of the rainbow fading out of the sky, and you will know how that mysterious symbol passed away.

"By Heaven! it is well-nigh gone!" said Aylmer to himself, in almost irrepressible ecstasy. "I can scarcely trace it now. Success! success! And now it is like the faintest rose color. The lightest flush of blood across her cheek would overcome it. But she is so pale!"

He drew aside the window-curtain and suffered the light of natural day to fall into the room and rest upon her cheek. At the same time he heard a gross, hoarse chuckle, which he had long known as his servant Aminadab's expression of delight.

"Ah, clod! ah, earthly mass!" cried Aylmer, laughing in a sort of frenzy, "you have served me well! Matter and spirit—earth and heaven—have both done their part in this! Laugh, thing of the senses! You have earned the right to laugh."

These exclamations broke Georgiana's sleep. She slowly unclosed her eyes and gazed into the mirror which her husband had arranged for that purpose. A faint smile flitted over her lips when she recognized how barely perceptible was now that crimson hand which had once blazed forth with such disastrous brilliancy as to scare away all their happiness. But then her eyes sought Aylmer's face with a trouble and anxiety that he could by no means account for.

"My poor Aylmer!" murmured she.

"Poor? Nay, richest, happiest, most favored!" exclaimed he. "My peerless bride, it is successful! You are perfect!"

"My poor Aylmer," she repeated, with a more than human tenderness, "you have aimed loftily; you have done nobly. Do not repent that, with so high and pure a feeling, you have rejected the best the earth could offer. Aylmer, dearest Aylmer, I am dying!"

Alas! it was too true! The fatal hand had grappled with the mystery of life, and was the bond by which an angelic spirit kept itself in union with a mortal frame. As the last crimson tint of the birthmark—that sole token of human imperfection—faded from her cheek, the parting breath of the now perfect woman passed into the atmosphere, and her soul, lingering a moment, near her husband, took its heavenward flight. Then a hoarse, chuckling laugh was heard again! Thus ever does the gross fatality of earth exult in its invariable triumph over the immortal essence which, in this dim sphere of half-development, demands the completeness of a higher state. Yet, had Aylmer reached a profounder wisdom, he need not thus have flung away the happiness which would have woven his mortal life of the selfsame texture with the celestial. The momentary circumstance was too strong for him; he failed to look beyond the shadowy scope of time, and, living once for all in eternity, to find the perfect future in the present.

# NOTES

[1] Published in the March, 1843, number of *The Pioneer*, edited by J. R. Lowell. Republished in *Mosses from an Old Manse* in 1846.

[2] 154:29 "Eve," of Powers. A noted American sculptor (1805-1873). "Eve," "The Fisher Boy," and "America" are some of his chief works.

[3] 168:28 Pygmalion. A sculptor and king of Cyprus.

[4] 181:16 recondite. Abstruse or secret.

[5] 168:27 corrosive. Destructive of tissue.

[6] 184:12 vitae. Of life.

[7] 166:3 infusion. The act of pouring in.

[8] 167:1 Albertus Magnus. A famous scholastic philosopher and member of the Dominican order (1193-1280).

[9] 167:1 Cornelius Agrippa. A German philosopher and student of alchemy and magic (1486-1535).

[10] 167:1 Paracelsus. A German-Swiss physician, and alchemist (1492-1541).

[11] 167:10 Royal Society. An association for the advancement of science, founded in London a little before 1660.

# BIOGRAPHY

Nathaniel Hawthorne was born in Salem, Massachusetts, July 4, 1804. His ancestors were prominent in the affairs of the colony: John Hawthorne was one of the judges who tried the witches in 1620; and another John Hawthorne was a member of the dignified school committee of Salem in 1796. Hawthorne's father, a ship captain, died in a foreign land when his son was only four years old; his mother lived for forty years after the death of her husband the life of a recluse in her own house. The family's star was in the decline and the people of Salem looked on Nathaniel as a lazy and very queer boy. He grew up in a unique solitude. During these years of seclusion Hawthorne acquired the habit of keeping silent on all occasions, and reading a few books frequently and thoroughly. The *Newgate Calendar* must have supplied him with many subtle suggestions for his later writings on sin and crime, for in almost all of his productions his imagination is tinged with, this old Puritanic philosophy and theology.

He entered Bowdoin College in 1821 and graduated from this institution in 1825. He had as classmates Longfellow, and Franklin Pierce, who afterward became president of the United States. After his graduation Hawthorne returned to Salem, where he lived with his mother and sisters in almost absolute seclusion for fourteen years. During this period he wrote daily, and spent his nights in burning what he had written in the daytime. He was clerk of the Boston Custom House from 1839 to 1841, when the Whig party removed him for being ultra-partisan in behalf of the Democrats. At this time Hawthorne wrote: "As to the Salem people, I really thought I had been exceedingly good-natured in my treatment of them. They certainly do not deserve good usage at my hands, after permitting me to be deliberately lied down, not merely once, but at two separate attacks, and on two false indictments, without hardly a voice being raised in my behalf." He married Sophia Peabody, July 9, 1842. From 1842 until 1846 they lived in Concord in the house formerly occupied by Emerson. These were the happiest years of his life. In 1846 he returned to Salem as surveyor in the Salem Custom House. He retired from this office in 1850 and lived in Lenox, Massachusetts, for two years. In 1852 he settled in Concord. President Pierce appointed him consul at Liverpool in 1853, and he served in this position until 1857.

After leaving Liverpool he travelled three years in England and on the continent. He returned to Concord in 1860. He died in the White Mountains, May 18, 1864. Although a silent man and a seeker of solitude during his life, few writers have ever experienced such wide publicity of their inmost lives as has Hawthorne since his death. The publication of his *Notes* has opened his desk and work-shop to every one, and has revealed to us a magnanimous, sympathetic, and pure man, who realized his responsibilities as a writer and improved all his literary opportunities.

## BIOGRAPHICAL REFERENCES

*History of American Literature*, Moses Coit Tyler.
*Introduction to American Literature*, Henry S. Pancoast.
*Studies in American Literature*, Charles Noble.
*Introduction to American Literature*, Brander Matthews.
"Gloom and Cheer in Hawthorne," *Critic*, 45: 28-36.
"Hawthorne and his Circle," *Nation*, 77: 410-411.
"Hawthorne as seen by his Publisher," *Critic*, 45: 51-55.

"Hawthorne from an English Point of View." *Critic*, 45: 60-66.
"Hawthorne's Last Years," *Critic*, 45: 67-71.
"Life of Hawthorne," *Atlantic Monthly*, 90: 563-567,

# CRITICISMS

Many influences in Hawthorne's environment served to condition and mold him as a writer. Salem had reached its highest prosperity in all lines and was just beginning its retrogression in Hawthorne's time; the primeval forests of Maine produced a subtle and lasting influence on him during his sojourn in Maine for his health; transcendentalism was the ruling thought at the time when Hawthorne was in his most plastic and solitary age; his interest in *Brook Farm* brought him in contact with all the good and bad points of that social movement; his life in the *Old Manse* in Concord and in the Berkshire Hills contributed largely to the deepening of his convictions and sympathies; and over all, like a sombre cloud, hung his ancestral Puritanic training which penetrated and suffused all his writings. He is the most native and the least imitative of all our fiction writers.

Hawthorne did not write on the common subjects and facts of his day, but chose to have his readers go with him, away from prosaic life, out into a world of mysteries where we may revel in all kinds of imaginary sports. By this process he succeeded in producing poetic effects from the most unpromising materials. His writings are fanciful. He enjoyed subjects that deal with the occult, such as mesmerism, hypnotism, and subtle suggestions. He harked back to the rigid beliefs and laws of the Puritans, but he and his subjects are spiritually advanced far above the crude, ponderous, and highly theological tenets of his forefathers.

Hawthorne is very provincial. He travelled little until he was fifty years old. He naturally loved the antique and poetic countries, but he always qualified his admiration of these foreign lands by praising something in his own New England. He conceded that there was little or nothing in this prosperous and crude country to inspire a writer to produce poetry, but his patriotism was so strong that he could never free himself wholly from its provincial effects. All his works were produced in the stress created by this pull of opposing forces—his high poetic ideals and his love of country.

In form he tends toward the polish of a classicist; in quality and freedom of thought he is very responsive to the mysteries of romanticism. He is introspective in his thinking and symbolical in his writing. Naturally he thinks abstractly, but is compelled to construct concrete methods of presenting his ideas. He never describes a strong emotion in detail, but delights in using suggestions and sidelights. His pure and refined manhood, his delicate fancy and deep interest in moral and religious questions, his conscience in its most artistic form, all are presented to the reader in the choicest garb of well chosen words and attuned to a subtle rhythm that adds beauty and attractiveness to his style.

## GENERAL REFERENCES

*Hours in a Library*, Leslie Stephen.
*A Literary History of America*, Barrett Wendell.
*American Literature*, William P. Trent.
*Makers of English Fiction*, W.J. Dawson.
*Leading American Novelists*, J. Erskine.
*Studies and Appreciations*, L.E. Gates.
"An Estimate," *Scribner's Magazine*, 43: 69-84.
"Unknown Quantity in Hawthorne's Personality," *Current Literature*, 42: 517-518.

## COLLATERAL READINGS

*Biographical Stories for Children*, Nathaniel Hawthorne.
*Mosses from an Old Manse*, Nathaniel Hawthorne.
*The Wonder Boot*, Nathaniel Hawthorne.
*The Blithedale Romance*, Nathaniel Hawthorne.
*Tanglewood Tales*, Nathaniel Hawthorne.
*Lady Eleanore's Mantle*, Nathaniel Hawthorne.
*The Great Stone Face*, Nathaniel Hawthorne.
*The Prophetic Pictures*, Nathaniel Hawthorne.
*The Necklace*, Guy de Maupassant.
*A Solitary*, Mary Wilkins Freeman.
*The Lady or the Tiger*, Frank R. Stockton.
*The Strange Ride*, Rudyard Kipling.
*Rikki-Tikki-Tavi*, Rudyard Kipling.
*They*, Rudyard Kipling.

*The Twelfth Guest*, Mary Wilkins Freeman.
*The Shadows on the Wall*, Mary Wilkins Freeman.

# ETHAN BRAND[1]

A Chapter From An Abortive Romance

*By Nathaniel Hawthorne (1804-1864)*

Bartram the lime-burner, a rough, heavy-looking man, begrimed with charcoal, sat watching his kiln, at nightfall, while his little son played at building houses with the scattered fragments of marble, when, on the hillside below them, they heard a roar of laughter, not mirthful, but slow, and even solemn, like a wind shaking the boughs of the forest.

"Father, what is that?" asked the little boy, leaving his play, and pressing betwixt his father's knees.

"O, some drunken man, I suppose," answered the lime-burner; "some merry fellow from the bar-room in the village, who dared not laugh loud enough within doors lest he should blow the roof of the house off. So here he is, shaking his jolly sides at the foot of Graylock."

"But, father," said the child, more sensitive than the obtuse, middle-aged clown, "he does not laugh like a man that is glad. So the noise frightens me!"

"Don't be a fool, child!" cried his father, gruffly. "You will never make a man, I do believe; there is too much of your mother in you. I have known the rustling of a leaf startle you. Hark! Here comes the merry fellow now. You shall see that there is no harm in him."

Bartram and his little son, while they were talking thus, sat watching the same lime-kiln that had been the scene of Ethan Brand's solitary and meditative life, before he began his search for the Unpardonable Sin. Many years, as we have seen, had now elapsed, since that portentous night when the IDEA was first developed. The kiln, however, on the mountain-side stood unimpaired, and was in nothing changed since he had thrown his dark thoughts into the intense glow of its furnace, and melted them, as it were, into the one thought that took possession of his life. It was a rude, round, towerlike structure, about twenty feet high, heavily built of rough stones, and with a hillock of earth heaped about the larger part of its circumference; so that the blocks and fragments of marble might be drawn by cart-loads, and thrown in at the top. There was an opening at the bottom of the tower, like an oven-mouth, but large enough to admit a man in a stooping posture, and provided with a massive iron door. With the smoke and jets of flame issuing from the chinks and crevices of this door, which seemed to give admittance into the hillside, it resembled nothing so much as the private entrance to the infernal regions, which the shepherds of the Delectable Mountains[2] were accustomed to show to pilgrims.

There are many such lime-kilns in that tract of country, for the purpose of burning the white marble which composes a large part of the substance of the hills. Some of them, built years ago, and long deserted, with weeds growing in the vacant round of the interior, which is open to the sky, and grass and wild flowers rooting themselves into the chinks of the stones, look already like relics of antiquity, and may yet be overspread with the lichens of centuries to come. Others, where the lime-burner still feeds his daily and night-long fire, afford points of interest to the wanderer among the hills, who seats himself on a log of wood or a fragment of marble, to hold a chat with the solitary man. It is a lonesome, and, when the character is inclined to thought, may be an intensely thoughtful, occupation; as it proved in the case of Ethan Brand, who had mused to such strange purpose, in days gone by, while the fire in this very kiln was burning.

The man who now watched the fire was of a different order, and troubled himself with no thoughts save the very few that were requisite to his business. At frequent intervals he flung back the clashing weight of the iron door, and, turning his face from the insufferable glare, thrust in huge logs of oak, or stirred the immense brands with a long pole. Within the furnace were seen the curling and riotous flames, and the burning marble, almost molten with the intensity of heat; while without, the reflection of the fire quivered on the dark intricacy of the surrounding forest, and showed in the foreground a bright and ruddy little picture of the hut, the spring beside its door, the athletic and coal-begrimed figure of the lime-burner, and the half-frightened child, shrinking into the protection of his father's shadow. And when again the iron door was closed, then reappeared the tender light of the half-full moon, which vainly strove to trace out the indistinct shapes of the neighboring mountains; and, in the upper sky, there was a flitting congregation of clouds, still faintly tinged with the rosy sunset, though thus far down into the valley the sunshine had vanished long and long ago.

The little boy now crept still closer to his father, as footsteps were heard ascending the hillside, and a human form thrust aside the bushes that clustered beneath the trees.

"Halloo! who is it?" cried the lime-burner, vexed at his son's timidity, yet half infected by it, "Come forward, and show yourself, like a man, or I'll fling this chunk of marble at your head !"

"You offer me a rough welcome," said a gloomy voice, as the unknown man drew nigh. "Yet I neither claim nor desire a kinder one, even at my own fireside."

To obtain a distincter view, Bartram threw open the iron door of the kiln, whence immediately issued a gush of fierce light, that smote full upon the stranger's face and figure. To a careless eye there appeared nothing very remarkable in his aspect, which was that of a man in a coarse, brown, country-made suit of clothes, tall and thin, with the staff and heavy shoes of a wayfarer. As he advanced, he fixed his eyes—which were very bright—intently upon the brightness of the furnace, as if he beheld, or expected to behold, some object worthy of note within it.

"Good evening, stranger," said the lime-burner; "whence come you, so late in the day?"

"I come from my search," answered the wayfarer; "for, at last, it is finished."

"Drunk!—or crazy!" muttered Bartram to himself. "I shall have trouble with the fellow. The sooner I drive him away, the better."

The little boy, all in a tremble, whispered to his father, and begged him to shut the door of the kiln, so that there might not be so much light; for that there was something in the man's face which he was afraid to look at, yet could not look away from. And, indeed, even the lime-burner's dull and torpid sense began to be impressed by an indescribable something in that thin, rugged, thoughtful visage, with the grizzled hair hanging wildly about it, and those deeply sunken eyes, which gleamed like fires within the entrance of a mysterious cavern. But, as he closed the door, the stranger turned towards him, and spoke in a quiet, familiar way, that made Bartram feel as if he were a sane and sensible man, after all.

"Your task draws to an end, I see," said he. "This marble has already been burning three days. A few hours more will convert the stone to lime."

"Why, who are you?" exclaimed the lime-burner. "You seem as well acquainted with my business as I am myself."

"And well I may be," said the stranger; "for I followed the same craft many a long year, and here, too, on this very spot. But you are a newcomer in these parts. Did you never hear of Ethan Brand?"

"The man that went in search of the Unpardonable Sin?" asked Bartram, with a laugh.

"The same," answered the stranger. "He has found what he sought, and therefore he comes back again,"

"What! then you are Ethan Brand himself?" cried the lime-burner, in amazement. "I am a newcomer here, as you say, and they call it eighteen years since you left the foot of Graylock, But, I can tell you, the good folks still talk about Ethan Brand, in the village yonder, and what a strange errand took him away from his lime-kiln. Well and so you have found the Unpardonable Sin?"

"Even so!" said the stranger, calmly.

"If the 'question is a fair one." proceeded Bartrarn, "where might it be?"

Ethan Brand laid his finger on his own heart.'

"Here!" replied he.

And then, without mirth in his countenance, but as if moved by an involuntary recognition of the infinite absurdity of seeking throughout the world for what was the closest of all things to himself, and looking into every heart, save his own, for what was hidden in no other breast, he broke into a laugh of scorn. It was the same slow, heavy laugh that had almost appalled the lime-burner when it heralded the wayfarer's approach.

The solitary mountain side was made dismal by it. Laughter, when out of place, mistimed, or bursting forth from a disordered state of feeling, may be the most terrible modulation of the human voice. The laughter of one asleep, even if it be a little child,—the madman's laugh,—the wild, screaming laugh of a born idiot,—are sounds that we sometimes tremble to hear, and would always willingly forget. Poets have imagined no utterance of fiends Or hobgoblins so fearfully appropriate as a laugh. And even the obtuse lime-burner felt his nerves shaken, as this strange man looked inward at his own heart, and burst into laughter that rolled away into the night, and was indistinctly reverberated among the hills.

"Joe," said he to his little son, "scamper down to the tavern in the village, and tell the jolly fellows there that Ethan Brand has come back, and that he has found the Unpardonable Sin!"

The boy darted away on his errand, to which Ethan Brand made no objection, nor seemed hardly to notice it. He sat on a log of wood, looking steadfastly at the iron door of the kiln. When the child was out of sight, and his swift and light footsteps ceased to be heard treading first on the fallen leaves and then on the rocky mountain path, the lime-burner began to regret his departure. He felt that the little fellow's presence had been a barrier between his guest and himself, and that he must now deal, heart to heart, with a man who, on his own confession, had committed the one only crime for which Heaven could afford no mercy. That crime, in its indistinct blackness, seemed to overshadow him. The lime-burner's own sins rose up within him, and made his memory riotous with a throng of evil shapes that asserted their kindred with the Master Sin, whatever it might be, which it was within the scope of man's corrupted nature to conceive and cherish. They were all of one family; they went to and fro between his breast and Ethan Brand's, and carried dark greetings from one to the other.

Then Bartram remembered the stories which had grown traditionary in reference to this strange man, who had come upon him like a shadow of the night, and was making himself at home in his old place, after so long absence that the dead people, dead and buried for years, would have had more right to be at home, in any familiar spot, than he. Ethan Brand, it was said, had conversed with Satan himself in the lurid blaze of this very kiln. The legend had been matter of mirth heretofore, but looked grisly now. According to this tale, before Ethan Brand departed on his search, he had been accustomed to evoke a fiend from the hot furnace of the lime-kiln, night after night, in order to confer with him about the Unpardonable Sin; the man and the fiend each laboring to frame the image of some mode of guilt which could neither be atoned for nor forgiven. And, with the first gleam of light upon the mountain-top, the fiend crept in at the iron door, there to abide the intensest element of fire, until again summoned forth to share in the dreadful task of extending man's possible guilt beyond the scope of Heaven's else infinite mercy.

While the lime-burner was struggling with the horror of these thoughts, Ethan Brand rose from the log, and flung open the door of the kiln. The action was in such accordance with the idea in Bartram's mind, that he almost expected to see the Evil One issue forth, red-hot from the raging furnace.

"Hold! hold!" cried he, with a tremulous attempt to laugh; for he was ashamed of his fears, although they overmastered him. "Don't, for mercy's sake, bring out your Devil now!"

"Man!" sternly replied Ethan Brand, "what need have I of the Devil? I have left him behind me, on my track. It is with such halfway sinners as you that he busies himself. Fear not, because I open the door. I do but act by old custom, and am going to trim your fire, like a lime-burner, as I was once."

He stirred the vast coals, thrust in more wood, and bent forward to gaze into the hollow prison-house of the fire, regardless of the fierce glow that reddened upon his face. The lime-burner sat watching him, and half suspected his strange guest of a purpose, if not to evoke a fiend, at least to plunge bodily into the flames, and thus vanish from the sight of man. Ethan Brand, however, drew quietly back, and closed the door of the kiln.

"I have looked," said he, "into many a human heart that was seven times hotter with sinful passions than yonder furnace is with fire. But I found not there what I sought. No, not the Unpardonable Sin!"

"What is the Unpardonable Sin?" asked the lime-burner; and then he shrank farther from his companion, trembling lest his question should be answered.

"It is a sin that grew within my own breast," replied Ethan Brand, standing erect, with a pride that distinguishes all enthusiasts of his stamp. "A sin that grew nowhere else! The sin of an intellect that triumphed over the sense of brotherhood with man and reverence for God, and sacrificed everything to its own mighty claims! the only sin that deserves a recompense of immortal agony! Freely, were it to do again, would I incur the guilt. Unshrinkingly I accept the retribution!"

"The man's head is turned," muttered the lime-burner to himself. "He may be a sinner, like the rest of us,—nothing more likely,—but, I'll be sworn, he is a madman too."

Nevertheless, he felt uncomfortable at his situation, alone with Ethan Brand on the wild mountain side, and was right glad to hear the rough murmur of tongues, and the footsteps of what seemed a pretty numerous party, stumbling over the stones and rustling through the under-brush. Soon appeared the whole lazy regiment that was wont to infest the village tavern, comprehending three or four individuals who had drunk flip beside the bar-room fire through all the winters, and smoked their pipes beneath the stoop through all the summers, since Ethan Brand's departure. Laughing boisterously, and mingling all their voices together in unceremonious talk, they now burst into the moonshine and narrow streaks of firelight that illuminated the open space before the lime-kiln. Bartram set the door ajar again, flooding the spot with light, that the whole company might get a fair view of Ethan Brand, and he of them.

There, among other old acquaintances, was a once ubiquitous[3] man, now almost extinct, but whom we were formerly sure to encounter at the hotel of every thriving village throughout the country. It was the stage-agent. The present specimen of the genus was a wilted and smoke-dried man, wrinkled and red-nosed, in a smartly cut, brown, bob-tailed coat, with brass buttons, who, for a length of time unknown, had kept his desk and corner in the bar-room, and was still puffing what seemed to be the same cigar that he had lighted twenty years before. He had great fame as a dry joker, though, perhaps, less on account of any intrinsic humor than from a certain flavor of brandy toddy and tobacco smoke, which impregnated all his ideas and expressions, as well as his person. Another well-remembered though strangely altered face was that of Lawyer Giles, as people still called him in courtesy; an elderly ragamuffin, in his soiled shirt-sleeves and tow-cloth trousers. This poor fellow had been an attorney, in what he called his better days, a sharp practitioner, and in great vogue among the village litigants; but flip, and sling, and toddy, and cocktails, imbibed at all hours, morning, noon, and night, had caused him to slide from intellectual to various kinds and degrees of bodily labor, till, at last, to adopt his own phrase, he slid into a soap vat. In other words, Giles was now a soap boiler, in a small way. He had come to be but the fragment of a human being, a part of one foot having been chopped off by an axe, and an entire hand torn away by the devilish grip of a steam engine. Yet, though the corporeal hand was gone, a spiritual member remained; for, stretching forth the stump, Giles steadfastly averred that he felt an invisible thumb and fingers with as vivid a sensation as before the real ones were amputated. A maimed and miserable wretch he was; but one, nevertheless, whom the world could not trample on, and had no right to scorn, either in this or any previous stage of his misfortunes, since he had still kept up the courage and spirit of a man, asked nothing in charity, and with his one hand—and that the left one—fought a stern battle against want and hostile circumstances.

Among the throng, too, came another personage, who, with certain points of similarity to Lawyer Giles, had many more of difference. It was the village doctor; a man of some fifty years, whom, at an earlier period of his life, we introduced as paying a professional visit to Ethan Brand during the latter's supposed insanity. He was now a purple-visaged, rude, and brutal, yet half-gentlemanly figure, with something wild, ruined, and desperate in his talk, and in all the details of his gesture and manners. Brandy possessed this man like an evil spirit, and made him as surly and savage as a wild beast, and as miserable as a lost soul; but there was supposed to be in him such wonderful skill, such native gifts of healing, beyond any which medical science could impart, that society caught hold of him, and would not let him sink out of its reach. So, swaying to and fro upon his horse, and grumbling thick accents at the bedside, he visited all the sick chambers for miles about among the mountain towns, and sometimes raised a dying man, as it were, by miracle, or quite as often, no doubt, sent his patient to a grave that was dug many a year too soon. The doctor had an everlasting pipe in his mouth, and, as somebody said, in allusion to his habit of swearing, it was always alight with hell-fire.

These three worthies pressed forward, and greeted Ethan Brand each after his own fashion, earnestly inviting him to partake of the contents of a certain black bottle, in which, as they averred, he would find something far better worth seeking for than the Unpardonable Sin. No mind, which has wrought itself by intense and solitary meditation into a high state of enthusiasm, can endure the kind of contact with low and vulgar modes of thought and feeling to which Ethan Brand was now subjected. It made him doubt—and, strange to say, it was a painful doubt,—whether he had indeed found the Unpardonable Sin and found it within himself. The whole question on which he had exhausted life, and more than life, looked like a delusion.

"Leave me," he said bitterly, "ye brute beasts, that have made yourselves so, shrivelling up your souls with fiery liquors! I have done with you. Years and years ago, I groped into your hearts, and found nothing there for my purpose. Get ye gone!"

"Why, you uncivil scoundrel," cried the fierce doctor, "is that the way you respond to the kindness of your best friends? Then let me tell you the truth. You have no more found the Unpardonable Sin than yonder boy Joe has. You are but a crazy fellow,—I told you so twenty years ago,—neither better nor worse than a crazy fellow, and a fit companion of old Humphrey, here!"

He pointed to an old man, shabbily dressed, with long white hair, thin visage, and unsteady eyes. For some years past this aged person had been wandering about among the hills, inquiring of all travellers whom he met for his daughter. The girl, it seemed, had gone off with a company of circus performers; and occasionally tidings of her came to the village, and fine stories were told of her glittering appearance as she rode on horseback in the ring, or performed marvellous feats on the tight rope.

The white-haired father now approached Ethan Brand, and gazed unsteadily into his face.

"They tell me you have been all over the earth," said he, wringing his hands with earnestness. "You must have seen my daughter, for she makes a grand figure in the world, and everybody goes to see her. Did she send any word to her old father, or say when she was coming back?"

Ethan Brand's eye quailed beneath the old man's. That daughter, from whom he so earnestly desired a word of greeting, was the Esther of our tale, the very girl whom, with such cold and remorseless purpose, Ethan Brand had made the subject of a psychological experiment, and wasted, absorbed, and perhaps annihilated her soul, in the process.

"Yes," murmured he, turning away from the hoary wanderer; "it is no delusion. There is an Unpardonable Sin!"

While these things were passing, a merry scene was going forward in the area of cheerful light, beside the spring and before the door of the hut. A number of the youth of the village, young men and girls, had hurried up the hillside, impelled by curiosity to see Ethan Brand, the hero of so many a legend familiar to their childhood. Finding nothing, however, very remarkable in his aspect,—nothing but a sunburnt wayfarer, in plain garb and dusty shoes, who sat looking into the fire, as if he fancied pictures among the coals,—these young people speedily grew tired of observing him. As it happened, there was other amusement at hand. An old German Jew, travelling with a diorama[4] on his back, was passing down, the mountain road towards the village just as the party turned aside from it, and, in hopes of eking out the profits of the day, the showman had kept them company to the lime-kiln.

"Come, old Dutchman," cried one of the young men, "let us see your pictures, if you can swear they are worth looking at!"

"O yes, Captain," answered the Jew,—whether as a matter of courtesy or craft, he styled everybody Captain,—"I shall show you, indeed, some very superb pictures!"

So, placing his box in a proper position, he invited the young men and girls to look through the glass orifices of the machine, and proceeded to exhibit a series of the most outrageous scratchings and daubings, as specimens of the fine arts, that ever an itinerant showman had the face to impose upon his circle of spectators. The pictures were worn out, moreover, tattered, full of cracks and wrinkles, dingy with tobacco smoke, and otherwise in a most pitiable condition. Some purported to be cities, public edifices, and ruined castles in Europe; others represented Napoleon's battles and Nelson's sea fights; and in the midst of these would be seen a gigantic, brown, hairy hand,—which might have been mistaken for the Hand of Destiny, though, in truth, it was only the showman's,—pointing its forefinger to various scenes of the conflict, while its owner gave historical illustrations. When, with much merriment at its abominable deficiency of merit, the exhibition was concluded, the German bade little Joe put his head into the box. Viewed through the magnifying glasses, the boy's round, rosy visage assumed the strangest imaginable aspect of an immense Titanic[5] child, the mouth grinning broadly, and the eyes and every other feature overflowing with fun at the joke. Suddenly, however, that merry face turned pale, and its expression changed to horror, for this easily impressed and excitable child had become sensible that the eye of Ethan Brand was fixed upon him through the glass.

"You make the little man to be afraid. Captain." said the German Jew, turning up the dark and strong outline of his visage, from his stooping posture, "But look again, and, by chance, I shall cause you to see somewhat that is very fine, upon my word!"

Ethan Brand gazed into the box for an instant, and then starting back, looked fixedly at the German. What had he seen? Nothing, apparently; for a curious youth, who had peeped in almost at the same moment, beheld only a vacant space of canvas.

"I remember you now," muttered Ethan Brand to the showman.

"Ah, Captain," whispered the Jew of Nuremburg, with a dark smile, "I find it to be a heavy matter in my show-box,—this Unpardonable Sin! By my faith, Captain, it has wearied my shoulders, this long day, to carry it over the mountain."

"Peace," answered Ethan Brand, sternly, "or get thee into the furnace yonder!"

The Jew's exhibition had scarcely concluded, when a great, elderly dog—who seemed to be his own master, as no person in the company laid claim to him—saw fit to render himself the object of public notice. Hitherto, he had shown himself a very quiet, well-disposed old dog, going round from one to another, and, by way of being sociable, offering his rough head to be patted by any kindly hand that would take so much trouble. But now, all of a sudden, this grave and venerable quadruped, of his own mere motion, and without the slightest suggestion from anybody else, began to run round after his tail, which, to heighten the absurdity of the proceeding, was a great deal shorter than it should have been. Never was seen such headlong eagerness in pursuit of an object that could not possibly be attained; never was heard such a tremendous outbreak of growling, snarling, barking, and snapping,—as if one end of the ridiculous brute's body were at deadly and most unforgivable enmity with the other. Faster and faster, round about went the cur; and faster and still faster fled the unapproachable brevity of his tail; and louder and fiercer grew his yells of rage and animosity; until, utterly exhausted, and as far from the goal as ever, the foolish old dog ceased his performance as suddenly as he had begun it. The next moment he was as mild, quiet, sensible, and respectable in his deportment, as when he first scraped acquaintance with the company. As may be supposed, the exhibition was greeted with universal laughter, clapping of hands, and shouts of encore, to which the canine performer responded by wagging all that there was to wag of his tail, but appeared totally unable to repeat his very successful effort to amuse the spectators. Meanwhile, Ethan Brand had resumed his seat upon the log, and moved, it might be, by a perception of some remote analogy between his own case and that of this self-pursuing cur, he broke into the awful laugh, which, more than any other token, expressed the condition of his inward being. From that moment, the merriment of the party was at an end; they stood aghast, dreading lest the inauspicious sound should be reverberated around the horizon, and that mountain would thunder it to mountain, and so the horror be prolonged upon their ears. Then, whispering one to another that it was late,—that the moon was almost down,—that the August night was growing chill,—they hurried homewards, leaving the lime-burner and little Joe to deal as they might with their unwelcome guest. Save for these three human beings, the open space on the hillside was a solitude, set in a vast gloom of forest. Beyond that darksome verge, the firelight glimmered on the stately trunks and almost black foliage of pines, intermixed with the lighter verdure of sapling oaks, maples, and poplars, while here and there lay the gigantic corpses of dead trees, decaying on the leaf-strewn soil. And it seemed to little Joe—a timorous and imaginative child—that the silent forest was holding, its breath, until some fearful thing should happen.

Ethan Brand thrust more wood into the fire, and closed the door of the kiln; then looking over his shoulder at the lime-burner and his son, he bade, rather than advised, them to retire to rest.

"For myself, I cannot sleep." said he, "I have matters that it concerns me to meditate upon. I will watch the fire, as I used to do in the old time."

"And call the Devil out of the furnace to keep you company, I suppose," muttered Bartram, who had been making intimate acquaintance with the black bottle above mentioned. "But watch, if you like, and call as many devils as you like! For my part, I shall be all the better for a snooze. Come, Joe!"

As the boy followed his father into the hut, he looked back at the wayfarer, and the tears came into his eyes, for his tender spirit had an intuition of the bleak and terrible loneliness in which this man had enveloped himself.

When they had gone, Ethan Brand sat listening to the crackling of the kindled wood, and looking at the little spirits of fire that issued through the chinks of the door. These trifles, however, once so familiar, had but the slightest hold of his attention, while deep within his mind he was reviewing the gradual but marvellous change that had been wrought upon him by the search to which he had devoted himself. He remembered how the night dew had fallen upon him,—how the dark forest had whispered to him,—how the stars had gleamed upon him,—a simple and loving man, watching his fire in the years gone by, and ever musing as it burned. He remembered with what tenderness, with what love and sympathy for mankind, and what pity for human guilt and woe, he had first begun to contemplate those ideas which afterwards became the inspiration of his life; with what reverence he had then looked into the heart of man, viewing it as a temple originally divine, and, however desecrated, still to be held sacred by a brother; with what awful fear he had deprecated the success of his pursuit, and prayed that the Unpardonable Sin might never be revealed to him. Then ensued that vast intellectual development, which, in its progress, disturbed the counterpoise between his mind and heart. The Idea that possessed his life had operated as a means of education; it had gone on cultivating his powers to the highest point of which they were susceptible; it had raised him from the level of an unlettered laborer to stand on a starlit eminence, whither the philosophers of the earth, laden with the lore of universities, might vainly strive to clamber after him. So much for the intellect! But where was the heart? That, indeed, had withered,—had contracted.—had hardened,—had perished! It had ceased to partake of the universal throb, He had lost his hold of the magnetic chain of humanity. He was no longer a brother-man, opening the chambers of the dungeons of our common nature by the key of holy sympathy, which gave him a right to share in all its secrets; he was now a cold observer, looking on mankind as the subject of his experiment, and, at length, converting man and woman to be his puppets, and pulling the wires that moved them to such degrees of crime as were demanded for his study.

Thus Ethan Brand became a fiend. He began to be so from the moment that his moral nature had ceased to keep the pace of improvement with his intellect. And now, as his highest effort and inevitable development,—as the bright and gorgeous flower, and rich, delicious fruit of his life's labor,—he had produced the Unpardonable Sin!

"What more have I to seek? what more to achieve?" said Ethan Brand to himself, "My task Is done, and well done!"

Starting from the log with a certain alacrity in his gait and ascending the hillock of earth that was raised against the stone circumference of the lime-kiln, he thus reached the top of the structure. It was a space of perhaps ten feet across, from edge to edge, presenting a view of the upper surface of the immense mass of broken marble with which the kiln was heaped. All these innumerable blocks and fragments of marble were red-hot and vividly on fire, sending up great spouts of blue flame, which quivered aloft and danced madly, as within a magic circle, and sank and rose again, with continual and multitudinous activity. As the lonely man bent forward over this terrible body of fire, the blasting heat smote up against his person with a breath that, it might be supposed, would have scorched and shrivelled him up in a moment.

Ethan Brand stood erect, and raised his arms on high. The blue flames played upon his face, and imparted the wild and ghastly light which alone could have suited its expression; it was that of a fiend on the verge of plunging into his gulf of intensest torment.

"O Mother Earth," cried he, "who art no more my Mother, and into whose bosom this frame shall never be resolved! O mankind, whose brotherhood I have cast off, and trampled thy great heart beneath my feet! O stars of heaven, that shone on me of old, as if to light me onward and upward!—farewell all, and forever. Come, deadly element of Fire,—henceforth my familiar frame! Embrace me, as I do thee!"

That night the sound of a fearful peal of laughter rolled heavily through the sleep of the lime-burner and his little son; dim shapes of horror and anguish haunted their dreams, and seemed still present in the rude hovel, when they opened their eyes to the daylight.

"Up, boy, up!" cried the lime-burner, staring about him. "Thank Heaven, the night is gone, at last; and rather than pass such another, I would watch, my lime-kiln, wide awake, for a twelvemonth. This Ethan Brand, with his humbug of an Unpardonable Sin, has done me no such mighty favor, in taking my place!"

He issued from the hut, followed by little Joe, who kept fast hold, of his father's hand. The early sunshine was already pouring its gold upon the mountain tops; and though the valleys were still in shadow, they smiled cheerfully in the promise of the bright day that was hastening onward. The village, completely shut in by hills, which swelled away gently about it, looked as if it had rested peacefully in the hollow of the great hand of Providence. Every dwelling was distinctly visible; the little spires of the two churches pointed upwards, and caught a fore-glimmering of brightness from the sun-gilt skies upon their gilded weathercocks. The tavern was astir, and the figure of the old, smoke-dried stage-agent, cigar in mouth, was seen beneath the stoop. Old Graylock was glorified with a golden cloud upon his head. Scattered likewise over the breasts of the surrounding mountains, there were heaps of hoary mist, in fantastic shapes, some of them far down into the valley, others high up towards the summits, and still others, of the same family of mist or cloud, hovering in the gold radiance of the upper atmosphere. Stepping from one to another of the clouds that rested on the hills, and thence to the loftier brotherhood that sailed in air, it seemed almost as if a mortal man might thus ascend into the heavenly regions. Earth was so mingled with sky that it was a day-dream to look at it.

To supply that charm of the familiar and homely, which Nature so readily adopts into a scene like this, the stage-coach was rattling down the mountain road, and the driver sounded his horn, while echo caught up the notes, and intertwined them into a rich and varied and elaborate harmony, of which the original performer could lay claim to little share. The great hills played a concert among themselves, each contributing a strain of airy sweetness.

Little Joe's face brightened at once.

"Dear father," cried he, skipping cheerily to and fro, "that strange man is gone, and the sky and the mountains all seem glad of it!"

"Yes," growled the lime-burner, with an oath, "but he has let the fire go down, and no thanks to him if five hundred bushels of lime are not spoiled. If I catch the fellow hereabouts again, I shall feel like tossing him into the furnace!"

With his long pole in his hand, he ascended to the top of the kiln. After a moment's pause, he called to his son.

"Come up here, Joe!" said he.

So little Joe ran up the hillock, and stood by his father's side. The marble was all burnt into perfect, snow-white lime. But on its surface, in the midst of the circle,—snow-white too, and thoroughly converted into lime,—lay a human skeleton, in the attitude of a person who, after long toil, lies down to long repose. Within the ribs—strange to say—was the shape of a human heart.

"Was the fellow's heart made of marble?" cried Bartram, in some perplexity at this phenomenon. "At any rate, it is burnt into what looks like special good lime; and, taking all the bones together, my kiln is half a bushel the richer for him."

So saying, the rude lime-burner lifted his pole, and, letting it fall upon the skeleton, the relics of Ethan Brand were crumbled into fragments.

# NOTES

[1] Written in 1848; published in Holden's *Dollar Magazine* in 1851.
[2] 182:26 Delectable Mountains. A range of mountains referred to in Bunyan's *Pilgrim's Progress*.
[3] 190:22 ubiquitous. Being present everywhere.
[4] 194:29 diorama. A series of paintings arranged for exhibition. See dictionary.
[5] 195:30 Titanic. Characteristic of the Titans; therefore large.


# COLLATERAL READINGS

*The Scarlet Letter*, Nathaniel Hawthorne.
*The House of Seven Gables*, Nathaniel Hawthorne.
*The Marble Faun*, Nathaniel Hawthorne.
*The Gray Champion*, Nathaniel Hawthorne.
*The Wedding Knell*, Nathaniel Hawthorne.
*The Great Carbuncle*, Nathaniel Hawthorne.
*Dr. Heidegger's Experiment*, Nathaniel Hawthorne.
*The Haunted Mind*, Nathaniel Hawthorne.
*Feathertop*, Nathaniel Hawthorne.
*Rip Van Winkle*, Washington Irving.
*The Elixir of Life*, Honoré de Balzac.
*The Leather Funnel*, A. Conan Doyle.
*The Return of Imray's Ghost*, Rudyard Kipling.
*A Gentle Ghost*, Mary Wilkins Freeman.

# THE SIRE DE MALETROIT'S DOOR[1]

*By Robert Louis Stevenson (1850-1894)*

Denis de Beaulieu was not yet two-and-twenty, but he counted himself a grown man, and a very accomplished cavalier into the bargain. Lads were early formed in that rough, warfaring epoch; and when one has been in a pitched battle and a dozen raids, has killed one's man in an honorable fashion, and knows a thing or two of strategy and mankind, a certain swagger in the gait is surely to be pardoned. He had put up his horse with due care, and supped with due deliberation; and then, in a very agreeable frame of mind, went out to pay a visit in the gray of the evening. It was not a very wise proceeding on the young man's part. He would have done better to remain beside the fire or go decently to bed. For the town was full of the troops of Burgundy and England under a mixed command; and though Denis was there on safe-conduct, his safe-conduct was like to serve him little on a chance encounter.

It was September, 1429; the weather had fallen sharp; a flighty piping wind, laden with showers, beat about the township; and the dead leaves ran riot along the streets. Here and there a window was already lighted up; and the noise of men-at-arms making merry over supper within came forth in fits and was swallowed up and carried away by the wind. The night fell swiftly: the flag of England, fluttering on the spire top, grew ever fainter and fainter against the flying clouds—a black speck like a swallow in the tumultuous, leaden chaos of the sky. As the night fell the wind rose, and began to hoot under archways and roar amid the tree-tops in the valley below the town.

Denis de Beaulieu walked fast and was soon knocking at his friend's door; but though he promised himself to stay only a little while and make an early return, his welcome was so pleasant, and he found so much to delay him, that it was already long past midnight before he said good-by upon the threshold. The wind had fallen again in the meanwhile; the night was as black as the grave; not a star, nor a glimmer of moonshine, slipped through the canopy of cloud. Denis was ill-acquainted with the intricate lanes of Chateau Landon; even by daylight he had found some trouble in picking his way; and in this absolute darkness he soon lost it altogether. He was certain of one thing only—to keep mounting the hill; for his friend's house lay at the lower end, or tail, of Chateau Landon, while the inn was up at the head, under the great church spire. With this clew to go upon he stumbled and groped forward, now breathing more freely in the open places where there was a good slice of sky overhead, now feeling along the wall in stifling closes. It is an eerie and mysterious position to be thus submerged in opaque blackness in an almost unknown town. The silence is terrifying in its possibilities. The touch of cold window bars to the exploring hand startles the man like the touch of a toad; the inequalities of the pavement shake his heart into his mouth; a piece of denser darkness threatens an ambuscade or a chasm in the pathway; and where the air is brighter, the houses put on strange and bewildering appearances, as if to lead him further from his way. For Denis, who had to regain his inn without attracting notice, there was real danger as well as mere discomfort in the walk; and he went warily and boldly at once, and at every corner paused to make an observation.

He had been for some time threading a lane so narrow that he could touch a wall with either hand, when it began to open out and go sharply downward. Plainly this lay no longer in the direction of his inn; but the hope of a little more light tempted him forward to reconnoitre. The lane ended in a terrace with a bartizan[2] wall, which gave an outlook between high houses, as out of an embrasure, into the valley lying dark and formless several hundred feet below. Denis looked down, and could discern a few tree-tops waving and a single speck of brightness where the river ran across a weir. The weather was clearing up, and the sky had lightened, so as to show the outline of the heavier clouds and the dark margin of the hills. By the uncertain glimmer, the house on his left hand should be a place of some pretensions; it was surmounted by several pinnacles and turret-tops; the round stern of a chapel, with a fringe of flying buttresses, projected boldly from the main block; and the door was sheltered under a deep porch carved with figures and overhung by two long gargoyles[3]. The windows of the chapel gleamed through their intricate tracery with a light as of many tapers, and threw out the buttresses and the peaked roof in a more intense blackness against the sky. It was plainly the hotel of some great family of the neighborhood; and as it reminded Denis of a town house of his own at Bourges, he stood for some time gazing up at it and mentally gauging the skill of the architects and the consideration of the two families.

There seemed to be no issue to the terrace but the lane by which he had reached it; he could only retrace his steps, but he had gained some notion of his whereabouts, and hoped by this means to hit the main thoroughfare and speedily regain the inn. He was reckoning without that chapter of accidents which was to make this night memorable above all others in his career; for he had not gone back above a hundred yards before he saw a light coming to meet him, and heard loud voices speaking together in the echoing narrows of the lane. It was a party of men-at-arms going the night round with torches. Denis assured himself that they had all been making free with the wine bowl, and were in no mood to be particular about safe-conducts or the niceties of chivalrous war. It, was as like as not that they would kill him like a dog and leave him where he fell. The situation was inspiriting but nervous. Their own torches would conceal him from sight, he reflected; and he hoped that they would drown the noise of his footsteps with their own empty voices. If he were but fleet and silent, he might evade their notice altogether.

Unfortunately, as he turned to beat a retreat, his foot rolled upon a pebble; he fell against the wall with an ejaculation, and his sword rang loudly on the stones. Two or three voices demanded who went there—some in French, some in English; but Denis made no reply, and ran the faster down the lane. Once upon the terrace, he paused to look back. They still kept calling after him, and just then began to double the pace in pursuit, with a considerable clank of armor, and great tossing of the torchlight to and fro in the narrow jaws of the passage.

Denis cast a look around and darted into the porch. There he might escape observation, or—if that were too much to expect—was in a capital posture whether for parley or defence. So thinking, he drew his sword and tried to set his back against the door. To his surprise it yielded behind his weight; and though he turned in a moment, continued to swing back on oiled and noiseless hinges until it stood wide open on a black interior. When things fall out opportunely for the person concerned, he is not apt to be critical about the how or why, his own immediate personal convenience seeming a sufficient reason for the strangest oddities and revolutions in our sublunary things; and so Denis, without a moment's hesitation, stepped within and partly closed the door behind him to conceal his place of refuge. Nothing was further from his thoughts than to close it altogether; but for some inexplicable reason—perhaps by a spring or a weight—the ponderous mass of oak whipped itself out of his fingers and clanked to, with a formidable rumble and a noise like the falling of an automatic bar. The round, at that very moment, debouched[4] upon the terrace and proceeded to summon him with shouts and curses. He heard them ferreting in the dark corners; the stock of a lance even rattled along the outer surface of the door behind which he stood; but these gentlemen were in too high a humor to be long delayed, and soon made off down a corkscrew pathway which had escaped Denis' observation, and passed out of sight and hearing along the battlements of the town.

Denis breathed again. He gave them a few minutes' grace for fear of accidents, and then groped about for some means of opening the door and slipping forth again. The inner surface was quite smooth, not a handle, not a moulding, not a projection of any sort. He got his finger nails round the edges and pulled, but the mass was immovable. He shook it, it was as firm as a rock, Denis de Beaulieu frowned, and gave vent to a little noiseless whistle. What ailed the door? he wondered. Why was it open? How came it to shut so easily and so effectually after him? There was something obscure and underhand about all this, that was little to the young man's fancy. It looked like a snare, and yet who could suppose a snare in such a quiet by-street and in a house of so prosperous and even noble an exterior? And yet—snare or no snare, intentionally or unintentionally—here he was, prettily trapped; and for the life of him he could see no way out of it again. The darkness began to weigh upon him. He gave ear; all was silent without, but within and close by he seemed to catch a faint sighing, a faint sobbing rustle, a little stealthy creak—as though many persons were at his side, holding themselves quite still, and governing even their respiration with the extreme of slyness. The idea went to his vitals with a shock, and he faced about suddenly as if to defend his life. Then, for the first time, he became aware of a light about the level of his eyes and at some distance in the interior of the house—a vertical thread of light, widening toward the bottom, such as might escape between two wings of arras over a doorway. To see anything was a relief to Denis; it was like a piece of solid ground to a man laboring in a morass; his mind seized upon it with avidity; and he stood staring at it and trying to piece together some logical conception of his surroundings. Plainly there was a flight of steps ascending from his own level to that of this illuminated doorway, and indeed he thought he could make out another thread of light, as fine as a needle and as faint as phosphorescence, which might very well be reflected along the polished wood of a handrail. Since he had begun to suspect that he was not alone, his heart had continued to beat with smothering violence, and an intolerable desire for action of any sort had possessed itself of his spirit. He was in deadly peril, he believed. What could be more natural than to mount the staircase, lift the curtain, and confront his difficulty at once? At least he would be dealing with something tangible; at least he would be no longer in the dark. He stepped slowly forward with outstretched hands, until his foot struck the bottom step; then he rapidly scaled the stairs, stood for a moment to compose his expression, lifted the arras and went in.

He found himself in a large apartment of polished stone. There were three doors, one on each of three sides, all similarly curtained with tapestry. The fourth side was occupied by two large windows and a great stone chimney-piece, carved with the arms of the Malétroits. Denis recognized the bearings, and was gratified to find himself in such good hands. The room was strongly illuminated; but it contained little furniture except a heavy table and a chair or two; the hearth was innocent of fire, and the pavement was but sparsely strewn with rushes clearly many days old.

On a high chair beside the chimney, and directly facing Denis as he entered, sat a little old gentleman in a fur tippet. He sat with his legs crossed and his hands folded, and a cup of spiced wine stood by his elbow on a bracket on the wall. His countenance had a strong masculine cast; not properly human, but such as we see in the bull, the goat, or the domestic boar; something equivocal and wheedling, something greedy, brutal and dangerous. The upper lip was inordinately full, as though swollen by a blow or a toothache; and the smile, the peaked eyebrows, and the small, strong eyes were quaintly and almost comically evil in expression. Beautiful white hair hung straight all round his head, like a saint's, and fell in a single curl upon the tippet. His beard and mustache were the pink of venerable sweetness. Age, probably in consequence of inordinate precautions, had left no mark upon his hands; and the Malétroit hand was famous. It would be difficult to imagine anything at once so fleshy and so delicate in design; the taper, sensual fingers were like those of one of Leonardo's[5] women; the fork of the thumb made a dimpled protuberance when closed; the nails were perfectly shaped, and of a dead, surprising whiteness. It rendered his aspect tenfold more redoubtable, that a man with hands like these should keep them devoutly folded like a virgin martyr— that a man with so intent and startling an expression of face should sit patiently on his seat and contemplates people with an unwinking stare, like a god, or a god's statue. His quiescence seemed ironical and treacherous, it fitted so poorly with his looks.

Such was Alain, Sire de Malétroit.

Denis and he looked silently at each other for a second or two.

"Pray step in," said the Sire de Malétroit. "I have been expecting you all the evening."

He had not risen, but he accompanied his words with a smile and a slight but courteous inclination of the head. Partly from the smile, partly from the strange musical murmur with which the sire prefaced his observation, Denis felt a strong shudder of disgust go through his marrow. And what with disgust and honest confusion of mind, he could scarcely get words together in reply.

"I fear," he said, "that this is a double accident. I am not the person you suppose me. It seems you were looking for a visit; but for my part, nothing was further from my thoughts—nothing could be more contrary to my wishes—than this intrusion."

"Well, well," replied the old gentleman indulgently, "here you are, which is the main point. Seat yourself, my friend, and put yourself entirely at your ease. We shall arrange our little affairs presently."

Denis perceived that the matter was still complicated with some misconception, and he hastened to continue his explanation.

"Your door," he began.

"About my door?" asked the other raising his peaked eyebrows. "A little piece of ingenuity." And he shrugged his shoulders. "A hospitable fancy! By your own account, you were not desirous of making any acquaintance. We old people look for such reluctance now and then; when it touches our honor, we cast about until we find some way of overcoming it. You arrive uninvited, but believe me, very welcome."

"You persist in error, sir," said Denis. "There can be no question between you and me. I am a stranger in this countryside. My name is Denis, damoiseau de Beaulieu. If you see me in your house it is only—"

"My young friend," interrupted the other, "you will permit me to have my own ideas on that subject. They probably differ from yours at the present moment," he added with a leer, "but time will show which of us is in the right."

Denis was convinced he had to do with a lunatic. He seated himself with a shrug, content to wait the upshot; and a pause ensued, during which he thought he could distinguish a hurried gabbling as of a prayer from behind the arras immediately opposite him. Sometimes there seemed to be but one person engaged, sometimes two; and the vehemence of the voice, low as it was, seemed to indicate either great haste or an agony of spirit. It occurred to him that this piece of tapestry covered the entrance to the chapel he had noticed from without.

The old gentleman meanwhile surveyed Denis from head to foot with a smile, and from time to time emitted little noises like a bird or a mouse, which seemed to indicate a high degree of satisfaction. This state of matters became rapidly insupportable; and Denis, to put an end to it, remarked politely that the wind had gone down.

The old gentleman fell into a fit of silent laughter, so prolonged and violent that he became quite red in the face. Denis got upon his feet at once, and put on his hat with a flourish.

"Sir," he said, "if you are in your wits, you have affronted me grossly. If you are out of them, I flatter myself I can find better employment for my brains than to talk with lunatics. My conscience is clear; you have made a fool of me from the first moment; you have refused to hear my explanations; and now there is no power under God will make me stay here any longer; and if I cannot make my way out in a more decent fashion, I will hack your door in pieces with my sword."

The Sire de Malétroit raised his right hand and wagged it at Denis with the fore and little fingers extended.

"My dear nephew," he said, "sit down."

"Nephew!" retorted Denis, "you lie in your throat;" and he snapped his fingers in his face.

"Sit down, you rogue!" cried the old gentleman, in a sudden, harsh voice like the barking of a dog. "Do you fancy," he went on, "that when I had made my little contrivance for the door I had stopped short with that? If you prefer to be bound hand and foot till your bones ache, rise and try to go away. If you choose to remain a free young buck, agreeably conversing with an old gentleman—why, sit where you are in peace, and God be with you."

"Do you mean, I am a prisoner?" demanded Denis.

"I state the facts," replied the other. "I would rather leave the conclusion to yourself."

Denis sat down again. Externally he managed to keep pretty calm, but within, he was now boiling with anger, now chilled with apprehension. He no longer felt convinced that he was dealing with a madman. And if the old gentleman was sane, what, in God's name, had he to look for? What absurd or tragical adventure had befallen him? What countenance was he to assume?

While he was thus unpleasantly reflecting, the arras that overhung the chapel door was raised, and a tall priest in his robes came forth, and, giving a long, keen stare at Denis, said something in an undertone to Sire de Malétroit.

"She is in a better frame of spirit?" asked the latter.

"She is more resigned, messire," replied the priest.

"Now the Lord help her, she is hard to please!" sneered the old gentleman. "A likely stripling—not ill-born—and of her own choosing, too? Why, what more would the jade have?"

"The situation is not usual for a young damsel," said the other, "and somewhat trying to her blushes."

"She should have thought of that before she began the dance! It was none of my choosing, God knows that; but since she is in it, by our Lady, she shall carry it to the end." And then addressing Denis, "Monsieur de Beaulieu," he asked, "may I present you to my niece? She has been waiting your arrival, I may say, with even greater impatience than myself."

Denis had resigned himself with a good grace—all he desired was to know the worst of it as speedily as possible; so he rose at once, and bowed in acquiescence. The Sire de Malétroit followed his example and limped, with the assistance of the chaplain's arm, toward the chapel door. The priest pulled aside the arras, and all three entered. The building had considerable architectural pretensions. A light groining sprang from six stout columns, and hung down in two rich pendants from the centre of the vault. The place terminated behind the altar in a round end, embossed and honeycombed with a superfluity of ornament in relief, and pierced by many little windows shaped like stars, trefoils, or wheels. These windows were imperfectly is glazed, so that the night air circulated freely in the chapel. The tapers, of which there must have been half a hundred burning on the altar, were unmercifully blown about; and the light went through many different phases of brilliancy and semi-eclipse. On the steps in front of the altar knelt a young girl richly attired as a bride. A chill settled over Denis as he observed her costume; he fought with desperate energy against the conclusion that was being thrust upon his mind; it could not—it should not—be as he feared.

"Blanche," said the sire, in his most flute-like tones, "I have brought a friend to see you, my little girl; turn round and give him your pretty hand. It is good to be devout; but it is necessary to be polite, my niece."

The girl rose to her feet and turned toward the newcomers. She moved all of a piece; and shame and exhaustion were expressed in every line of her fresh young body; and she held her head down and kept her eyes upon the pavement, as she came slowly forward. In the course of her advance her eyes fell upon Denis de Beaulieu's feet—feet of which he was justly vain, be it remarked, and wore in the most elegant accoutrement even while travelling. She paused—started, as if his yellow boots had conveyed some shocking meaning—and glanced, suddenly up into the wearer's countenance. Their eyes met; shame gave place to horror and terror in her looks; the blood left her lips, with a piercing scream she covered her face with her hands and sank upon, the chapel floor.

"That is not the man!" she cried. "My uncle, that is not the man!"

The Sire de Malétroit chirped agreeably. "Of course not," he said; "I expected as much. It was so unfortunate you could not remember his name."

"Indeed," she cried, "indeed, I have never seen this person till this moment—I have never so much as set eyes upon him—I never wish to see him again. Sir," she said, turning to Denis, "if you are a gentleman, you will hear me out. Have I ever seen you—have you ever seen me—before this accursed hour?"

"To speak for myself, I have never had that pleasure," answered the young man. "This is the first time, messire, that I have met with your engaging niece."

The old gentleman shrugged his shoulders.

"I am distressed to hear it," he said. "But it is never too late to begin. I had little more acquaintance with my own late lady ere I married her; which proves," he added, with a grimace, "that these impromptu marriages may often produce an excellent understanding in the long run. As the bridegroom is to have a voice in the matter, I will give him two hours to make up for lost time before we proceed with the ceremony." And he turned toward the door, followed by the clergyman.

The girl was on her feet in a moment. "My uncle, you cannot be in earnest," she said. "I declare before God I will stab myself rather than be forced on that young man. The heart rises at it; God forbids such marriages; you dishonor your white hair. Oh, my uncle, pity me! There is not a woman in all the world but would prefer death to such a nuptial. Is it possible," she added, faltering—"is it possible that you do not believe me—that you still think this"—and she pointed at Denis with a tremor of anger and contempt—"that you still think *this* to be the man?"

"Frankly," said the old gentleman, pausing on the threshold, "I do. But let me explain to you once for all, Blanche de Malétroit, my way of thinking about this affair. When you took it into your head to dishonor my family and the name that I have borne, in peace and war, for more than threescore years, you forfeited, not only the right to question my designs, but that of looking me in the face. If your father had been alive, he would have spat on you and turned you out of doors. His was the hand of iron. You may bless your God you have only to deal with the hand of velvet, mademoiselle. It was my duty to get you married without delay. Out of pure goodwill, I have tried to find your own gallant for you. And I believe I have succeeded. But before God and all the holy angels, Blanche de Malétroit, if I have not, I care not one jack-straw. So let me recommend you to be polite to our young friend; for, upon my word, your next groom may be less appetizing."

And with that he went out, with the chaplain at his heels; and the arras fell behind the pair.

The girl turned upon Denis with flashing eyes.

"And what, sir," she demanded, "may be the meaning of all this?"

"God knows," returned Denis, gloomily, "I am a prisoner in this house, which seems full of mad people. More I know not; and nothing do I understand."

"And pray how came you here?" she asked.

He told her as briefly as he could. "For the rest," he added, "perhaps you will follow my example, and tell me the answer to all these riddles, and what, in God's name, is like to be the end of it."

She stood silent for a little, and lie could see her lips tremble and her tearless eyes burn with a feverish lustre. Then she pressed her forehead in both hands.

"Alas, how my head aches!" she said, wearily—"to say nothing of my poor heart! But it is due to you to know my story, unmaidenly as it must seem. I am called Blanche de Malétroit; I have been without father or mother for—oh! for as long as I can recollect, and indeed I have been most unhappy all my life. Three months ago a young captain began to stand near me every day in church. I could see that I pleased him; I am much to blame, but I was so glad that any one should love me; and when he passed me a letter, I took it home with me and read it with great pleasure. Since that time he has written many. He was so anxious to speak with me, poor fellow! and kept asking me to leave the door open some evening that we might have two words upon the stair. For he knew how much my uncle trusted me." She gave something like a sob at that, and it was a moment before she could go on. "My uncle is a hard man, but he is very shrewd," she said, at last. "He has performed many feats in war, and was a great person at court, and much trusted by Queen Isabeau in old days. How he came to suspect me I cannot tell; but it is hard to keep anything from his knowledge; and this morning, as we came from mass, he took my hand into his, forced it open, and read my little billet, walking by my side all the while.

"When he finished, he gave it back to me with great politeness. It contained another request to have the door left open; and this has been the ruin of us all. My uncle kept me strictly in my room until evening, and then ordered me to dress myself as you see me—a hard mockery for a young girl, do you not think so? I suppose, when he could not prevail with me to tell him the young captain's name, he must have laid a trap for him; into which, alas! you have fallen in the anger of God. I looked for much confusion; for how could I tell whether he was willing to take me for his wife on these sharp terms? He might have been trifling with me from the first; or I might have made myself too cheap in his eyes. But truly I had not looked for such a shameful punishment as this? I could not think that God would let a girl be so disgraced before a young man. And now I tell you all; and I can scarcely hope that you will not despise me."

Denis made her a respectful inclination.

"Madam," he said, "you have honored me by your confidence. It remains for me to prove that I am not unworthy of the honor. Is Messire de Malétroit at hand?"

"I believe he is writing in the *salle[6]* without," she answered.

"May I lead you thither, madam?" asked Denis, offering his hand with his most courtly bearing.

She accepted it; and the pair passed out of the chapel, Blanche in a very drooping and shamefast condition, but Denis strutting and raffling in the consciousness of a mission, and the boyish certainty of accomplishing it with honor.

The Sire Malétroit rose to meet them with an ironical obeisance.

"Sir," said Denis, with the grandest possible air, "I believe I am to have some say in the matter of this marriage; and let me tell you at once, I will be no party to forcing the inclination of this young lady. Had it been freely offered to me, I should have been proud to accept her hand, for I perceive she is as good as she is beautiful; but as things are, I have now the honor, messire, of refusing."

Blanche looked at him with gratitude in her eyes; but the old gentleman only smiled and smiled, until his smile grew positively sickening to Denis.

"I am afraid," he said, "Monsieur de Beaulieu, that you do not perfectly understand the choice I have offered you. Follow me, I beseech you, to this window." And he led the way to one of the large windows which stood open on the night. "You observe," he went on, "there is an iron ring in the upper masonry, and reeved through that, a very efficacious rope. Now, mark my words: if you should find your disinclination to my niece's person insurmountable, I shall have you hanged out of this window before sunrise. I shall only proceed to such an extremity with the greatest regret, you may believe me. For it is not at all your death that I desire, but my niece's establishment in life. At the same time, it must come to that if you prove obstinate. Your family, Monsieur de Beaulieu, is very well in its way; but if you sprung from Charlemagne[7], you should not refuse the hand of a Malétroit with impunity—not if she had been as common as the Paris road—not if she was as hideous as the gargoyle over my door. Neither my niece nor you, nor my own private feelings, move me at all in this matter. The honor of my house has been compromised; I believe you to be the guilty person, at least you are now in the secret; and you can hardly wonder if I request you to wipe out the stain. If you will not, your blood be on your own head! It will be no great satisfaction to me to have your interesting relics kicking their heels in the breeze below my windows, but half a loaf is better than no bread, and if I cannot cure the dishonor, I shall at least stop the scandal."

There was a pause.

"I believe there are other ways of settling such imbroglios among gentlemen," said Denis. "You wear a sword, and I hear you have used it with distinction."

The Sire de Malétroit made a signal to the chaplain, who crossed the room with long silent strides and raised the arras over the third of the three doors. It was only a moment before he let it fall again; but Denis had time to see a dusky passage full of armed men.

"When I was a little younger, I should have been delighted to honor you, Monsieur de Beaulieu," said Sire Alain: "but I am now too old. Faithful retainers are the sinews of age, and I must employ the strength I have. This is one of the hardest things to swallow as a man grows up in years; but with a little patience, even this becomes habitual. You and the lady seem to prefer the *salle* for what remains of your two hours; and as I have no desire to cross your preference, I shall resign it to your use with all the pleasure in the world. No haste!" he added, holding up his hand, as he saw a dangerous look come into Denis de Beaulieu's face. "If your mind revolt against hanging, it will be time enough two hours hence to throw yourself out of the window or upon the pikes of my retainers. Two hours of life are always two hours. A great many things may turn up in even as little a while as that. And, besides. If I understand her appearance, my niece has something to say to you. You will not disfigure your last hours by a want of politeness to a lady?"

Denis looked at Blanche, and she made him an imploring gesture.

It is likely that the old gentleman was hugely pleased at this symptom of an understanding; for he smiled on both, and added sweetly: "If you will give me your word of honor, Monsieur de Beaulieu, to await my return at the end of the two hours before attempting anything desperate, I shall withdraw my retainers, and let you speak in greater privacy with mademoiselle."

Denis again glanced at the girl, who seemed to beseech him to agree.

"I give you my word of honor," he said.

Messire de Malétroit bowed, and proceeded to limp about the apartment, clearing his throat the while with that odd musical chirp which had already grown so irritating in the ears of Denis de Bealieu. He first possessed himself of some papers which lay upon the table; then he went to the mouth of the passage and appeared to give an order to the men behind the arras; and lastly he hobbled out through the door by which Denis had come in, turning upon the threshold to address a last smiling bow to the young couple, and followed by the chaplain with a hand lamp.

No sooner were they alone than Blanche advanced toward Denis with her hands extended. Her face was flushed and excited, and her eyes shone with tears.

"You shall not die!" she cried, "you shall marry me after all."

"You seem to think, madam," replied Denis, "that I stand much in fear of death."

"Oh, no, no," she said, "I see you are no poltroon[8]. It is for my own sake—I could not bear to have you slain for such a scruple."

"I am afraid," returned Denis, "that you underrate the difficulty, madam. What you may be too generous to refuse, I may be too proud to accept. In a moment of noble feeling toward me, you forget what you perhaps owe to others."

He had the decency to keep his eyes on the floor as he said this, and after he had finished, so as not to spy upon her confusion. She stood silent for a moment, then walked suddenly away, and falling on her uncle's chair, fairly burst out sobbing. Denis was in the acme of embarrassment. He looked round, as if to seek for inspiration, and, seeing a stool, plumped down upon it for something to do. There he sat, playing with the guard of his rapier, and wishing himself dead a thousand times over, and buried in the nastiest kitchen-heap in France. His eyes wandered round the apartment, but found nothing to arrest them. There were such wide spaces between the furniture, the light fell so badly and cheerlessly over all, the dark outside air looked in so coldly through the windows, that he thought he had never seen a church so vast, nor a tomb so melancholy. The regular sobs of Blanche de Malétroit measured out the time like the ticking of a clock. He read the device upon the shield over and over again, until his eyes became obscured; he stared into shadowy corners until he imagined they were swarming with horrible animals; and every now and again he awoke with a start, to remember that his last two hours were running, and death was on the march.

Oftener and oftener, as the time went on, did his glance settle on the girl herself. Her face was bowed forward and covered with her hands, and she was shaken at intervals by the convulsive hiccough of grief. Even thus she was not an unpleasant object to dwell upon, so plump and yet so fine, with a warm brown skin, and the most beautiful hair, Denis thought, in the whole world of womankind. Her hands were like her uncle's: but they were more in place at the end of her young arms, and looked infinitely soft and caressing. He remembered how her blue eyes had shone upon him, full of anger, pity, and innocence. And the more he dwelt on her perfections, the uglier death looked, and the more deeply was he smitten with penitence at her continued tears. Now he felt that no man could have the courage to leave a world which contained so beautiful a creature; and now he would have given forty minutes of his last hour to have unsaid his cruel speech.

Suddenly a hoarse and ragged peal of cockcrow rose to their ears from the dark valley below the windows. And this shattering noise in the silence of all around was like a light in a dark place, and shook them both out of their reflections.

"Alas, can I do nothing to help you?" she said, looking up.

"Madam," replied Denis, with a fine irrelevancy, "if I have said anything to wound you, believe me, it was for your own sake and not for mine."

She thanked him with a tearful look.

"I feel your position cruelly," he went on. "The world has been bitter, hard on you. Your uncle is a disgrace to mankind. Believe me, madam, there is no young gentleman in all France but would be glad of my opportunity, to die in doing you a momentary service."

"I know already that you can be very brave and generous," she answered. "What I *want* to know is whether I can serve you—now or afterward," she added, with a quaver.

"Most certainly," he answered, with a smile. "Let me sit beside you as if I were a friend, instead of a foolish intruder; try to forget how awkwardly we are placed to one another; make my last moments go pleasantly; and you will do me the chief service possible."

"You are very gallant," she added, with a yet deeper sadness—"very gallant—and it somehow pains me. But draw nearer, if you please; and if you find anything to say to me, you will at least make certain of a very friendly listener. Ah! Monsieur de Beaulieu," she broke forth—"ah! Monsieur de Beaulieu, how can I look you in the face?" And she fell to weeping again with a renewed effusion.

"Madam," said Denis, taking her hand in both of his, "reflect on the little time I have before me, and the great bitterness into which I am cast by the sight of your distress. Spare me, in my last moments, the spectacle of what I cannot cure even with the sacrifice of my life."

"I am very selfish," answered Blanche. "I will be braver, Monsieur de Beaulieu, for your sake. But think if I can do you no kindness in the future—if you have no friends to whom I could carry your adieux. Charge me as heavily as you can; every burden will lighten, by so little, the invaluable gratitude I owe you. Put it in my power to do something more for you than weep."

"My mother is married again, and has a young family to care for. My brother Guichard will inherit my fiefs; and if I am not in error, that will content him amply for my death. Life is a little vapor that passeth away, as we are told by those in holy orders. When a man is in a fair way and sees all life open in front of him, he seems to himself to make a very important figure in the world. His horse whinnies to him; the trumpets blow and the girls look out of window as he rides into town before his company; he receives many assurances of trust and regard—sometimes by express in a letter—sometimes face to face, with persons of great consequence falling on his neck. It is not wonderful if his head is turned for a time. But once he is dead, were he as brave as Hercules[9] or as wise as Solomon[10], he is soon forgotten. It is not ten years since my father fell, with many other knights around him, in a very fierce encounter, and I do not think that any one of them, nor so much as the name of the fight, is now remembered. No, no, madam, the nearer you come to it, you see that death is a dark and dusty corner, where a man gets into his tomb and has the door shut after him till the judgment day. I have few friends just now, and once I am dead I shall have none."

"Ah, Monsieur de Beaulieu!" she exclaimed, "you forget Blanche de Malétroit."

"You have a sweet nature, madam, and you are pleased to estimate a little service far beyond its worth."

"It is not that," she answered. "You mistake me if you think I am easily touched by my own concerns. I say so because you are the noblest man I have ever met; because I recognize in you a spirit that would have made even a common person famous in the land."

"And yet here I die in a mousetrap—with no more noise about it than my own squeaking," answered he.

A look of pain crossed her face and she was silent for a little while. Then a light came into her eyes, and with a smile she spoke again.

"I cannot have my champion think meanly of himself. Any one who gives his life for another will be met in paradise by all the heralds and angels of the Lord God. And you have no such cause to hang your head. For—Pray, do you think me beautiful?" she asked, with a deep flush.

"Indeed, madam, I do," he said.

"I am glad of that," she answered heartily. "Do you think there are many men in France who have been asked in marriage by a beautiful maiden— with her own lips—and who have refused her to her face? I know you men would half despise such a triumph; but believe me, we women know more of what is precious in love. There is nothing that should set a person higher in his own esteem; and we women would prize nothing more dearly."

"You are very good," he said; "but you cannot make me forget that I was asked in pity and not for love."

"I am not so sure of that," she replied, holding down her head. "Hear me to an end, Monsieur de Beaulieu. I know how you must despise me; I feel you are right to do so; I am too poor a creature to occupy one thought of your mind, although, alas! you must die for me this morning. But when I asked you to marry me, indeed, and indeed, it was because I respected and admired you, and loved you with my whole soul, from the very moment that you took my part against my uncle. If you had seen yourself, and how noble you looked, you would pity rather than despise me. And now," she went on, hurriedly checking him with her hand, "although I have laid aside all reserve and told you so much, remember that I know your sentiments toward me already. I would not, believe me, being nobly born, weary you with importunities into consent. I too have a pride of my own: and I declare before the holy mother of God, if you should now go back from your word already given, I would no more marry you than I would marry my uncle's groom."

Denis smiled a little bitterly.

"It is a small love," he said, "that shies at a little pride."
She made no answer, although she probably had her own thoughts.
"Come hither to the window," he said with a sigh. "Here is the dawn."
And indeed the dawn was already beginning. The hollow of the sky was full of essential daylight, colorless and clean; and the valley underneath was flooded with a gray reflection. A few thin vapors clung in the coves of the forest or lay along the winding course of the river. The scene disengaged a surprising effect of stillness, which was hardly interrupted when the cocks began once more to crow among the steadings[11]. Perhaps the same fellow who had made so horrid a clangor in the darkness not half an hour before, now sent up the merriest cheer to greet the coming day. A little wind went bustling and eddying among the tree-tops underneath the windows. And still the daylight kept flooding insensibly out of the east, which was soon to grow incandescent and cast up that red-hot cannon-ball, the rising sun.
Denis looked out over all this with a bit of a shiver. He had taken her hand, and retained it in his almost unconsciously.
"Has the day begun already?" she said; and then illogically enough: "the night has been so long! Alas! what shall we say to my uncle when he returns?"
"What you will," said Denis, and he pressed her fingers in his.
She was silent.
"Blanche," he said, with a swift, uncertain, passionate utterance, "you have seen whether I fear death. You must know well enough that I would as gladly leap out of that window into the empty air as to lay a finger on you without your free and full consent. But if you care for me at all do not let me lose my life in a misapprehension; for I love you better than the whole world; and though I will die for you blithely, it would be like all the joys of Paradise to live on and spend my life in your service."
As he stopped speaking, a bell began to ring loudly in the interior of the house; and a clatter of armor in the corridor showed that the retainers were returning to their post, and the two hours were at an end.
"After all that you have heard?" she whispered, leaning toward him with her lips and eyes.
"I have heard nothing," he replied.
"The captain's name was Florimond de Champdivers," she said in his ear.
"I did not hear it," he answered, taking her supple body in his arms, and covered her wet face with kisses.

A melodious chirping was audible behind, followed by a beautiful chuckle, and the voice of Messire de Malétroit wished his new nephew a good morning.


# NOTES

[1] Published in 1878. Acknowledgment is due to the Charles Scribner's Sons Company, Publishers, for the use of the text of their edition of Stevenson's works.

[2] 207:18 bartizan. A small overhanging turret with loop-holes and embrasures projecting from the parapet of a medieval building.

[3] 208:1 gargoyles. Mouths of spouts, in antic shapes.

[4] 209:30 debouched. Passed out.

[5] 212:29 Leonardo. (1452-1519.) A famous Italian painter, architect, sculptor, scientist, engineer, mechanician, and musician.

[6] 222:7 salle. French word for hall or room.

[7] 223:13 Charlemagne. (742 or 747-814.) A great king of the Franks and emperor of the Romans.

[8] 225:25 poltroon. A coward, a dastard.

[9] 229:12 Hercules. A mighty hero in Greek and Roman mythology.

[10] 229:13 Solomon. Son of David. King of Israel, 993-953 B.C.

[11] 231: 26 steadings. A farmstead—barns, stables, cattle-sheds, etc.


# BIOGRAPHY

Robert Louis Stevenson was born November 13, 1850, in Edinburgh. He was an only child. On his mother's side he came from a line of Scotch philosophers and ministers; on his father's, from a line of active workers and scientists. His grandfather, Robert Stevenson, and his father, Thomas Stevenson, gained world-wide reputations in engineering.

Robert inherited from his mother throat and lung troubles. His health was very poor from his birth and his life was preserved only by the careful watchfulness of his mother and his devoted nurse, Alison Cunningham. As a child he was very lovable and possessed a very active imagination.

He went to school in Edinburgh between the years 1858-1867. He first attended a preparatory school, then the Edinburgh academy. He spent considerable time at his maternal grandfather's home. It was there that he first tasted the delights of romance. In his school work he was none too studious, but all his teachers were charmed by his pleasing manner and general intelligence. Though an idler in other things, he worked constantly on the art of writing. Throughout his study in Edinburgh University and his unsuccessful efforts in engineering and the practice of law, literature became more and more a passion with him.

The period between 1875 and 1879 was one of improved health and considerable literary activity. During this time he published *A Lodging for the Night, Will o' the Mill, The New Arabian Nights*, and an *Inland Voyage*. While in southern Europe he met and fell in love with Mrs. Osbourne. So after she returned to her home in California, Stevenson received the news that she was seriously ill. He immediately sailed for San Francisco, travelling as a steerage passenger because of lack of funds and a desire for literary material. Out of this experience grew a number of stories and essays. Exposure on the voyage affected his health and caused a very dangerous illness. After his recovery he married Mrs. Osbourne and returned to England with his wife and stepson.

For a few years his work was more or less spasmodic on account of his bitter struggle with poor health, in 1883 he achieved success by the publication of *Treasure Island. Markheim* appeared in 1884. *Kidnapped* and *Dr. Jekyll and Mr. Hyde* were published in 1886.

After the death of his father in 1887, Stevenson and his family sailed to America, where they settled in the Adirondacks for the winter of 1888. Here his health was good and he wrote a number of essays for *Scribner's Magazine*. In the spring of the same year they started on a cruise of the south seas. They visited many of the southern islands and settled at Vailima, Samoa. Stevenson was interested in the Samoaas and took an active part in their political affairs. The tropical climate agreed with him and his creative power was renewed. He wrote a number of short stories, a series of letters on the South Seas, and the novel *David Balfour*.

Political reverses and failing strength took away for a time his power to write. He was again stimulated, however, by the love and appreciation of his Samoan followers, and started on what promised to be his period of highest achievement. This promise was soon blighted by his untimely death from a stroke of apoplexy, December 13, 1894. He was buried in Samoa.

# BIOGRAPHICAL REFERENCES

*Life of Robert Louis Stevenson*, 2 vols., Graham Balfour.
*Robert Louis Stevenson*, Isobel Strong.
*Memories and Portraits*, Robert Louis Stevenson.
*Friends on the Shelf*, Bradford Torrey.
"Personal Recollections," Edmund Gosse, *Century Magazine*, 50:447.
"Character Sketch," *Atlantic Monthly*, 89:89-99.
"The Real Stevenson," *Atlantic Monthly*, 85:702-5.
*A Bibliography of the Works of Robert Louis Stevenson*, W.F. Prideaux.

# CRITICISMS

Fundamentally Stevenson's style is marked by a conscious aim to entertain. His engaging humor, free of all affectation, sentimentality, and exaggeration, is spontaneous and natural. His most original writing is *The Child's Garden of Verses*. His touch is light and his thought is clear and lucid. *Across the Plains* is written in his most straightforward and natural style.

Stevenson was a careful writer, doing with great skill any established piece of art. He practised diligently, and gained, as he himself states, his high rank by constantly drilling himself in the art of writing. This imitation of form to the point of perfection, rather than an expression of a great and moving idea, gives an air of insincerity to some of Stevenson's works. Yet, although seemingly artificial, he never chose words for the sake of mere sounds, but for their accuracy in truth and fitness. He was as an ephemeral shadow with an optimistic and real spirit. He infused an intimacy and spirituality into his writings that prove delightful to all his readers.

The subject of Markheim, a man failing through weakness, was a favorite topic for Stevenson. Markheim is almost an ideal specimen of the impressionistic short-story. It has a plot in which Hawthorne might justly have revelled, a treatment as intellectual as that of Poe, descriptions not unlike those of Flaubert's, and a moral ending true to the Puritanic type. The movement of the story is swift and possesses perfect unity. The surprise at the end comes as a shock although the author has consistently and logically constructed his plot.

# GENERAL REFERENCES

*Emerson and Other Essays*, John Jay Chapman.
*Robert Louis Stevenson*, L. Cope Cornford.
*Modern Novelists*, William Lyon Phelps.
*Makers of English Fiction*, W.J. Dawson.
"Art of Stevenson," *North American Review*, 171: 348-358.
"Criticism," *Dial*, 30:345. May 18, 1901.

# COLLATERAL READINGS

*The Suicide Club (New Arabian Nights)*, Robert Louis Stevenson.
*Story of the Physician and the Saratoga Trunk*, Robert Louis Stevenson.
*The Adventure of the Hansom Cab*, Robert Louis Stevenson.
*The Rajah's Diamond*, Robert Louis Stevenson.
*The Story of the House with the Green Blinds*, Robert Louis Stevenson.
*The Adventure of Prince Florizel and the Detective*, Robert Louis Stevenson.
*A Lodging for the Night*, Robert Louis Stevenson,
*Providence and the Guitar*, Robert Louis Stevenson.
*In the Valley*, Robert Louis Stevenson.
*With the Children of Israel*, Robert Louis Stevenson.
*The Lotus and the Cockleburrs*, "O. Henry."
*Two Bites at a Cherry*, Thomas Bailey Aldrich.
*The Notary of Perigueux*, Henry W. Longfellow.

# MARKHEIM[1]

*By Robert Louis Stevenson (1850-1894)*

"Yes," said the dealer, "our windfalls[2] are of various kinds. Some customers are ignorant, and then I touch a dividend[3] on my superior knowledge. Some are dishonest," and here he held up the candle, so that the light fell strongly on his visitor, "and in that case," he continued, "I profit by my virtue."

Markheim had but just entered from the daylight streets, and his eyes had not yet grown familiar with the mingled shine and darkness in the shop. At these pointed words, and before the near presence of the flame, he blinked painfully and looked aside.

The dealer chuckled. "You come to me on Christmas Day," he resumed, "when you know that I am alone in my house, put up my shutters, and make a point of refusing business. Well, you will have to pay for that; you will have to pay for my loss of time, when I should be balancing my books; you will have to pay, besides; for a kind of manner that I remark in you to-day very strongly. I am the essence of discretion, and ask no awkward questions; but when a customer cannot look me in the eye, he has to pay for it." The dealer once more chuckled; and then, changing to his usual business voice, though still with a note of irony, "You can give, as usual, a clear account of how you came into the possession of the object?" he continued. "Still your uncle's cabinet? A remarkable collector, sir!"

And the little pale, round-shouldered dealer stood almost on tiptoe, looking over the top of his gold spectacles, and nodding his head with every mark of disbelief. Markheim returned his gaze with one of infinite pity, and a touch of horror.

"This time," said he, "you are in error. I have not come to sell, but to buy. I have no curios to dispose of; my uncle's cabinet is bare to the wainscot: even were it still intact, I have done well on the Stock Exchange, and should more likely add to it than otherwise, and my errand to-day is simplicity itself. I seek, a Christmas present for a lady," he continued, waxing more fluent as he struck into the speech he had prepared; "and certainly I owe you every excuse for thus disturbing you upon so small a matter. But the thing was neglected yesterday; I must produce my little compliment at dinner; and, as you very well know, a rich marriage is not a thing to be neglected."

There followed a pause, during which the dealer seemed to weigh this statement incredulously. The ticking of many clocks among the curious lumber of the shop, and the faint rushing of the cabs in a near thoroughfare, filled up the interval of silence.

"Well, sir," said the dealer, "be it so. You are an old customer after all; and if, as you say, you have the chance of a good marriage, far be it from me to be an obstacle. Here is a nice thing for a lady, now," he went on, "this hand glass—fifteenth century, warranted; comes from a good collection, too; but I reserve the name, in the interests of my customer, who was just like yourself, my dear sir, the nephew and sole heir of a remarkable collector."

The dealer, while he thus ran on in his dry and biting voice, had stooped to take the object from its place; and, as he had done so, a shock had passed through Markheim, a start both of hand and foot, a sudden leap of many tumultuous passions to the face. It passed as swiftly as it came, and left no trace beyond a certain trembling of the hand that now received the glass.

"A glass," he said hoarsely, and then paused, and repeated it more clearly. "A glass? For Christmas? Surely not."

"And why not?" cried the dealer. "Why not a glass?"

Markheim was looking upon him with an indefinable expression. "You ask me why not?" he said. "Why, look here—look in it—look at yourself! Do you like to see it? No! nor I—nor any man."

The little man had jumped back when Markheim had so suddenly confronted him with the mirror; but now, perceiving there was nothing worse on hand, he chuckled. "Your future lady, sir, must be pretty hard favored," said he.

"I ask you," said Markheim, "for a Christmas present, and you give me this—this damned reminder of years and sins and follies—this hand-conscience! Did you mean it? Had you a thought in your mind? Tell me. It will be better for you if you do. Come, tell me about yourself, I hazard a guess now, that you are in secret a very charitable man?"

The dealer looked closely at his companion. It was very odd, Markheim did not appear to be laughing; there was something in his face like an eager sparkle of hope, but nothing of mirth.

"What are you driving at?" the dealer asked.

"Not charitable?" returned the other, gloomily. "Not charitable; not pious; not scrupulous; unloving; unbeloved; a hand to get money, a safe to keep it. Is that all? Dear God, man, is that all?"

"I will tell you what it is," began the dealer, with some sharpness, and then broke off again into a chuckle. "But I see this is a love match of yours, and you have been drinking the lady's health."

"Ah!" cried Markheim, with a strange curiosity, "Ah, have you been in love? Tell me about that."

"I!" cried the dealer. "I in love! I never had the time, nor have I the time to-day for all this nonsense. Will you take the glass?"

"Where is the hurry?" returned Markheim. "It is very pleasant to stand here talking; and life is so short and insecure that I would not hurry away from any pleasure—no, not even from so mild a one as this. We should, rather cling, cling to what little we can get, like a man at a cliff's edge. Every second is a cliff, if you think upon it—a cliff a mile high—high enough, if we fall, to dash us out of every feature of humanity. Hence it is best to talk pleasantly. Let us talk of each other; why should we wear this mask? Let us be confidential. Who knows, we might become friends?"

"I have just one word to say to you," said the dealer. "Either make your purchase, or walk out of my shop."

"True, true," said Markheim. "Enough fooling. To business. Show me something else."

The dealer stooped once more, this time to replace the glass upon the shelf, his thin blond hair falling over his eyes as he did so. Markheim moved a little nearer, with one hand in the pocket of his greatcoat; he drew himself up and filled his lungs; at the same time many different emotions were depicted together on his face—terror, horror, and resolve, fascination, and a physical repulsion; and through a haggard lift of his upper lip, his teeth looked out.

"This, perhaps, may suit," observed the dealer; and then, as he began to re-arise, Markheim bounded from behind upon his victim. The long, skewer-like[4] dagger flashed and fell. The dealer straggled like a hen, striking his temple on the shelf, and then tumbled on the floor in a heap.

Time had some score of small voices in that shop, some stately and slow as was becoming to their great age, others garrulous and hurried. All these told out the seconds in an intricate chorus of tickings. Then the passage of a lad's feet, heavily running on the pavement, broke in upon these smaller voices and startled Markheim into the consciousness of his surroundings. He looked about him awfully. The candle stood on the counter, its flame solemnly wagging in a draught; and by that inconsiderable movement, the whole room was filled with noiseless bustle and kept heaving like a sea: the tall shadows nodding, the gross blots of darkness swelling and dwindling as with respiration, the faces of the portraits and the china gods changing and wavering like images in water. The inner door stood ajar, and peered into that leaguer[5] of shadows with a long slit of daylight like a pointing finger.

From these fear-stricken rovings, Markheim's eyes returned to the body of his victim, where it lay both humped and sprawling, incredibly small and strangely meaner than in life. In these poor, miserly clothes, in that ungainly attitude, the dealer lay like so much sawdust. Markheim had feared to see it, and, lo! it was nothing. And yet, as he gazed, this bundle of old clothes and pool of blood began to find eloquent voices. There it must lie; there was none to work the cunning hinges or direct the miracle of locomotion—there it must lie till it was found. Found! aye, and then? Then would this dead flesh lift up a cry that would ring over England, and fill the world with the echoes of pursuit. Ay, dead or not, this was still the enemy. "Time was that when the brains were out[6]," he thought; and the first word struck into his mind. Time, now that the deed was accomplished—time, which had dosed for the victim, had become instant and momentous for the slayer.

The thought was yet in his mind, when, first one and then another, with every variety of pace and voice—one deep as the bell from a cathedral turret, another ringing on its treble notes the prelude of a waltz—the clocks began to strike the hour of three in the afternoon.

The sudden outbreak of so many tongues in that dumb chamber staggered him. He began to bestir himself, going to and fro with the candle, beleaguered by moving shadows, and startled to the soul by chance reflections. In many rich mirrors, some of home designs, some from Venice or Amsterdam, he saw his face repeated and repeated, as it were an army of spies; his own eyes met and detected him; and the sound of his own steps, lightly as they fell, vexed the surrounding quiet. And still as he continued to fill his pockets, his mind accused him, with a sickening iteration[7], of the thousand faults of his design. He should have chosen a more quiet hour; he should have prepared an alibi; he should not have used a knife; he should have been more cautious, and only bound and gagged the dealer, and not killed him; he should have been more bold, and killed the servant also; he should have done all things otherwise; poignant regrets, weary, incessant toiling of the mind to change what was unchangeable, to plan what was now useless, to be the architect of the irrevocable past. Meanwhile, and behind all this activity, brute terrors, like the scurrying of rats in a deserted attic, filled the more remote chambers of his brain with riot; the hand of the constable would fall heavy on his shoulder, and his nerves would jerk like a hooked fish; or he beheld, in galloping defile, the dock, the prison, the gallows, and the black coffin. Terror of the people in the street sat down before his mind like a besieging army. It was impossible, he thought, but that some rumor of the struggle must have reached their ears and set on edge their curiosity; and now, in all the neighboring houses, he divined them sitting motionless and with uplifted ear—solitary people, condemned to spend Christmas dwelling alone on memories of the past, and now startlingly recalled from that tender exercise: happy family parties, struck into silence round the table, the mother still with raised finger; every degree and age and humor, but all, by their own hearths, prying and hearkening and weaving the rope that was to hang him. Sometimes it seemed to him he could not move too softly; the clink of the tall Bohemian goblets rang out loudly like a bell; and alarmed by the bigness of the ticking, he was tempted to stop the clocks. And then, again, with a swift transition of his terrors, the very silence of the place appeared a source of peril, and a thing to strike and freeze the passer-by; and he would step more boldly, and bustle aloud among the contents of the shop, and imitate, with elaborate bravado, the movements of a busy man at ease in his own house.

But he was now so pulled about by different alarms that, while one portion of his mind was still alert and cunning, another trembled on the brink of lunacy. One hallucination in particular took a strong hold on his credulity. The neighbor hearkening with white face beside his window, the passer-by arrested by a horrible surmise on the pavement—these could at worst suspect, they could not know; through the brick walls and shuttered windows only sounds could penetrate. But here, within the house, was he alone? He knew he was; he had watched the servant set forth sweethearting, in her poor best, "out for the day" written in every ribbon and smile. Yes, he was alone, of course; and yet, in the bulk of empty house about him, he could surely hear a stir of delicate footing—he was surely conscious, inexplicably conscious, of some presence. Ay, surely; to every room and corner of the house his imagination followed it; and now it was a faceless thing, and yet had eyes to see with; and again it was a shadow of himself; and yet again behold the image of the dead dealer, reinspired with cunning and hatred.

At times, with a strong effort, he would glance at the open door which still seemed to repel his eyes. The house was tall, the skylight small and dirty, the day blind with fog; and the light that filtered down to the ground story was exceedingly faint, and showed dimly on the threshold of the shop. And yet, in that strip of doubtful brightness, did there not hang wavering a shadow?

Suddenly, from the street outside, a very jovial gentleman began to beat with a staff on the shop door, accompanying his blows with shouts and railleries[8] in which the dealer was continually called upon by name. Markheim, smitten into ice, glanced at the dead man. But no! he lay quite still; he was fled away far beyond earshot of these blows and shoutings; he was sunk beneath seas of silence; and his name, which would once have caught his notice above the howling of a storm, had become an empty sound. And presently the jovial gentleman desisted from his knocking and departed.

Here was a broad hint to hurry what remained to be done, to get forth from, this accusing neighborhood, to plunge into a bath of London multitudes, and to reach, on the other side of day, that haven of safety and apparent, innocence——-his bed. One visitor had come: at any moment it another might follow and be more obstinate. To have done the deed, and yet not to reap the profit, would be too abhorrent a failure. The money, that was now Markheim's concern: and as a means to that, the keys.

He glanced over his shoulder at the open door, where the shadow was still lingering and shivering; and with no conscious repugnance of the mind, yet with a tremor of the belly, he drew near the body of his victim. The human character had quite departed. Like a suit half-stuffed with bran, the limbs lay scattered, the trunk doubled, on the floor; and yet the thing repelled him. Although so dingy and inconsiderable to the eye, he feared it might have more significance to the touch. He took the body by the shoulders, and turned it on its back. It was strangely light and supple, and the limbs, as if they had been broken, fell into the oddest postures. The face was robbed of all expression; but it was as pale as wax, and shockingly smeared with blood about one temple. That was, for Markheim, the one displeasing circumstance. It carried him back, upon the instant, to a certain fair day in a fishers' village: a gray day, a piping wind, a crowd upon the street, the blare of brasses, the booming of drums, the nasal voice of a ballad singer; and a boy going to and fro, buried over head in the crowd and divided between interest and fear, until, coming out upon the chief place of concourse, he beheld a booth and a great screen with pictures, dismally designed, garishly[9] colored: Brownrigg[10] with her apprentice; the Mannings[11] with their murdered guest; Weare in the death grip of Thurtell[12]; and a score besides of famous crimes. The thing was as clear as an illusion; he was once again that little boy; he was looking once again, and with the same sense of physical revolt, at these vile pictures; he was still stunned by the thumping of the drums. A bar of that day's music returned upon his memory; and at that, for the first time, a qualm came over him, a breath of nausea, a sudden weakness of the joints, which he must instantly resist and conquer.

He judged it more prudent to confront than to flee from these considerations; looking the more hardily in the dead face, bending his mind to realize the nature and greatness of his crime. So little a while ago that face had moved with every change of sentiment, that pale mouth had spoken, that body had been all on fire with governable energies; and now, and by his act, that piece of life had been arrested, as the horologist[13], with interjected finger, arrests the beating of the clock. So he reasoned in vain; he could rise to no more remorseful consciousness; the same heart which had shuddered before the painted effigies of crime, looked on its reality unmoved. At best, he felt a gleam of pity for one who had been endowed in vain with all those faculties that can make the world a garden of enchantment, one who had never lived and who was now dead. But of penitence, no, not a tremor.

With that, shaking himself clear of these considerations, he found the keys and advanced toward the open door of the shop. Outside, it had begun to rain smartly; and the sound of the shower upon the roof had banished silence. Like some dripping cavern, the chambers of the house were haunted by an incessant echoing, which filled the ear and mingled with the ticking of the clocks. And, as Markheim approached the door, he seemed to hear, in answer to his own cautious tread, the steps of another foot withdrawing up the stair. The shadow still palpitated loosely on the threshold. He threw a ton's weight of resolve upon his muscles, and drew back the door.

The faint, foggy daylight glimmered dimly on the bare floor and stairs; on the bright suit of armor posted, halbert in hand, upon the landing; and on the dark wood carvings and framed pictures that hung against the yellow panels of the wainscot. So loud was the beating of the rain through all the house that, in Markheim's ears, it began to be distinguished into many different sounds. Footsteps and sighs, the tread of regiments marching in the distance, the chink of money in the counting, and the creaking of doors held stealthily ajar, appeared to mingle with the patter of the drops upon the cupola and the gushing of the water in the pipes. The sense that he was not alone grew upon him to the verge of madness. On every side he was haunted and begirt by presences. He heard them moving in the upper chambers; from the shop, he heard the dead man getting to his legs; and as he began with a great effort to mount the stairs, feet fled quietly before him and followed stealthily behind. If he were but deaf, he thought, how tranquilly he would possess his soul! And then again, and hearkening with ever fresh attention, he blessed himself for that unresting sense which held the outposts and stood a trusty sentinel upon his life. His head turned continually on his neck; his eyes, which seemed starting from their orbits, scouted on every side, and on every side were half rewarded as with the tail of something nameless vanishing. The four-and-twenty steps to the first floor were four-and-twenty agonies.

On that first story the doors stood ajar, three of them like three ambushes, shaking his nerves like the throats of cannon. He could never again, he felt, be sufficiently immured and fortified from men's observing eyes; he longed to be home, girt in by walls, buried among bed-clothes, and invisible to all but God. And at that thought he wondered a little, recollecting tales of other murderers and the fear they were said to entertain of heavenly avengers. It was not so, at least, with him. He feared the laws of nature, lest, in their callous and immutable procedure, they should preserve some damning evidence of his crime. He feared tenfold more, with a slavish, superstitious terror, some scission[14] in the continuity of man's experience, some wilful illegality of nature. He played a game of skill, depending on the rules, calculating consequence from cause; and what if nature, as the defeated tyrant overthrew the chessboard, should break the mould of their succession? The like had befallen Napoleon (so writers said) when the winter changed the time of its appearance. The like might befall Markheim: the solid walls might become transparent and reveal his doings like those of bees in a glass hive; the stout planks might yield under his foot like quicksands and detain him in their clutch; aye, and there were soberer accidents that might destroy him: if, for instance, the house should fall and imprison him beside the body of his victim; or the house next door should fly on fire, and the firemen invade him from all sides. These things he feared; and, in a sense, these things might be called the hands of God reached forth against sin. But about God himself he was at ease; his act was doubtless exceptional, but so were his excuses, which God knew; it was there, and not among men, that he felt sure of justice.

When he got safe into the drawing-room, and shut the door behind him, he was aware of a respite from alarms. The room was quite dismantled, uncarpeted besides, and strewn with packing cases and incongruous furniture; several great pier glasses, in which he beheld himself at various angles, like an actor on a stage; many pictures, framed and unframed, standing, with their faces to the wall; a fine Sheraton[15] sideboard, a cabinet of marquetry[16], and a great old bed, with tapestry hangings. The windows opened to the floor; but by great good fortune the lower part of the shutters had been closed, and this concealed him from the neighbors. Here, then, Markheim drew in a packing case before the cabinet, and began to search among the keys. It was a long business, for there were many; and it was irksome, besides; for, after all, there might be nothing in the cabinet, and time was on the wing. But the closeness of the occupation sobered him. With the tail of his eye he saw the door—even glanced at it from time to time directly, like a besieged commander pleased to verify the good estate of his defences. But in truth he was at peace. The rain falling in the street sounded natural and pleasant. Presently, on the other side, the notes of a piano were wakened to the music of a hymn, and the voices of many children took up the air and words. How stately, how comfortable was the melody! How fresh the youthful voices! Markheim gave ear to it smilingly, as he sorted out the keys; and his mind was thronged with answerable ideas and images; church-going children and the pealing of the high organ; children afield, bathers by the brookside, ramblers on the brambly common, kite-flyers in the windy and cloud-navigated sky; and then, at another cadence of the hymn, back again to church, and the somnolence of summer Sundays, and the high, genteel voice of the parson (which he smiled a little to recall), and the painted Jacobean[17] tombs, and the dim lettering of the Ten Commandments in the chancel.

And as he sat thus, at once busy and absent, he was startled to his feet. A flash of ice, a flash of fire, a bursting gush of blood, went over him, and then he stood transfixed and thrilling. A step mounted the stair slowly and steadily, and presently a hand was laid upon the knob, and the lock clicked, and the door opened.

Fear held Markheim in a vice. What to expect he knew not, whether the dead man walking, or the official ministers of human justice, or some chance witness blindly stumbling in to consign him to the gallows. But when a face was thrust into the aperture, glanced round the room, looked at him, nodded and smiled as if in friendly recognition, and then withdrew again, and the door closed behind it, his fear broke loose from his control in a hoarse cry. At the sound of this the visitant returned.

"Did you call me?" he asked pleasantly, and with that he entered the room, and closed the door behind him.

Markheim stood and gazed at him with all his eyes. Perhaps there was a film upon his sight, but the outlines of the newcomer seemed to change and waver like those of the idols in the wavering candlelight of the shop: and at times he thought he knew him; and at times he thought he bore a likeness to himself; and always, like a lump of living terror, there lay in his bosom the conviction that this thing was not of the earth and not of God.

And yet the creature had a strange air of the commonplace, as he stood looking on Markheim with a smile; and when he added: "You are looking for the money, I believe?" it was in the tones of everyday politeness.

Markheim made no answer.

"I should warn you," resumed the other, "that the maid has left her sweetheart earlier than usual and will soon be here. If Mr. Markheim be found in this house, I need not describe to him the consequences."

"You know me?" cried the murderer.

The visitor smiled. "You have long been a favorite of mine," he said; "and I have long observed and often sought to help you."

"What are you?" cried Markheim: "the devil?"

"What I may be," returned the other, "cannot affect the service I propose to render you."

"It can," cried Markheim; "it does! Be helped by you? No, never; not by you! You do not know me yet; thank God, you do not know me!"

"I know you," replied the visitant, with a sort of kind severity or rather firmness. "I know you to the soul."

"Know me!" cried Markheim. "Who can do so? My life is but a travesty[18] and slander on myself. I have lived to belie my nature. All men do; all men are better than this disguise that grows about and stifles them. You see each dragged away by life, like one whom bravos have seized and muffled in a cloak. If they had their own control—if you could see their faces, they would be altogether different, they would shine out for heroes and saints! I am worse than most; myself is more overlaid; my excuse is known to me and God. But, had I the time, I could disclose myself."

"To me?" inquired the visitant.

"To you before all," returned the murderer. "I supposed you were intelligent. I thought—since you exist—you would prove a reader of the heart. And yet you would propose to judge me by my acts! Think of it; my acts! I was born and I have lived in a land of giants; giants have dragged me by the wrists since I was born out of my mother—the giants of circumstance. And you would judge me by my acts! But can you not look within? Can you not understand that evil is hateful to me? Can you not see within me the clear writing of conscience, never blurred by any wilful sophistry[19] although too often disregarded? Can you not read me for a thing that surely must be common as humanity—the unwilling sinner?"

"All this is very feelingly expressed," was the reply, "but it regards me not. These points of consistency are beyond my province, and I care not in the least by what compulsion you may have been dragged away, so as you are but carried in the right direction. But time flies; the servant delays, looking in the faces of the crowd and at the pictures on the hoardings, but still she keeps moving nearer; and remember, it is as if the gallows itself were striding toward you through the Christmas streets! Shall I help you—I, who know all? Shall I tell you where to find the money?"

"For what price?" asked Markheim.

"I offer you the service for a Christmas gift," returned the other.

Markheim could not refrain from smiling with a kind of bitter triumph, "No," said he, "I will take nothing at your hands; if I were dying of thirst, and it was your hand that put the pitcher to my lips, I should find the courage to refuse. It may be credulous, but I will do nothing to commit myself to evil."

"I have no objection to a death-bed repentance," observed the visitant.

"Because you disbelieve their efficacy[20]!" Markheim cried.

"I do not say so," returned the other; "but I look on these things from a different side, and when the life is done my interest falls. The man has lived to serve me, to spread black looks under color of religion, or to sow tares[21] in the wheat field, as you do, in a course of weak compliance with desire. Now that he draws so near to his deliverance, he can add but one act of service—to repent, to die smiling, and thus to build up in confidence and hope the more timorous of my surviving followers. I am not so hard a master. Try me. Accept my help. Please yourself in life as you have done hitherto; please yourself more amply, spread your elbows at the board; and when the night begins to fall and the curtains to be drawn, I tell you, for your greater comfort, that you will find it even easy to compound your quarrel with your conscience, and to make a truckling peace with God. I came but now from such a death-bed, and the room was full of sincere mourners, listening to the man's last words; and when I looked into that face, which had been set as a flint against mercy, I found it smiling with hope."

"And do you, then, suppose me such a creature?" asked Markheim. "Do you think I have no more generous aspirations than to sin, and sin, and sin, and, at last, sneak into heaven? My heart rises at the thought. Is this, then, your experience of mankind? or is it because you find me with red hands that you presume such baseness? and is this crime of murder indeed so impious as to dry up the very springs of good?"

"Murder is to me no special category[22]," replied the other. "All sins are murder, even all life is war. I behold your race, like starving mariners on a raft, plucking crusts out of the hands of famine and feeding on each other's lives. I follow sins beyond the moment of their acting; I find in all that the last consequence is death; and to my eyes, the pretty maid who thwarts her mother with such taking graces on a question of a ball, drips no less visibly with human gore than such a murderer as yourself. Do I say that I follow sins? I follow virtues also; they differ not by the thickness of a nail, they are both scythes for the reaping angel of Death. Evil, for which I live, consists not in action but in character. The bad man is dear to me; not the bad act, whose fruits, if we could follow them far enough down the hurtling[23] cataract of the ages, might yet be found more blessed than those of the rarest virtues. And it is not because you have killed a dealer, but because you are Markheim, that I offered to forward your escape."

"I will lay my heart open to you," answered Markheim. "This crime on which you find me is my last. On my way to it I have learned many lessons; itself is a lesson, a momentous lesson. Hitherto I have been driven with revolt to what I would not; I was a bondslave to poverty, driven and scourged. There are robust virtues that can stand in these temptations; mine was not so: I had a thirst of pleasure. But to-day, and out of this deed, I pluck both warning and riches—both the power and a fresh resolve to be myself. I become in all things a free actor in the world; I begin to see myself all changed, these hands the agents of good, this heart at peace. Some thing comes over me out of the past; something of what I have dreamed on Sabbath evenings to the sound of the church organ, of what I forecast when I shed tears over noble books, or talked, an innocent child, with my mother. There lies my life; I have wandered a few years, but now I see once more my city of destination."

"You are to use this money on the Stock Exchange, I think?" remarked the visitor; "and there, if I mistake not, you have already lost some thousands?"

"Ah," said Markheim, "but this time I have a sure thing."

"This time, again, you will lose," replied the visitor, quietly.

"Ah, but I keep back the half!" cried Markheim.

"That also you will lose," said the other.

The sweat started upon Markheim's brow. "Well, then, what matter?" he exclaimed. "Say it be lost, say I am plunged again in poverty, shall one part of me, and that the worse, continue until the end to override the better? Evil and good ran strong in me, hailing me both ways. I do not love the one thing, I love all. I can conceive great deeds, renunciations, martyrdoms; and though I be fallen to such a crime as murder, pity is no stranger to my thoughts. I pity the poor; who knows their trials better than myself? I pity and help them; I prize love, I love honest laughter; there is no good thing nor true thing on earth but I love it from my heart. And are my vices only to direct my life, and my virtues to lie without effect, like some passive lumber of the mind? Not so; good, also, is a spring of acts."

But the visitant raised his finger. "For six-and-thirty years that you have been in this world," said he, "through many changes of fortune and varieties of humor, I have watched you steadily fall. Fifteen years ago you would have started at a theft. Three years back you would have blenched at the name of murder. Is there any crime, is there any cruelty or meanness, from which you still recoil?—five years from now I shall detect you in the fact! Downward, downward lies your way; nor can anything but death avail to stop you."

"It is true," Markheim said huskily, "I have in some degree complied with evil. But it is so with all: the very saints, in the mere exercise of living, grow less dainty, and take on the tone of their surroundings."

"I will propound to you one simple question," said the other; "and as you answer, I shall read to you your moral horoscope. You have grown in many things more lax; possibly you do right to be so; and at any account, it is the same with all men. But granting that, are you in any one particular, however trifling, more difficult to please with your own conduct, or do you go in all things with a looser rein?"

"In any one?" repeated Markheim, with an anguish of consideration. "No," he added, with despair, "in none! I have gone down in all."

"Then," said the visitor, "content yourself with what you are, for you will never change; and the words of your part on this stage are irrevocably written down."

Markheim stood for a long while silent, and indeed it was the visitor who first broke the silence. "That being so," he said, "shall I show you the money?"

"And grace?" cried Markheim.

"Have you not tried it?" returned the other. "Two or three years ago, did I not see you on the platform of revival meetings, and was not your voice the loudest in the hymn?"

"It is true," said Markheim; "and I see clearly what remains for me by way of duty. I thank you for these lessons from my soul; my eyes are opened, and I behold myself at last for what I am."

At this moment, the sharp note of the door-bell rang through the house; and the visitant, as though this were some concerted signal for which he had been waiting, changed at once in his demeanor.

"The maid!" he cried. "She has returned, as I forewarned you, and there is now before you one more difficult passage. Her master, you must say, is ill; you must let her in, with an assured but rather serious countenance— no smiles, no overacting, and I promise you success! Once the girl within, and the door closed, the same dexterity that has already rid you of the dealer will relieve you of this last danger in your path. Thenceforward you have the whole evening—the whole night, if needful—to ransack the treasures of the house and to make good your safety. This is help that comes to you with the mask of danger. Up!" he cried: "up, friend; your life hangs trembling in the scales: up, and act!"

Markheim steadily regarded his counsellor. "If I be condemned to evil acts," he said, "there is still one door of freedom open—I can cease from action. If my life be an ill thing, I can lay it down. Though I be, as you say truly, at the beck of every small temptation, I can yet, by one decisive gesture, place myself beyond the reach of all. My love of good is damned to barrenness; it may, and let it be! But I have still my hatred of evil; and from that, to your galling disappointment, you shall see that I can draw both energy and courage."

The features of the visitor began to undergo a wonderful and lovely change: they brightened and softened with a tender triumph; and, even as they brightened, faded and dislimned[24]. But Markheim did not pause to watch or understand the transformation. He opened the door and went downstairs very slowly, thinking to himself. His past went soberly before him; he beheld it as it was, ugly and strenuous like a dream, random as chance-medley—a scene of defeat. Life, as he thus reviewed it, tempted him no longer; but on the farther side he perceived a quiet haven for his bark. He paused in the passage, and looked into the shop, where the candle still burned by the dead body. It was strangely silent. Thoughts of the dealer swarmed into his mind, as he stood gazing. And then the bell once more broke out into impatient clamor.

He confronted the maid upon the threshold with something like a smile. "You had better go for the police," said he: "I have killed your master."

# NOTES

[1] Written in 1884. This story is used by permission of and special arrangement with the Charles Scribner's Sons Company, Publishers.

[2] 237:1 windfalls. Unexpected gains.

[3] 237:3 dividend. His knowledge a business asset that draws interest.

[4] 241:22 skewer-like. Like a wooden pin now used to fasten meat.

[5] 242:11 leaguer. Place besieged with shadows.

[6] 242:27 Time was that when the brains were out. See Macbeth, Act III, sc. 4, line 78.

[7] 243:16 iteration. Repetition.

[8] 246:25 railleries. Merry jesting or ridicule.

[9] 247:7 garishly. A blinding, gaudy effect.

[10] 247:7 Brownrigg. A notorious murderess living in England in the middle of the eighteenth century. She was hanged and her skeleton is still preserved.

[11] 247:8 Mannings. Marie Manning and her husband murdered a former suitor. They were given, a death sentence.

[12] 247:9 Thurtell. A gambler who quarrelled with Weare and killed him after he had professed peace. He designed his own gallows.

[13] 247:25 horologist. One who makes timepieces.

[14] 249:27 scission. A cleaving or a dividing.

[15] 250:25 Sheraton. Next to Chippendale the greatest furniture designer and cabinet-maker.

[16] 250:25 marquetry. An inlay of some thin material in the surface of a piece of furniture or other object.

[17] 251:23 Jacobean. Pertaining to the time of James I of England.

[18] 253:12 travesty. A grotesque imitation.

[19] 254:3 sophistry. Methods of the Greek sophists.

[20] 254:29 efficacy. Effective energy.

[21] 255:5 sow tares, etc. See Matthew XII, 24-30.

[22] 255:29 category. A class, condition, or predicament.

[23] 256:14 hurtling. Rushing headlong or confusedly.

[24] 280:10 dislimned. Erased or effaced.

# COLLATERAL READINGS

*Treasure Island*, R.L. Stevenson.
*Kidnapped*, R.L. Stevenson.
*Dr. Jekyll and Mr. Hyde*, R.L. Stevenson.
*Prince Otto*, R.L. Stevenson.
*Across the Plains*, R.L. Stevenson.
*Travels with a Donkey*, R.L. Stevenson.
*An Inland Voyage*, R.L. Stevenson.
*Essays on Burns and Thoreau*, R.L. Stevenson.
*Virginibus Puerisque*, R.L. Stevenson.
*The Child's Garden of Verses*, R.L. Stevenson.
*The Masque of the Red Death*, Edgar Allan Poe.
*The Pit and the Pendulum*, Edgar Allan Poe.
*A Coward*, Guy de Maupassant.
*The Substitute*, François Coppée.
*The Revolt of Mother*, Mary Wilkins Freeman.
*Flute and Violin*, James Lane Alien.
*A Lear of the Steppes*, Ivan Turgeneff.
*Rappacini's Daughter*, Nathaniel Hawthorne.

www.ingramcontent.com/pod-product-compliance
Lightning Source LLC
Chambersburg PA
CBHW051433130726
47987CB00005B/2028